FIRE
WATER

A PETER BARTHOLOMEW MYSTERY

SALLY GUNNING

POCKET STAR BOOKS

New York   London   Toronto   Sydney   Tokyo   Singapore

This book is a work of fiction. Names, characters, places and incidents are products of the author's imagination or are used fictitiously. Any resemblance to actual events or locales or persons, living or dead, is entirely coincidental.

An *Original* Publication of POCKET BOOKS

A Pocket Star Book published by
POCKET BOOKS, a division of Simon & Schuster Inc.
1230 Avenue of the Americas, New York, NY 10020

ISBN: 0-671-01737-3

First Pocket Books printing June 1999

10 9 8 7 6 5 4 3 2 1

POCKET STAR BOOK and colophon are registered trademarks of Simon & Schuster Inc.

Cover art by Ben Perini

Printed in the U.S.A.

For Tom
'Nuff said.

AUTHOR'S NOTE

In the course of my research on rumrunners I found two books that were so helpful I would like to mention them here—Scott Corbett's *The Sea Fox*, and Everett S. Allen's *The Black Ships*. I'm also indebted to Robert Louis Stevenson for *A Child's Garden of Verses*, my father's copy of which still opens to "The Lamplighter."

Many thanks to Dr. Thomas Schmidt, Catherine Vickery, and Ruth Shalline of Breakwater Dental for coming up with the nice selection of dental anomalies. My thanks also to my sister Jan Carlson for help with rules, to Chris Dolan for explaining how police radios do (and don't) work, to Nancy Thacher Reid for the sparking anecdote, and to my nephew Alex Carlson for sorting out the marine dilemmas. Any errors I take credit for myself.

FIRE
WATER

PETER BARTHOLOMEW stood on the bank of the creek and watched the five-year-old Lucy Suggs as she scrabbled in the mud like a terrier after a bone. He had no idea what she was after— fiddler crabs, shells, more mud? Whatever she was after, he hoped they didn't run out of it soon. For the first time since she'd arrived a month ago, the kid was having some good old-fashioned, unorchestrated fun, the kind of fun kids whose mothers hadn't just died probably had on a regular basis. For the past month Pete had stood on his head, literally, just to get Lucy to let go with a good old ear-to-ear grin, but this was different. With no pushing or prodding on Pete's part, here she was, small shoulders knotted with effort, hair spiked with globs of wet sand, cheeks pink, eyes glowing.

When she finally looked up at him every one of her milk teeth showed. "I'm finding treasure."

"Wow." The word had recently become Pete's favorite conversational tool. Lucy liked hyperbole.

A simple "oh," and she'd fix him with those huge, dark eyes until he came up with the rest. Now she shot him one of those looks that told him she was feeling pretty pleased with herself, and, impossible as it might seem, pretty pleased with him, too.

Not that the little girl had had much choice. Minutes before the mother had died, she'd pointed Lucy in Pete's direction and mouthed two words at him. *Keep her.* So they'd kept her. And how many childless thirty-eight-year-old men, newly remarried to their ex-wives, could expertly field a five-year-old dropped into their laps? Not too many, he was sure.

Pete and Lucy sighed in unison, for different reasons. Lucy went back to her digging, and Pete went back to what he'd been doing before Lucy's unaccustomed glee had captured his attention—looking around. Fifty yards in front of Pete was Nashtoba Sound, and fifty yards behind him was his cottage. A month ago, in the height of a hurricane, sound and cottage had met, and although the marsh in between had been designed to survive any amount of wind and water unscathed, the same couldn't be said for the creek. The recent storm had sent it ripping into its banks with new confidence, and everywhere Pete looked he saw raw peaty edges. The biggest of these natural excavations was at the very spot where Lucy was hard at work. Pete used to be able to hop the creek here to make the beach. Not so now. He was eyeballing the span to the far bank when Lucy gave a disgusted grunt.

"It's a *rock*. A giant old *rock*."

Pete looked down. Lucy had clawed a hole the

size of a small cave in the creek wall and was leaning over at a precarious angle. It was warm for October, and low tide, the water shin deep at best, but Pete didn't relish the thought of explaining to Connie that he'd had to fish Lucy out of the creek, no matter what the water level. Connie had surprised him by turning out to be the more nervous child-rearer, but the arrival of Lucy had changed them both, Pete knew. They were no longer so ready to rush out and meet life's little adventures head-on. They were more often on their guard, more often on edge.

And always exhausted.

If only I were ten years younger, thought Pete. If only kids came with safety features, like cars. Hazard lights. Air bags. Bumpers. Even now he could see that another big gob of bank was ready to go and if he didn't move fast Lucy was going to . . . "Whoa, there." Pete reached out and nabbed Lucy by the back of the overalls only seconds before the ground underneath her caved in.

"There it is! Look, it's a big old ball! *Get* it, Pete! There it goes! It's whooshing away! *Pete!*"

Lucy hopped up and down, flimsy denim tugging against Pete's vicelike fingers. The ball had indeed tumbled into the creek and, the current being at full ebb, was rolling along the bottom end over end, toward the open sea. But Pete stood frozen on the bank, feeling himself curiously divided. In the old, pre-Lucy days Pete would have waded into the creek, captured Lucy's "treasure," and borne it proudly home. The new Pete wanted nothing more than to turn his back, march Lucy through the mud to the cottage, and leave the ball to wash up on someone else's beach, disrupt someone else's life for once. Hadn't he already done his share and more?

But even as his mind stood divided, his muscles seemed to unite against him. He scooped up Lucy, planted her safely ten feet behind him, plunged into the creek unmindful of jeans or sneakers, and slogged after the ball.

Which was no ball, he'd seen that much right off. He reached into the icy water, fished it out, and bundled it into his sweatshirt with his body carefully positioned between it and the little girl.

Lucy's treasure was not a giant rock, not a big ball, but a mud-stained human skull.

4

※2※

FOR A MINUTE Police Chief Willy McOwat thought it was someone's bad joke. He'd been out on the marsh since dawn with a team of state investigators, watching them slosh through the mud, sifting and seining and meticulously bagging anything that faintly resembled human bone. When the gray orb rose out of the muck the chief glared at the annoyingly trim but satisfyingly filthy state trooper who'd unearthed it. "What's this?"

"I believe it's the skull, sir."

Willy squinted at the trooper. Nothing in the chiseled features moved. So it wasn't his joke. Then whose? The chief investigator, John Rocco, whose nickname was Rocky, of course, charged to the fore. He wasn't as trim as the trooper, but neither was he as filthy. "You got some problem here?"

"We do." Willy pointed to the skull. "As far as I know, it's supposed to be on somebody's desk awaiting the dental expert." He leaned over and removed the skull from the trooper's fingers. No, it

5

was no joke. He could see the neat, round hole in the back of this skull. Yesterday's skull had been cracked vertically between the eyes. So Pete had outdone himself, this time, two bodies for the price of one?

An electronic beep suddenly violated the primal air. It wasn't Willy's—the Nashtoba police, all two of them, still used antiquated radios that cut out every time a seagull flew by. It was the chief investigator who reached for an inside pocket and withdrew the state-of-the-art portable phone. By the time he put it back, he was smiling. "We've got the first one. Gotta love those dental pros. The guy found a funny tooth, a retained, bonded baby tooth. Figured the local dentists might remember one of those. Called around and found a guy over in Weams Point, not only remembered the funny tooth but the name that went with it. Pulled the file and it was a perfect match. One Susan Jameson, white female, early twenties when she went in the ground, been in there at least ten years. Guess that puts it before your time. Want us to take it from here, Chief?"

"No thanks."

It wasn't the answer Rocky Rocco had been expecting. Willy could feel the eyes, like bullets in his back, as he handed over the skull and slogged back the way he'd come. Willy didn't mind. He was used to bullets in the back by now.

Willy knocked first, opened the door second, and hallooed third, as was his usual custom here. A "Yo!" echoed from the kitchen. He navigated through a living room full of toys and traversed the hall with the ease of a frequent flyer. He pushed open the kitchen door and was met with a domestic scene that he'd come of late to envy—Pete and Connie Bartholomew draped on either side of the kitchen table, two heads meeting companionably in the middle, Pete's dark and rumpled, Connie's gold and . . . well, yes, rumpled, too, but rumples had never hurt Connie any. Willy found himself pausing uncharacteristically in the doorway. The tranquility he saw before him had been long enough in coming, and he felt reluctant to disturb it. Hadn't they been twice robbed of their honeymoon? Didn't they deserve these few precious minutes alone without the police chief barging in? But Connie looked up and shot him a welcoming grin, quickly changed to a warning shake of the head as he opened his mouth. The chair at the end of the table scraped backward, and a smaller, even more disheveled head appeared.

"Apples, peaches, pears!" shouted Lucy.

"Peanuts, pineapples, croutons," said Pete.

"Am I interrupting something?" asked Willy.

"Yes, thank God," said Connie. "They've been doing it for days. There's no end to it. No point, either. At least not as far as I can tell. Lemons, limes, oranges—"

"We *did* lemons," said Lucy.

"And nobody but me ever seems to get hungry." Connie pointed to a half-full pizza box on the kitchen counter, but Willy looked at Lucy, not the pizza. The little girl had come to his friends thin, but she seemed to be getting thinner. And why not?

7

According to Pete's reports she hardly ever ate. Or slept. Or laughed. Or almost never laughed, Willy amended, as Pete tossed out, "Picked pickled peppers," and Lucy giggled.

Willy listened patiently to a few more food groups before he cut in. "We've got something."

Pete turned at once to Lucy. "Okay, pal, time for toothbrush and pajamas. I'll be up in a minute."

Lucy scampered for the stairs, and once she was out of sight, four eyes swung toward Willy.

"What?" said Connie.

"We've found a second body. Or a second skull, anyway. This one looks like it took a bullet in the back of the head."

"No," said Connie.

"Afraid so," said Willy. "And we've got an ID on the first one. Does the name Susan Jameson ring a bell?"

Clinically, Willy supposed, he'd have to label the two reactions interesting. Pete went into that unfocused trance that meant he wouldn't see or hear anything for awhile. Connie focused on Pete, and, Willy guessed, saw plenty. She stood up. "I'll do Lucy." She left the room, straight and proud. Too straight and proud. Once she was out of sight Willy said, "Well?"

It took awhile, but finally Pete snapped into focus. "It can't be. Not Susan Jameson."

"You knew her?"

"I knew her."

"When did you see her last?"

"Fifteen years ago."

8

"And she was how old?"

"Twenty-one. Just turned. I was twenty-three. It was my second full season for Factotum. We were looking for help. I met Susan on the beach. It was—"

And the eyes went again, this time back fifteen years . . .

It was like something out of a state-of-the-art preteen fantasy. Late on a hot July day, the sand frying the soles of his feet, the dirt and grime from a long day of mucking out Percy Cobb's barns running off him in rivers. Some dumb idea of his, this person-employed-to-do-all-kinds-of-work. Better to have said he'd do yard work, home repair, paint jobs, even wallpaper. And he didn't mind the taxi runs. Or reading old Sarah the newspaper. Or the tutoring, or even the grocery shopping. But no barns. No chicken coops, either. The chicken coop was last month, and he could still smell the stink of it, even through the cows. So no barns. No coops. He'd tell Rita first thing in the morning. Pete dropped his towel and ran the last twenty feet to the water, pushed off and dove.

And when he surfaced there she was.

The fantasy.

Only she was no fantasy. Just the most beautiful woman he'd ever seen, stark naked, rising out of the water ten feet away from him.

"Hello," she said.

"Hello," said Pete. Sort of. The only trouble was, it came out more like, "Gobbo."

"Excuse me?"

"I . . . nothing. Hello. I said 'hello.' You said 'hello.' So I said 'hello.' " Moron.

9

She smiled. "Oh. Hello."

"Yeah, hello," said Pete. Idiot.

"I don't think I've ever been so hot in my entire life. Aren't you hot?"

"Sure. Hot. Real hot."

The woman eased under the water, treading backward, and Pete took the opportunity to get a grip. It was just a perfectly proportioned, wet, naked woman, with long, streaming red hair and green eyes.

Man, he loved green eyes.

"You're from around here?" she asked.

"Sure. Right here. And you? Are you from here?"

Right. As if somebody like this would be from here.

"No, I'm . . . well, actually, I guess I'll be leaving soon. As soon as I can get enough money. I was planning to stay, but—" She flipped onto her stomach and breast-stroked toward him, stood up again, held out a hand. "I'm Susan Jameson."

He was going to have a heart attack. He really was. He was going to need artificial respiration. Did she know artificial respiration? If this was a fantasy, she would. And it had to be fantasy. If he reached out for her he'd find nothing but air. He knew that.

He extended his hand.

And felt it pressed and held by cool, wet fingers.

"You're—?"

Moron. Idiot. "Pete Bartholomew."

"And you live—?"

Pete pointed. "Right there. See that cottage on the other side of the marsh?"

She smiled. "So you should have me arrested for trespassing. I didn't have a place to stay last night so I slept on the beach. And I suppose it's against the rules to go skinny dipping? But I was so hot, and I don't have a bathing suit, and there was no one around."

"That's okay," said Pete magnanimously.

They turned, as if by mutual accord, and left the water. She had a backpack and a rough-looking blanket that she would have used for a towel if Pete hadn't handed her his. She thanked him and began to dry off. Pete looked away. Mostly. She put on a short, stretchy dress, no underwear, bent forward and began to comb out her hair. There was at least a yard of it.

Pete swallowed. "So you're looking for a place to stay?"

"Place, job, you name it. I have no money. If you want to know the whole sad story, I came here with a guy. But things didn't work out, if you know what I mean." Susan Jameson's voice, which was soft and low, got a hair louder and harder. "There are things I don't let anyone do to me, no matter if it means I starve to death on a deserted beach in the middle of nowhere. I'll get by. Maybe I'll forget about bus fare, just hitch a ride back."

"Back where?"

Susan flipped her hair back and straightened. Her face was flushed a deep, dusty rose. It made her eyes look even greener. She laughed. "Now that you mention it, back nowhere. There's no one left where I came from. And I'm not going back where he came from, that's for sure. I guess I'll just hit the road and see where I land." She handed back Pete's towel. "Thanks. I'm kind of turned around. Can you point me to the nearest road from here?"

Pete picked up her backpack. "Come on." He led her

across the beach, over the marsh, up to his house. His intention was to get out a map, plot her route home, take her to the bus station, give her bus fare. But to where? Over a couple of Budweisers she told him more. Parents dead in a plane crash. No other family. Friends that had drifted off in the face of this all-consuming relationship. This relationship that had just come undone.

She sat on Pete's screen porch, looked out over the water, and sighed.

"So go ahead," she said finally. "Tell me your story. No, wait, I bet I can guess. You have this great job, a great family, a girlfriend who treats you like a king, more friends than you know what to do with."

"Great job," said Pete, and he told her about Factotum. About advertising in high school as a person employed to do all kinds of work. About finding out there were lots of people even on a small island with all kinds of work that needed doing. About deciding to stick with this crazy odd-jobbing after college. He even told her about some of the things they did, omitting the chickens and the cows.

"And family?" asked Susan.

"Sister in summer school in Maine, trying to make up a lost semester. Parents currently in Virginia, retreating state by state from New England weather. I figure they should hit Florida in time to retire there."

"And girlfriends?"

"None at present." And none for some time, either. There had been a college thing that hadn't survived the travel, then a rehash of a high school disaster, then nothing. He hadn't thought he'd changed while he was away

12

at school, but it turned out he'd at least expanded a little. The people who'd stayed here hadn't.

Susan Jameson smiled at him. The smile was as perfect as the rest of her.

And somehow or other Pete found himself offering Susan Jameson a meal, a job, and his spare bedroom.

In that order.

✦3✦

W<small>ILL</small> M<small>C</small>O<small>WAT</small> cleared his throat. "Interesting. And she worked for you how long?"

"Only a month. Five weeks, maybe. One night she went to stay with some friends and she never came back. She was like that. Free spirit. I got a postcard a few days later from Weams Point. No return address. That was the last I heard of her. But that's why this can't be Susan Jameson. She *left* here."

He sounded desperate. A little too desperate, thought Willy. There's something he's not telling, here. "I don't suppose you've still got that postcard."

"Yeah, I do."

"You do?" This came from behind them. Willy turned and saw Connie in the doorway.

Uh-oh.

Pete stood up. "I'll get it."

"While you're up there, do Leerie."

Pete left the room. Connie dropped hard into the chair across from Willy.

14

"Leerie?"

" 'The Lamplighter.' That poem by Robert Louis Stevenson. Pete knows the whole thing by heart. Thank God, since she won't go to sleep without it. Or with it, sometimes, especially if I try to read it to her."

"Things still a little rocky?"

"Things still very rocky. With an occasional glimpse of verdant pasture. Like the fact that she seems to have no idea what she found out there. She thinks you're looking for her treasure."

"I wish," said Willy.

He waited.

"So I guess he told you about Susan Jameson," said Connie finally.

"You knew her?"

"That neo-hippy slut? Sure I knew her."

Willy cleared his throat. "Anything else you can tell me about her?"

"I'd say that about covers it."

"Pete says she was only here about a month."

"Really? It just seemed longer."

"She was that bad?"

"Yes, but he was worse."

"Why don't you take it from the top," said Willy.

The sign said Factotum *in big letters, and below that, in smaller ones,* Person Employed to Do All Kinds of Work. *Since the door was open, Connie walked in. And stopped. The under layer to the room seemed to be a bunch of old, rattan furniture with faded, splashy cushions, an ancient floor lamp, an old sea chest for a coffee table, a fireplace that had been well used. Once. Now it*

*was blocked by a pile of paint cans, some boat cushions,
and what looked like part of a child's swing set. The
couch and coffee table were buried under old books. The
two chairs were buried under gardening implements and
a roll of chicken wire. To Connie's immediate right a
woman sat behind a desk that contained the only spot of
order in the room. The woman looked pretty well ordered,
too. She was maybe ten years older than Connie. Or
maybe not. Maybe it was just the neat black bob, the
Peter Pan collar, the shell pink nail polish . . . that was
as far as Connie got before some guy walked into the
room, but Connie barely noticed him. Nothing special,
maybe six feet tall in his shoes, dark hair with a hint of
reddish underglow. That was the hair on his head. The
hair on his arms glinted like gold in the light from the
window. He had a deep tan on the more horizontal of
his surfaces, less deep on the vertical ones. He wore old
jeans and a faded T-shirt that was too small, pulling at
his shoulders some. Low-cut basketball sneakers, no
socks. These perfectly ordinary, plumbable brown eyes,
but for some reason, the minute they fixed on her, she
felt like some demand had just been placed on her.*

So she said, "What do you want?"

*The eyes widened. "You're the one standing in my
living room."*

Connie shot a look around. "Living room?"

*A brief flash of teeth. "Yeah. Once. Now it's Factotum.
You've got some work you need done?"*

"No, I thought you did. I saw the ad."

"The what?"

*"The ad. Person to do everything. No experience
necessary."*

"Oh!" This from the black bob, hustling out from

16

behind the desk. "Thank goodness someone saw it. I was beginning to think it had sunk without a trace among the personals. I'm Rita Peck. I answer the phone. And place the ads. This is the boss, Peter Bartholomew."

The boss didn't say much. He stood rooted, listening, or maybe not listening, as Rita Peck rambled on, explaining about Factotum, about what they did. It would have been a hell of a lot quicker, thought Connie, if she'd listed what they didn't do. Which wasn't much, by the sound of it. Right now, for example, the boss was on his way to read the newspaper to an old lady whose eyesight couldn't handle the small print.

"Why don't you take her along, Pete?" said the bob. "Show her the kind of thing we do."

"That's okay," said Connie.

"So you don't want the job," said Peter Bartholomew.

"I didn't say that."

"Maybe she's busy," said the bob.

"I'm not busy," said Connie. "I just — " She stopped. What the hell was the matter with her? It was this guy. Every time she looked over at him, he was looking back at her.

But not like most guys looked at her.

"Come or don't come," he said finally. "I don't care."

"Well, I sure don't."

"Fine," said the bob. "So go ahead. You'll love Sarah."

So Connie went.

"And he hired you," said Willy.

Connie grinned. "Sarah did, actually. Pete told me to read her the paper. It was supposed to be some kind of test. So I picked this long article about septic tanks, just to bug him, and every time he tried to cut me off, Sarah said, 'Go on, dear. Peter, you may leave the room if you can't mind your manners.' He sat there scowling, Sarah sat there beaming. When I got through she listed off what she wanted me to do as if he'd already hired me."

Which told Willy a few things about Pete and Connie, but not too much about Susan Jameson. Willy cast about for a way to bring Connie gently back on track and finally settled on, "Was this before or after he'd hired Susan Jameson?"

Connie looked nonplused. "Oh, right. Sarah hired me, then about a week later, Pete hired Susan Jameson." The thought seemed to give Connie pause. "And I'll tell you why he hired her, too. Because of that thing that happened when he met me."

"What thing?" Had Willy missed something? Apparently.

"I just told you. The minute we met. He couldn't keep his eyes off me. And he knew I knew it, too. So he hired Susan Jameson just to show me."

"I understand Susan Jameson was rather striking."

"*Striking?* She was *naked*, that's what she was. That's the trouble with you men. That's the extent of your artistic appreciation. Put Golda Meir in the middle of the road with no clothes on and you'd call *her* striking."

Willy decided it was time to move on. Quickly. "So this Susan Jameson arrived out of the blue, worked for a month, left out of the blue. And in the interim—"

18

"In the interim she screwed his brains out. But I suppose he told you that part."

Willy cleared his throat. "No. Not exactly."

A thumping sound echoed from upstairs. Connie sat up, on instant red alert, seemed to diagnose the sound as non-Lucy, settled back. "Pete. Hall closet. Looking for that postcard. Can you believe he saved it?"

"It could be worse. He could know just where to find it. Under his pillow, for example."

At least that got a smile. But Willy had to admit that if he were Connie, he might have wished it took a little longer for Pete to find a fifteen-year-old postcard. He gallumped down the stairs and slapped it on the table in front of Willy. The picture side showed an aerial view of Cape Hook, the oddly shaped peninsula off which the island of Nashtoba hung like a good luck charm. At least it was Willy's good luck charm. He'd come here two years ago from the sweat and grime of a metropolis homicide division looking for a kinder, gentler life. He'd found that life. He'd also found a few more homicides. Not that this one was a homicide. He thought of the odd, vertical crack in Susan Jameson's skull. Not yet, anyway.

Willy picked up the card and flipped it over. It was postmarked Weams Point, the town at the extreme tip of the Cape Hook peninsula, an hour's ride from Nashtoba, the same town in which Susan's dentist had resided. The card was dated August tenth, fifteen years and three months ago. The message was printed in block letters, back-slanting. The signature was large and loopy. The message:

Pete, Guess we're a no go. Time to move on. Thanks for everything. Susan.

"I'm hungry."

Willy turned around and saw another domestic scene he could envy—a little girl in a long white nightgown, rubbing sleepy eyes, standing in the doorway.

Pete got up and reached for the pizza box.

"You're not giving her that now," said Connie.

"Why not?"

"You know what happens when you eat pizza at this hour."

"Yeah, but she's got a newer stomach."

"Give her a glass of milk."

"And a cookie," said Lucy.

Pete poured the milk and dispensed the cookies, but it was Connie who picked up the loot and herded Lucy toward the door. "We'll eat these upstairs while you reminisce. No sense exposing the child to pornography."

Willy listened as they disappeared through the door.

Lucy: "Who's Poor Noddy?"

Connie: "The brother of Wee Willy Winky."

Willy smiled and returned to business reluctantly. "I get the idea Susan Jameson didn't stay in that spare room forever."

"About five minutes."

"Jesus," said Willy.

❖4❖

PETE COULDN'T SLEEP. First he blamed Connie, lying wide awake beside him. Her eyes were shut tight and she didn't move a muscle, but Pete could tell she was awake all the same. Connie awake gave off these waves like radar. So they were both lying there awake. And the odds were good they were both thinking about the same thing.

Susan.

Dead.

He couldn't believe she was dead. He'd held her skull in his hands the day before, and he still couldn't believe it. Not Susan. Not dead. That mud-stained piece of bone wasn't Susan. Susan was that red hair and those green eyes and that body in that dress. That body not in that dress. She was the living, breathing voice that had spoken from the dark in his doorway the very first night she'd spent under his roof. *The thing of it is, I've never been able to sleep alone.*

Willy hadn't believed it. But then again, Pete

hadn't believed it, either. Even when he'd found her in his arms, found her flesh against his flesh . . .

Pete tossed back the covers and sat up. He was one sick individual. Here he was, only a few hours after finding out Susan Jameson was dead, wallowing in flesh-filled fantasies. But that was the thing about Susan Jameson, even back then, even during the odd intervals over the fifteen years when his thoughts had turned to her. It still seemed like fantasy.

And flesh.

Pete twisted around to look at Connie. Eyes still shut, body still motionless. And still awake. Funny how he'd met the two women together. Or almost together. Connie first, but Susan the very week after. One a dream, the other closer to nightmare . . .

Pete was late for Sarah's. He hated being late in general, but he especially hated being late for Sarah's. It had something to do with the way her face always looked when she saw him. He could tell she watched for him, waited for him, listened for him. So he hated to be late and he had no time for whoever this was, standing in the living room. He didn't even have time to look, let alone talk. He had to keep moving.

So he moved. And he didn't look. All he caught were those eyes. Soft green, like saltwater over a sandbar. But other than that strange green, the rest of her was all gold—gold hair, gold skin, long gold limbs. Unfussy. Unfettered. The shorts, the shirt, they weren't the kind you were supposed to notice. So he didn't. And he sure

*didn't say anything. So what was she driving at with
this, "What do you want?"*

And the next thing he knew they were arguing.

*What was this? He had no time for this. As soon as
Rita jumped in, he tried to move toward the door, but
he couldn't seem to get there. And when he did get there
he had her with him.*

What was this?

*Okay, so he would run her out to Sarah's, let that old
curmudgeon argue with her. That should do it. They'd
come back, she'd suddenly remember she was on her way
to Nairobi to marry a big game hunter.*

So good luck to him.

But she hadn't left for Nairobi. She hadn't married any big game hunter—although there were
times over the course of the next twelve years when
Pete had cause to wish she had. Like when she'd
run off with Glen Newcomb, for example. But how
had he gotten on that old track? He'd been thinking
about Susan Jameson, not Connie.

He heard a half-swallowed snort beside him
and turned.

"I'm sorry," said Connie. "I know she's dead and
it's horrible. But I can't help it. You were such a
schmuck about her."

"A what? I was such a what?"

"You heard me. She strolls in, snaps you up,
dumps you—"

"*Dumps* me?"

"Yes, dumps you. Or didn't you read your own
postcard? 'Guess we're a no go.' Translation: Bye-
bye, Bozo."

Pete got up.

"Where are you going?"

"To check on Lucy. She went right to sleep. It's not like her."

"So you're going to wake her up?"

"I am going to check on her," said Pete evenly.

And he'd been no schmuck about Susan Jameson, either.

"Oh, he was such a schmuck over that woman," said Rita. "But what could I say? I wasn't a partner then, only his paid secretary. And you know Pete. Any stray dog."

Willy sat perched on the corner of Rita's desk in the Factotum office as she burrowed in the file cabinet to her lower left. Although he suspected that Rita hadn't changed much in the intervening fifteen years, Factotum certainly had. It had started in Pete's parents' garage, moved with Pete to the cottage on the marsh, and eventually taken over the cottage. When an old boat barn had washed up during the recent hurricane and been abandoned by its rightful owners, Pete had moved it onto the southwest corner of his property, done some hasty remodeling, moved Factotum into the bottom and his sister Polly into the top. Rita had spent the past few weeks busily lining her new nest and establishing her usual order, but Rita's order could never quite offset Pete's chaos. The shelves and cabinets were already crammed, and the middle of the room was already cluttered. Willy could identify the fertilizer spreader, the pile of newspapers, the seatless deck chairs, even the partially deflated rubber raft, but was stymied by the pile of funny shaped canvas and the huge, orange . . . something. All in all, though, Rita seemed pleased with the arrangement. So was Willy, but for different reasons.

Willy forced his mind off Polly and returned his attention to Rita. She didn't seem to be having much luck with his first request—to find a sample of Susan Jameson's handwriting.

"I must have kept a copy of her W-2," Rita said now. "But honestly. Fifteen years ago—"

"All right," said Willy. "Why don't you work on answering my second question."

Rita popped upright. "Oh. What do I remember about Susan. Well, let me see. She was his third one that summer."

"Third girlfriend?"

"*Pete?* Lord, no. Third stray dog. First he hired a high schooler named Hugh Peletier. Connie called him Baby Hughie. His parents were the type who seemed to limp from crisis to crisis to disaster. I swear, half the time it was Hughie's paycheck that fed that family. A *padded* paycheck, I might add. That Pete. I swear to you, it's a miracle we're still in business. I think that's why he insisted on making me a partner. He knew he would never be able to stay afloat the way he was going. Now where was I? Oh, yes, the second stray dog, Tim St. George. He looked better but was in fact much worse—someone Pete met through an old college chum, if I remember. He showed up in June, just to say hi, apparently, and the next thing I knew, Pete had signed him on for the summer. At least it was supposed to be for the summer. We couldn't get rid of him. He stayed and stayed and stayed. I think it was October before he finally left. And he was no Employee of the Year, I must tell you. He tried, I'll give him that, but he kept getting, I don't know, *fogged in*. And we were busy. So I put an ad in the paper and that's how we ended up hiring Connie. I should do it again right now, actually. We've gotten nothing done since Lucy came. Not that I blame them. That little girl is the priority. But in the meantime, Andy's on vacation, off hunting with his cousin Walt, which means that's the last we'll see of him. Either he'll shoot himself or he'll get lost in the woods, you mark my words. *Honestly*. And I've got a business to run."

"So Susan came between this St. George and Connie?" prompted Willy.

"What? Oh. Yes. Now Connie got a few things done, let me tell you. She and Hughie. And there was absolutely no need for Pete to go hiring Susan Jameson. But talk about your stray dogs. No job, no place to stay, no money, hadn't eaten in two days. Oh, I was beside myself. You should have seen him that morning."

"Why?"

"Well," said Rita primly, "I mean, *honestly*. There they were, still practically dripping from the shower, as if they'd shared the same towel or something, and Pete wearing this brand-new chambray shirt I'd given him. And the jeans without the holes. And a pair of boat shoes. *Boat shoes*, mind you, not those ratty old sneakers . . ."

*   *   *

But the spiffy look couldn't camouflage the sleepless shadows under the eyes and he looked . . . well, he looked as if someone had dropped an electric razor in his bathwater.

"Rita," he said, beaming at her, "I'd like you to meet Susan Jameson. I've just hired her. Susan, this is Rita Peck."

He stepped back, displaying Susan in all her glory, and Rita had to admit she was stunning. A kinky waterfall of red hair, creamy skin, emerald green eyes, and one of those bodies that Rita had always believed only occurred after extensive plastic surgery. She gave Rita one of those flawless smiles that you saw in the glossy magazines. Rita listened to her sing Pete's praises. The meeting on the beach, the day that had begun with no friends, no bed, no job, no money. The day that ended with . . . here a shy smile . . . the day that had ended with Pete. When she said his name it was as if she'd taken the Lord's name in vain. To Pete's credit, he did look momentarily chagrined. And far be it from Rita to put the kibosh on happy beginnings. And let's be fair. Just because the woman looked like she should be posing for a centerfold, it didn't mean she couldn't do a good day's work with the best of them.

"But if she did, I never saw it," said Rita.

"And when did you see her last?"

"If you mean the exact date, I'm afraid I can't help you. But I'm sure my ex-husband has it etched permanently in his memory. And Pete, of course. I do remember the day Pete came in, around mid-August if I had to guess, and told me she'd be gone for a few days. Then two days later Pete got

that postcard. That was the last we heard of her."
Rita looked out the window. "I must say I was
relieved. There was something not quite right
about her."

"In what sense?"

"Well, they weren't . . . she wasn't . . ." Rita
glared defiantly. "She was too darned sexy, for one
thing. Of course if I said that to my ex-husband
he'd say there's no such thing. And I suppose you'd
agree with him."

"Not necessarily," said Willy. He was starting to
suspect that if he wasn't careful, this Susan Jameson
could get even him into trouble.

So he took the stairs to Polly's apartment cautiously. But that was how he'd been taking them
for the entire four days she'd been living there.
When he'd first met Polly she'd been moving at
a dead run from anything with a Y chromosome
attached, hot off an abusive relationship that had
by sheer luck ended up with the man dead, not
her. It had taken Polly a good long time to see Willy
as a person, not a gender, longer still to bring it
back the other way so she could see the man, but
for some reason, once she'd finally seen him whole,
they'd stalled there.

Like now. She opened the door, saw him and
beamed, then realized she was beaming and raced
for the rocking chair. Not the couch, the chair. So
Willy took the couch, the very couch he and Pete
had lugged up the stairs for her the week before.
Willy looked around and recognized a few other
additions she'd pilfered from Pete and Connie—a
braided rug, a floor lamp, a lobster trap coffee table.

"I'm afraid this visit's official," he began, and tried not to notice her reaction—half relief, half disappointment. "We've IDed the first body. A Susan Jameson. Do you remember her?"

Polly's eyes grew round. "Susan Jameson? *Yes*, I remember her. Susan. Wow. She had this thing with my brother one summer. It was nauseating. She dissolved all his brain cells. He couldn't do fractions. He—" Polly raked through her dark curls, the usual sign that she was also raking her memory. "Susan Jameson. Boy, do I remember her. I was on my way back to Maine from this guy's house in New Jersey . . ."

It was a risky maneuver, but Polly decided to do it anyway, to make a brief stopover to see her brother. She'd have to remember to tell him that first thing—that she was just passing through—otherwise he'd put her to work picking corn or walking somebody's dog or assembling lawn furniture. Polly had had enough of Factotum. After all, she'd worked there all last summer. And besides, if she didn't get back to start her course on Monday she'd have to tack on a whole extra semester. So she walked in fast, trying to look like she was in a hurry, and there was Pete, standing in the middle of the kitchen looking like he'd never been in a hurry in his life, with some half-naked redhead hanging off him.

"Hi," said Polly.

Pete jumped.

The redhead took a half step back, but kept a hand in Pete's rear pants pocket.

Like, gag me, thought Polly.

29

"Polly," said Pete. "Where'd you come from? This is Susan Jameson. Susan, this is my sister, Polly."

"You didn't even have to tell me," said Susan. "You're the spitting image. And every bit as cute."

Like, double-gag me.

"I can't stay," said Polly. "I've got, like, one hour, max. Just wanted to check in and—"

That was as far as she got before all hell broke loose. Or so it seemed to Polly.

A tall sun-streaked blonde strode in and stopped about a foot in front of Pete, ignoring the redhead completely. "What kind of Mickey Mouse operation is this? I've been hacking through brush for six hours. Tim was supposed to meet me with a truck at the end of Platt Road an hour ago. Where is he?"

"What are you asking me for?" Pete snapped, and Polly looked at her brother in surprise. In about a millionth of a second his face had gone from something off cloud nine to something out of the Tower of London.

"I'm asking you because I was told you were the boss around here. If you're not, just say so and I'll ask Rita. At least she seems to know what she's doing."

Susan Jameson moved closer to Pete, if that were possible. She really wasn't half-naked, Polly realized. It was just that the shorts were so short. And the tank top couldn't quite reach them. Polly had never been that enamored with her own belly button, but to each her own, she supposed.

"Excuse me," said red to blonde, "but you seem to be bleeding."

Again the blonde ignored her, but Polly looked where

the finger pointed and saw a long, bare, badly scratched leg. She went to the sink, ripped off a few paper towels, and handed them to the bleeding woman. "Hi. I'm Pete's sister, Polly."

The blonde shot her a slightly less hostile look than she'd delivered up to now. "Connie Benz. I work here. I'm apparently the only one who does."

"Hold it," Pete began, but he couldn't get any further, either, before the door opened again.

Polly turned, and there was the answer to her dreams, standing there.

But Connie, at least, didn't seem too impressed. She descended on the newcomer like a banshee. "Where the hell have you been? I've been waiting on Platt Road for an hour."

The man stepped into the room. He actually got better as he got closer. He looked at Pete, puzzled. "Platt Road? I thought you said Fort Road."

"Platt Road," said Pete. "That's okay, Tim. We'll try again tomorrow."

Connie whirled on Pete. "What's this royal we crap? You try again tomorrow if you want to. I'm supposed to be in Arapo."

Pete ignored her. Or at least he looked like he wanted to. And everyone seemed to be ignoring the redhead, which probably didn't happen to her too often.

Polly went up to Tim and held out her hand. "Hi. I'm Pete's sister, Polly."

He smiled. "Pleased to meet you, Pete's sister, Polly. I'm Pete's thorn in the side, Tim St. George. Here for a while, are you?"

"Yes," said Polly.

* * *

"I was a little boy crazy back then," Polly explained. "And he was enough to drive *you* crazy. Really. You should have seen him. He was like something out of Chippendale's."

"Chippendale's?"

"You know. Those male strippers."

Willy reminded himself that this was one of the things that had first drawn him to Pete's sister—a certain conversational openness oblivious of effect. "If we could get back to Susan Jameson."

"Oh, right. I don't know, I don't remember much else about her. Just that she acted like Pete was—"

"Tim St. George?"

Polly giggled. "Exactly."

"Can you recall any conversations you might have had with her? Any plans she might have mentioned? Any acquaintances in the area?"

"She had this boyfriend. Before Pete, I mean. The only reason I know about him is he tried to pick me up."

"Quite the Summer of Love."

Polly giggled again. "Really. He came sniffing around one day. You'd have to ask Pete for the details, but I guess the guy decided to reclaim his lost property. Pete told him to shove off, and on his way out he happened to see me and we got talking. He wanted me to go away with him, can you believe it? To Gull Island. I said no, of course."

"Because of this St. George?"

Polly shot him an offended look. "Because of my general principles. I wasn't *that* boy crazy. Hard as you may find that to believe."

"Not hard." It was that other Polly that was hard

to believe. Willy could only hope that somewhere between the two lay the real Polly. He flipped his notebook to a clean page. "Do you recall the name of this former boyfriend?"

"Oh, right. You cops like those old boyfriends, don't you? Roger Coolidge. That was his name. I never forget a conquest, no matter how temporary."

Willy wrote down the name and shut the notebook. "If you remember anything else—"

"I know, I know. Call you. Even if it's the dead of night. Neither rain nor snow—"

"I think you're confusing me with your mailman. But that's not to say you can't call me in the dead of night."

Mistake.

Polly scuttled back further in the rocker. "So is that the end of the official interrogation?"

"For now," said Willy formally. And he had no time for the unofficial. Two bodies. And still he stood and walked toward the lone picture on the wall—a black-and-white photograph of James Dean. It wasn't the picture that interested him, it was its location—halfway between couch and chair.

Polly slid out of the chair and came to stand beside him. "So I suppose you've got a million things to do now?"

"A million and one. Now if I could only remember what they were."

She smiled up at him, temporarily forgetting to run for cover, and Willy almost forgot the rule he'd made for himself. *Go slow here.* He'd never had a Summer of Love. He'd never had much of a fall or winter or spring, for that matter. But this woman,

33

he hoped, was going to be his lifetime of it. And obviously she wasn't ready for what he was ready for. So let her pick her pace. There would be no coercion here.

Willy brushed his lips to her left eyebrow and got out of there.

❖5❖

"**W**HO?" SAID PETE, slapping peanut butter on crackers. He had his mind on other things. Like packing Lucy's snack for kindergarten. Like getting her to the bus on time.

Like Susan Jameson.

"Manuel Rose," said Willy. "I'm told he usually went by the name of Manny. A trawl fisherman, supposedly lost at sea in the early 1930s. Which makes that bullet in the back of the head most interesting."

As if a bullet in the back of a head wasn't interesting enough already. From upstairs Pete heard Connie calling to Lucy. Something about there being no time for bubbles. Or was it rubles? With Connie it was never safe to assume.

"And Susan?" Pete listened to his own voice. Was it cool? Detached? At least fifteen years worth of detached, anyway?

Sure.

Maybe.

35

"They used computerized axial tomography on the skull."

"CT scan? What they use to find tumors in live people?"

"Right. Nifty idea of some forensic anthropologist they called in. He found bone fragmentation in the forehead consistent with a blow from a sharp, handheld object."

Pete set the peanut butter knife on the counter. He breathed in and out twice. When he spoke again his voice was good and even, he was sure of it. "Meaning somebody hit her."

"That's what it looks like."

"Killed her."

"Apparently."

"On purpose?"

"The hitting, yes. The killing, not necessarily."

"But once she was dead they didn't exactly come rushing up to my house to call the police, now, did they?"

"Well, no," said Willy.

Pete picked up the knife and threw it into the sink. He must have used more force than he meant to; it ricocheted off the enamel, sailed through the air, and clattered onto the floor close enough to the chief to cause him to leap backward.

"Jesus," said Willy. "Two murders are enough for one week. Calm down, will you?"

"I am calm." But this time Pete didn't need to pause to listen to his own voice. He knew he was neither cool nor detached. He zipped Lucy's crackers into a plastic bag, snapped a banana out of the bunch, opened the refrigerator.

"We need to go over a few things," said Willy.

"Such as?"

"Such as these friends she went to stay with."

"I don't know who they were. She left a note. Said she'd met up with some friends and was going to stay with them for a few days."

"Did you save that note?"

"It wasn't the kind of note you'd save."

"Not like the postcard?"

Pete didn't answer.

"How was this note different from the postcard?"

Pete slammed the refrigerator door. Or he tried to. Refrigerator doors didn't slam, he discovered. So he opened it again, just to have somewhere to look. "For one thing, that note was scribbled on a piece of Kleenex. For another, I didn't think it was the last I'd see of her. She said she'd be back in a few days."

"And you knew nothing of these friends. Never heard her mention any names, addresses, places she might have lived? She had a dentist in Weams Point. The postcard came from there. It never occurred to you that—"

"I didn't know anything about any dentist. She told me she wasn't from here."

Willy stood up. "I'll have to talk to her family."

"Susan had no family. I told you that. Or weren't you listening?"

Willy didn't answer him. When Pete looked up he saw the chief watching him curiously. "Look," said Willy finally. "I didn't exactly get the idea the other day that I had to tiptoe around your feelings. If I'm wrong, correct me."

"Why, so you can run home for your ballet shoes?"

"I've got questions I have to ask. If you—"

"So ask."

"Were you in love with her?"

It wasn't a question Pete had expected. And it wasn't one he felt like he wanted to answer, either. He stalled, and eventually he heard something that might save him. Feet on stairs, some soft, some loud. The kitchen door opened. He watched Connie zero in on the empty snack pack on the counter, at Pete standing idle in front of the refrigerator.

"What is this? You said you'd do snack. We're late already."

"I did snack." Pete extracted a box of juice from the refrigerator, threw it and the crackers and the banana in the pack, and zipped it closed.

"Cookies!" said Lucy.

Pete opened the cupboard. No cookies.

"Didn't you buy cookies?" he said to Connie.

Willy reached into his shirt pocket and pulled out a lollipop. "Will this do?" He tossed it on the counter. Pete opened the pack and zipped it in before Connie could say anything. Connie didn't go for lollipops, but Pete couldn't remember the reason. He scooped up bag and Lucy and ran.

He was getting faster. He actually caught the bus at the corner. He waved till it was out of sight, which was probably just the wrong thing to do. He couldn't even see the kid, couldn't tell if she was waving back or hiding from the guy making a fool of himself out in the street, but whatever instinct he possessed about these things, it told him to keep waving. Who else was there to wave at her?

After the bus had disappeared Pete took his time walking home, partly so he could catch his breath, partly so he could do some thinking without anyone watching. And the more he thought the slower he went, until finally he was standing stock-still in the middle of the road. If he could just explain it to Connie. . . . But he couldn't explain what he didn't understand himself, now, could he? The pit in his stomach. The questions in his head. Someone had killed Susan Jameson. Someone had buried her here, on his marsh. For fifteen years she had been lying out there. And no matter how hard he tried, he couldn't reconcile the fact of her death with the fantasy . . .

He walked in calling her name. No answer. He made a quick foray through the tiny cottage. No Susan. The disappointment was like death. She was gone. He stepped out on the porch and came back to life. There she was, out on the marsh, like one of those snowy egrets that landed there now and then, her red hair aflame, her white dress fluorescent from the late-day sun. He walked out to meet her. She saw him but ran on ahead of him, plopping and plooshing through the low spots, muddy to the calves, not caring that the brand-new dress was splattered, stopping and calling out to him every time she came upon a shell or a flower or a new kind of grass. And every time he told her what something was—ribbed mussel, sea lavender, spartina—she'd smile back at him like he'd created them himself, sprinkled them over the marsh just to make her happy.

Happy.

That was what it was, Pete decided. She'd been here for three whole days and for every minute of it he'd been happy. It was some kind of record. And in all due modesty, nothing he'd done so far seemed to have disappointed her any.

Like now.

He caught up with her along the dune, in a gentle hollow the wind had carved out for them. When she looked up at him it was as if she'd waded through all those bad times just so she could land there in that hollow, just so they could make love in the cool sand with the sun's last best efforts washing over them.

Willy squinted out the window at Pete. The man was beginning to concern him.

"Now what's he doing?" said Connie from behind him.

"Standing in the road. Maybe I should get him."

"Leave him alone. Maybe if he gets hit it'll knock his brains back into him. So I heard your question. Let me know if he answers you."

"I was hoping you'd know the answer."

"It doesn't matter what I know. It's what he thinks that matters. So what's happened?"

Willy told her. Manny Rose *and* Susan Jameson. Murdered.

Connie opened and closed her mouth, issuing no sound. The minute Lucy had arrived, Connie had announced she was going to clean up her language. She'd made a valiant effort, but it seemed to have reduced her vocabulary considerably.

"A word of warning," said Willy. "Our friend

isn't handling this latest news about Susan too gracefully."

"Tell me about it." After a second Connie added, "And what do you think that means, exactly?"

"Dunno. Maybe he killed her."

"Thanks."

"Has he talked to you about her?"

"A little. Not much. I admit it might have gone better if I hadn't called him a schmuck."

Willy grinned. He was relieved to see she was able to grin back at him. And finally she asked him the question that Willy had perhaps naively expected someone to ask a while ago. "So what were Susan Jameson and Manny Rose doing in the same hole on the marsh?"

"Search me. But Manny Rose was in it for fifty years before Susan joined him."

Connie pondered that in silence, but seemed to get nowhere. "So what's next?" she asked finally.

"The Widow Rose."

"She's still alive?"

"So I'm told," said Willy.

Alive, yes, thought Willy, but barely. He walked along the sterile halls trying not to look left or right at the hunched forms in wheelchairs, the motionless shapes just visible through open doors, laid out between crisp sheets. When the nurse stopped in front of one particular door and waved him ahead of her, he had to fight off an urge to pivot and run.

Alice Rose? He peered down at the shrivelled skin over shrunken flesh over gnarled bone. At ninety-two she was hardly less of a skeleton than her husband Manny. She lay on her back with her eyes closed, so still and colorless that Willy was tempted to call for the coroner.

"I don't know why you bother," said the nurse at Willy's elbow. "She never speaks. Hasn't for years and years. Did a little when she first came, but one day she looked up at Mr. Finnell and said, 'I'm losing my marbles, aren't I?' Hasn't said another word since."

"Let's try, shall we?"

The nurse cupped the frail shoulder and shook it gently. "Alice. Wake up, Alice. You have a visitor."

The widow's eyes snapped open, brown and bright, suddenly filling the wasted form with life.

"This is Police Chief McOwat," said the nurse. "He'd like to speak with you for a moment."

The only response was some blinking.

"Mrs. Rose," said Willy unhopefully, "do you understand who I am?"

Nothing.

"I'm Police Chief McOwat. We've found your husband's body, Mrs. Rose."

The eyes closed.

"Mrs. Rose?"

Nothing.

"See?" said the nurse. "I told you not to bother. Besides, what difference could it make to her now?"

It might not have made a difference to *her*, thought Willy, but it could have made a big difference to *him*.

Once outside the nursing home he breathed deeply, got into his Ford Explorer, and sat there. He pulled out his notebook, leafed through, re-

viewed his options. He still had to talk to Factotum's old employees, Tim St. George and Hugh
Peletier. Maybe even Rita Peck's ex-husband. If
Susan Jameson was etched into the man's brain the
way Rita had implied, he should be useful.

But in the end, it was his own curiosity that
got him.

He tracked down Tim St. George in the hospital
in Bradford, on the mainland peninsula, and what
he found there gave him a moment's pause. Not
the man's looks. Whatever Polly's opinion might
have been, Willy found him uninspiring. He was
probably around Willy's age, early forties, although
a less-trained eye might have placed him younger.
Average height—average, at least, if you came at it
from the perspective of Willy's six feet four inches.
Mouse-colored hair trimmed a little too nineties for
Willy's taste; he preferred a good run-in every few
weeks with a pair of clippers. And yes, the man
was in shape, neatly squared off like a piece of furniture, but it had been Willy's experience that sheer
mass came in handy from time to time. No, it
wasn't the looks that gave Willy pause, it was the
profession. Tim St. George was a doctor. An inter-
nist, to be exact.

And Willy was forced to cool his heels in the
hospital corridors for twenty minutes, waiting until
the good doctor could see him.

But Tim St. George finally led him to a private
office that wasn't much to Willy's taste, either, full
of lots of metal and very little wood. Willy sank

into one chair that looked like a pants presser. Tim St. George draped himself over the other.

"I apologize for the delay. I'm sure you know how it is. We have a gentleman with pancreatitis, liver failure, emphysema, diabetes. We admit him and all we manage to do for him is to give him pneumonia." He smiled, tired but friendly. "Now. How may I help you?"

"By possessing a good memory. We've looked into some events that occurred fifteen years ago, prompted by the recent recovery of the body of one Susan Jameson. I believe you worked with her at Peter Bartholomew's odd-job company, Factotum."

The change in St. George's face was probably only visible to someone who was looking for it, like Willy. But that was part of what this guy did, Willy imagined—looked blank-faced at a patient while he thought, *You poor bugger, you'll be dead by Labor Day*.

"I worked for Pete one summer years ago. I remember that, surely."

"Fifteen years ago. And do you remember Susan Jameson?"

"Vaguely."

Now there's a new one, thought Willy. He decided he'd better make sure they were on the same page. "Could you describe her for me?"

"I remember she had the kind of skin that should avoid the sun. She got a bad burn one day and I recall thinking, 'In twenty years we'll be talking melanoma.'"

"And . . . the rest of her?" asked Willy lamely.

"Well, let's see. She had the hair that went with

44

the skin. Red. Long. Attractive woman. What happened to her? Or did you say?"

Willy studied St. George curiously. He knew doctors became numb to many things, but he'd imagined they'd at least pay attention when you told them you'd just found an old acquaintance's dead body. "Pete and his young ward found her skull out on the marsh in front of his cottage. It had been there a long time. Which is why we're so interested in the particular summer in question."

"Pete and his ward?"

"A five-year-old girl. He and his wife took her in when her mother got killed."

St. George smiled. "So Pete has a wife. And a ward."

"You might remember the wife, actually. Connie Benz."

There was a pause. "Yes, I do remember her."

"They got married a month ago."

If you didn't count the first time twelve years ago.

St. George's smile went the same kind of wistful Willy had felt on his own face of late. "I'm surprised it took them that long. Although I do seem to recall there was a period when his attentions were—" he stopped.

"Elsewhere?"

"No. No, not at all. If you see them, please do give them my best. Was there anything else?"

"Yes," said Willy. Obviously. What was it with this clown? "Susan Jameson," he prompted him.

"If you mean where was I fifteen years ago when she died, I'm afraid I can't help you. And let's face it, it would be quite a stretch if I could, don't you think?"

Yes, thought Willy, especially since they didn't know when she'd died. But did St. George? "I'd appreciate anything about her you can remember. Strictly for the purposes of background."

"I see. All right." St. George's even features crumpled slightly as he concentrated. "It's a long time ago. But you understand that, obviously. Let's see. I suppose my overriding impression, other than the things I've already mentioned, was of an impulsive nature. But I base it on nothing more than her methods of arrival and departure. Touching down out of the blue, disappearing the same way some months later."

"Some months?"

"Or however many weeks. I have no idea, really. I was what you would call a summer hire, I left after Labor Day. I do recall a decent interval between our departures, if that helps you any."

Tim St. George snuck a look at his watch, again the kind of look someone else might have missed. Another doctor move. Time's up. Next patient, please.

Willy ignored it.

"Can you recall any conversations you might have had with her previous to her departure?"

"I can't recall any conversations with her at all. What with all the coming and going."

"And what with her being involved with someone else," added Willy.

Was that a wince? If it was, it was quickly smiled over. "So you know about her and Pete. Or was that one of those trick statements to break through my deflective maneuvers?"

"No trick. Pete came clean on his own."

"And you say he was the one who discovered the body. And obviously informed you immediately. So he's not on your suspect list anyway." Another smile, but tiring fast now, confined to the mouth only.

See, Polly? thought Willy. It wasn't just the cops who turned to the boyfriends first. You found a murdered woman, that's where you looked. Husbands. Boyfriends. The odds were good she'd been killed by one of them. Hell, the statistics were in the paper every day. And Tim St. George, not knowing how well Willy knew Pete, had felt the urge to protect his old boss, Susan Jameson's last known boyfriend.

So, enough. Willy stood up, handing St. George a card. "If you remember anything else, I'd appreciate a call. No matter how trivial it might seem to you. You never know with these things."

"No, I don't suppose you do."

Willy walked to the door.

"You say he's still right there, in that same cottage on the marsh?"

"Pete? Still there. Still odd-jobbing. Still hiring every loose screw he—" Willy stopped. Large foot in large mouth on that one.

But St. George only smiled. "He did tend toward a rather motley crew, didn't he? And I was as motley as the rest of them. Please do be sure to give them my best wishes."

"Sure," said Willy.

❖6❖

CONNIE WAS ON her knees on the bathroom floor, mopping up the aftermath of Lucy's bath, when she heard him coming up the stairs. Finally. He stopped at the bathroom door, but she was the one who spoke first. "There has to be a way to wash a kid and leave the water in the tub."

"Define schmuck," Pete answered her.

"Somebody who can't see beyond the end of his—"

"All right, I get the picture."

Connie straightened. It was a much more painful procedure since Lucy'd come to live with them. There were times when it was simply easier to pick her up and move her than to apply the rules of reason, but that method wasn't going to work forever. Hell, even now the kid could have jumped out the window in the time it took Connie to unlock her vertebrae. . . . But the minute Connie caught a good look at Pete's face her mental Lucy digressions ceased. She'd never seen this particular look before. It was a mix of the one she'd seen on Lucy when they gave her her first helium balloon, combined with the one when the kid in the parking lot snatched it away from her. And toss in a little of the snatcher. So would somebody please tell her what was going on around here? She tried to remember what Willy had said. He'd tried to warn her, but to do what, exactly?

"Look," she said finally, "I'm sorry. I guess this must be doing some weird things to you. It's bad enough for me and I wasn't the one who was—" She paused. "What were you two, anyway?"

"We were . . . involved."

"Involved. Now there's a word that could use some defining."

"I know how you'd define it. But we did other things, too."

"Like what, for instance?"

"Walking. Talking. We shared many of the same interests, actually."

With considerable effort, Connie restrained a snort. "Such as?"

"Nashtoba. Nature. History."

"*History?*"

"I was a history major, in case you've forgotten. Hard to believe, I know, a woman actually interested in my field of endeavor."

Connie managed to let that one go, too. Barely. And since Pete didn't disappear, she decided he must want to keep at it for some reason. So she said, "Not so hard to believe. Especially since I've been thinking maybe she didn't dump you."

"Generous of you."

"No, I mean it. Or if she did dump you, she changed her mind. She was found out on that marsh, wasn't she? Why else would she come back if it wasn't for you? The old change of heart. It's happened before. It's gotten to be a real thing with you. No matter how hard they try, your women just can't seem to leave you."

Pete's face changed drastically and instantly. For the better, Connie was happy to note. He took a step nearer, brushed back her hair, kissed her on the temple. "And for one particular doomed effort I'm eternally grateful."

Which was all well and good, thought Connie, but she knew Pete, and he still had a "but" hanging around in there somewhere. Or maybe it was an "and." On the whole, she figured, an "and" would be better. "And?" she prompted.

"I want to go to Weams Point."

She should have figured. The last known address of Susan Jameson and all that rot. She pulled away from him. "So go."

"You'll meet the bus?"

"I'll meet the bus."

He would have hit the door right then if Connie hadn't grabbed him by the shirt. "Just for the record, you've noticed how great I'm being about all this?"

He actually grinned. "Duly noted."

"But if she were still alive I'd have you castrated before you left the house. So duly note that."

The grin faded.

As soon as Pete's truck pulled out, Connie looked at the clock. An hour and a half till bus time. She could faintly remember a time in her life when whole days went by without her once looking at the clock. Now, it was always either breakfasttime, bathtime, bustime, bedtime. Bedtime. She could go to bed now and sleep till Monday. Now that she thought about it, she couldn't remember the last time she and Pete had climbed into bed to do anything but fall unconscious. She couldn't remember the last time she'd climbed out of it when her body was actually ready to.

Connie heard a door downstairs and looked at the clock in panic. Had she daydreamed away an hour and a half? Had she missed the bus? No. She heard the familiar "Halloo" echo up the stairs.

Willy.

She hallooed back, and he came up the stairs by twos, meeting her in the hallway.

"If you're looking for Pete, he's in Weams Point. A sudden, burning desire to trace Susan Jameson's final movements. Or so I gather."

Willy squinted at her. It was his version of the traditional raised eyebrow. More or less.

"How was the Widow Rose?" she asked politely.

"Non compos mentis."

"What does that mean when it's in living language?"

"It means she's past caring why or where we found her husband's body. She hasn't spoken in years. And she didn't speak to me. The St. George fellow spoke, but he was useless." Willy paused. "You remember this St. George?"

What was it with these guys? Obviously poor old Manny Rose was going to get a half hour of lip service while they chased around avenging this piece of white trash. "I remember him," said Connie. She could tell Willy was waiting for her to say more.

So she said nothing.

The hell with him.

She supposed it was in the interest of evening things up that she found herself ten minutes later sitting in a small, straight chair across the bed from Alice Rose. But once she saw the tiny shell of a woman in the railed bed she had a feeling she was right to come. She still remembered her own first introduction to the police chief—his size alone, emphasized when in uniform, had sent her into the particular brazen hussy mode she used when most intimidated. And much bigger men and women than Alice Rose had decided not to mess with him.

"Mrs. Rose, my name is Connie Bartholomew."

Nothing.

"I try to tell you people," said the nurse.

"Would you excuse us, please?" said Connie.

The nurse huffed out of the room. Connie drew her chair closer and laid a hand across the old woman's swollen, twisted knuckles. The touch at least served to bring the eyes into focus on Connie's face. "Mrs. Rose, I know you don't know me. I'm not even sure why I'm here. I guess I thought I ought to make sure you understood about your husband. About how they found him. It was my husband who found him. I don't know if you know Pete. He lives out there in that cottage on the marsh. He's lived there for, oh, sixteen years, at least. I haven't been there as long. Well, sort of off and on, actually." She rambled on. She doubted Alice had a clue what she was saying. Half the time Connie didn't have a clue what she was saying. But Alice's eyes remained fixed on her face, and eventually it dawned on Connie that every time she said the name "Manny" the fingers under her hand twitched.

"Mrs. Rose," she said finally. "You understand me, don't you? You know what I'm saying? You understand where Manny is?"

The puckered mouth opened like a baby bird's beak, looking for regurgitated worm. She made a squawk that sounded like worm coming the other way, followed by what sounded like "Run, geek."

"What?" said Connie.

"Glem." Another squawk, this one loud enough to bring the sound of footsteps. The black eyes darted to the door. "Won't talk, glem," said Alice Rose. "Won't talk. Geep money."

"What?" said Connie again.

"What's going on?" said the nurse behind them. "Is she choking? Here we go, dear, upsy daisy." The nurse raised the head of the bed and Alice came with it, black eyes still fixed on Connie.

Connie refused to relinquish the disfigured hand. She tried again and again, mentioning Manny's name.

And got nothing.

Pete didn't leave Nashtoba too often these days, mostly because he hadn't found much out there to improve on his own backyard. But each time he

did cross the old wood causeway that connected
Nashtoba to the mainland peninsula, he felt less
and less like he belonged there. Even that small
leap sped up the world too much for his liking,
crowded it with buildings, people, cars. But at least
this time he could avoid the highway west toward
real civilization, and head in the other direction to
the tip of Cape Hook. It was an hour ride to Weams
Point, but the further out he went, the more it got
like Nashtoba.

Until you got to Weams Point itself.

He supposed that at one time you would have
called Weams Point the metropolis of Cape Hook,
but a metropolis based on sea routes, not land ones.
Every kid in Weams Point was born with his hand
not far from a tiller, but they still told stories about
the first horse that had arrived there, how everyone
assumed you'd steer him by the tail, the closest
thing they could find to a rudder. It was only a
matter of time before the artists discovered the pic-
turesque seafaring village with the cheap, off-season
rents, and as the fishing industry had declined,
more and more of the locals turned to tourism. Pete
never knew what in particular had attracted Weams
Point's gay community, unless it was the simple
fact that the Weams Pointers tended to live and let
live. And there you had the interesting mix that
made up the modern-day Weams Point.

There were two roads through town—Front
Street, which ran along the waterfront, and Back
Street, which didn't. Front Street was crowded with
shops and galleries and eateries. Back Street was
just as structurally crowded, with residences and

quiet inns, but without the summer hordes. At this time of year, however, both streets were equally deserted. But Pete knew where a person in need of information should go, and he went there.

There were plenty of places in Weams Point that opened their doors Memorial Day weekend and shut up tight as a clam come Labor Day, but the Galley wasn't one of them. The Galley was busy all day, all night, all year. It was kept dark in the Galley, Pete supposed, so the fishermen fresh off the water at six in the morning wouldn't feel so strange ordering a shot and a beer, to them their evening cocktail. The breakfasters in the booths behind them didn't seem to mind the scent of whiskey in the air, and, conversely, the evening revelers didn't blink when the coffee and eggs went back and forth as fast as the drinks. There were no frills at the Galley, but there was a woman with a good fast draw at the bar and another who served up plenty of good, hot food in the kitchen.

Pete went straight for the bar, where two old men sat watching World Series highlights on television. Pete sat three stools away from the nearest occupant. It never paid to crowd a New Englander. The bartender had been there forever—a big, black-haired, blue-eyed woman who Pete happened to know was named Eileen Carey but, for reasons that were never clear to Pete, went by the name of Patsy. She slapped a cardboard coaster down and cocked an eyebrow.

"Ballantine," said Pete. "And a Reuben. "

Patsy nodded in approval. Anyone who ordered the Reuben knew what he was doing.

Pete had given some thought as to the best way to attack his quest for information, and he'd settled on the dumb-direct. "I'm looking for Susan Jameson," he said as Patsy plonked his Ballantine in front of him.

"Too late." She disappeared into the kitchen.

Pete waited, sipping his Ballantine.

"Susan got dug up someplace over on Nashtoba last weekend," said a voice three stools to his right.

Pete turned from the neck only. Not only didn't it pay to crowd but it also didn't pay to look too eager. "That so?"

It was the dirty canvas coat, greasy gray hair, faded blue baseball cap with the logo Bob's Excavating that answered him. "But you're looking in the wrong place, anyway. Susan ain't been here in more'n a decade."

"Decade and a half," said a white crew cut in bib-overalls. "You ask Rosella, she'll tell you."

Bob's Excavating guffawed. "Right, you do that. You ask Rosella."

"Rosella?"

"Her sister. Corner of Back Street and Governor Bradford. White house, black shutters."

It was a setup if Pete ever heard one, but all he said was, "Thanks, I'll do that."

Pete's sandwich came, and it was even better than he'd remembered. He ate in silence, waiting. They had more to tell, and if he knew his old geezers, they were busting to tell it.

"You knew these Jamesons pretty good, didn't you?" said Bibs to Bob's Excavating.

"The parents, sure. Pretty good. Pretty good. Damn shame."

"First trip, wunnit?"

"First trip. And the damn plane explodes under 'em. Left the two girls alone."

"No more family," said Bibs.

"No family. And then those girls not speaking. How long that went on for?"

"Still going," said Patsy, collecting Pete's empty plate.

Bibs nodded sagely. "Silence beyond the grave."

And speaking of silence seemed to remind them they should be doing more of it.

They returned, in unison, to the television.

So Susan Jameson had a sister right here in Weams Point. A sister she didn't speak to. Maybe that explained why she'd never mentioned her. Pete stepped out of the Galley and onto Back Street and looked to the right, in the direction of Governor Bradford Lane. There it was—white house, black shutters. He marched up the steps, lifted and dropped the brass knocker.

He could hear heavy footsteps. He saw a closed blind to the right of the door flutter. He saw the tarnished brass doorknob turning, a crack of darkness, a round, white face, graying red hair.

Susan Jameson's sister.

It had to be.

But could it be?

The woman was . . . well, what was the point in hedging? The woman was just about the least attractive woman Pete had ever seen. It wasn't just the folds of white flesh or the unkempt hair or the grimy polyester pantsuit. This went beyond skin deep. This went to something way down behind the eyes.

There was nothing in there.

"Rosella?" asked Pete.

Without a word she turned and waddled down the hall. Since nobody told him not to, Pete followed. She turned into a shuttered room, the only light a flickering TV screen. She collapsed heavily onto a couch that was threadbare in one large swath where she sat. She picked up the TV remote and began to click through the channels.

Pete cleared his throat. "You are Rosella? Susan Jameson's sister?"

She looked at him. Sort of. Pete supposed he could even make a case for the fact that she nodded.

He decided the only way he was going to get anywhere here was to blast right through the dead cells. "I'm Peter Bartholomew," he said. "I've just found your sister's body."

She changed channels.

❖7❖

WILLY McOWAT DIDN'T have to wait as long for the Summer of Love's last remaining Factotum employee, Hugh Peletier, but that was all that could be said for him. He'd come up in the world since his days at Factotum—he was the owner of Bradford Marina on the mainland peninsula, which didn't sound like much until Willy found out that Bradford Marina owned a quarter of the Bradford waterfront.

Willy stood on the dock and waited while a hireling went to fetch Peletier. When the man appeared, he had a long, ugly fishing gaff slung over his shoulder. Accident or design? Willie decided to reserve judgment. Hugh Peletier couldn't have been much more than thirty if he'd been in high school fifteen years ago, but he looked older. No more than five feet ten and slight, but the kind of slight that was all coiled steel wire. He stopped in front of the chief and shot out his chin in a gesture Willy knew well, the type of gesture used to balance old chips on the shoulder. "You looking for me?"

"If you're Hugh Peletier. If you used to work at Factotum."

"You got some problem?"

"Yes, as a matter of fact. A dead body. Susan Jameson. Remember her?"

Yes, obviously. Hugh Peletier swallowed several times.

"Her body was found last Sunday on the marsh in front of your old place of employment. It had been there some time. I'd be interested in anything you can tell me about her."

"Such as?"

"Let's start with the last time you saw her."

A half-second hesitation there. "Who knows? She came, she left, I hardly knew her. She was out of my league."

"Meaning?"

"Meaning the Susan Jamesons in this world don't notice grubby little high school kids like me."

"Who do they notice?"

"How should I know?"

"You weren't aware of a relationship between Susan Jameson and Peter Bartholomew?"

More chin action. "You go ask him about that, why don't you?"

"I have."

"So what are you asking me for?"

"Because you were there. I'll ask you again. Who noticed Susan? Other than your boss. This St. George fellow?"

Peletier laughed. "The old college pal? Mucking with Pete's girl? Wrong profile. Strictly the all-for-one-and-one-for-all school."

"And you?"

"You mean if she'd noticed me, would I have done something about it? Sure."

Willy studied the little pit bull in front of him. This, at least, he believed. But there was more, here, he was sure. He looked around the dock. "Guess things worked out all right for you in the long run."

The chin again. "You got some problem with that?"

Willy decided to reserve judgment there, too. He handed Peletier his card. "If you recall anything about Susan Jameson that might aid the investigation, I'd appreciate a call."

"Like where I buried her, you mean?"

"I have the *where*, Mr. Peletier. It's the *why* I'm after."

"Don't you mean *who*?"

Willy just smiled. With punks like Baby Hughie, it was the worst thing you could do to them.

But as Willy drove away, he pondered. Was this the second of Pete's old employees seemingly hell-bent on protecting him from suspicion, or did Hughie like obstructing justice on general principle?

The latter, most likely.

Rita Peck had just returned the fertilizer spreader to the shed, stashed the newspapers, and kicked the rubber raft when she happened to look up and see the woman in the doorway. She could tell she'd been thinking way too much about Susan Jameson by the fact that the red hair nearly gave her a heart attack. But this was no Susan Jameson. For one thing, her eyes were hazel, not green. For another, she was about five feet ten inches tall and thin as a rail. And for yet another, she was apparently more inclined to conceal flesh than to reveal it, since most of it was covered with a bulky sweater and a pair of baggy denim overalls.

"I'm Phoebe Small," she said in a way that allowed little inclination for any jokes about the height. "I heard rumors you were hiring."

"It's under discussion," said Rita. She introduced herself. Phoebe Small stepped forward and shook her hand vigorously. "Do you know what kinds of things we do here?" asked Rita.

"Everything, I'm told. Sounds interesting." She looked around, and Rita looked with her. In addition to the larger things in the middle of the room, like the deflated rubber raft and the ripped sails and the broken deck chairs and the giant, half-painted papier-mâché pumpkin, there was an entire wall of shelves filled with things like unframed pictures, unpainted shutters, unwired lamps, unpatched bicycle tires.

They certainly needed help, thought Rita, discouraged. She returned to the study of the newcomer. "How old are you, if I may ask?"

"I don't think you're supposed to, actually."

Oh, really? And what was the big secret? She was a decade or two younger than Rita, and you didn't see Rita quibbling about it, especially not with total strangers. "I believe I am allowed to ask what you've been doing up to now?"

"School, mainly."

So she was one of those perpetual students who collected useless degrees until the parents finally pulled the plug. And was this what they needed? No. What they needed was someone easygoing and personable, with a wide variety of work experience and not one kernel of professional or financial ambition. Another Pete, for example. And where in the world would she ever find another one of those?

The door banged behind them twice, in quick succession, and Rita turned to see Pete, Connie, and Lucy all bunched up in front of it, staring. The red hair? Probably. Rita introduced them. Pete and Connie stepped forward to shake Phoebe's hand. Neither of them said anything about the height-name business, either. Phoebe seemed to know better than to accost Lucy, but she did wink at her.

"So why don't you tell us something about yourself," said Rita.

"Yikes. Okay, let's see. I grew up in Elder Bay. Went to school in Boston. I probably can't do all kinds of work, but I'll try anything once. Except raw fish. I'm great at puzzles. I'm terrible at Parcheesi. I'm also terrible at poker, but I love it anyway. I also love ballet." And here she executed a quick series of pliés and relevés, finishing off with a camped-up pirouette that was obviously for the little girl's benefit. Sure enough, it set Lucy giggling.

Once Rita had sufficiently recovered from the impromptu dance recital, she opened her mouth to ask the usual questions. Driver's license? Skill with tools? Paintbrushes? Gardening implements? Animals? And what exactly was all this schooling in, anyway?

But Pete beat her to it. "Why are you terrible at Parcheesi?"

"I don't know. I can never keep up those barricades. And I hate to send people back."

"And poker?"

"Oh, that's different. That's because I won't fold. I mean, what's the fun if you're not even playing?"

Rita raised an eyebrow at Pete, but he didn't see it. Would it have mattered if he had?

"When can you start?" he asked.

"Yikes," said Phoebe again. "Can you give me an hour?"

"Sure," said Pete, beaming at her.

Rita made a valiant attempt to hide her displeasure. Connie didn't bother.

Willy was stretched on Polly's couch with his notebook, trying to pretend he was working, but in actual fact he was watching Polly in the kitchen, measuring out coffee. There was a knock at the door, and Polly went to answer it. When Willy heard the brother's voice, his old-fashioned instinct shot him upright.

"Sorry to bug you," said Pete. "Rita finally found this and she left it with me to drop by the station, but I got hung up with Lucy. I saw your car was here—" His voice trailed off awkwardly.

Willy reached out and took the paper he offered. A copy of Susan Jameson's W-2.

"It was the only sample of Susan's writing Rita could find. You've still got that postcard?"

"I've got it. Want me to laminate it before I give it back?"

Pete ignored him. "I've got a piece of information for you, if you're interested. Susan Jameson apparently grew up in Weams Point, where she has an estranged sister named Rosella. The family home is on the corner of Back Street and Governor Bradford. The sister still lives there. And she was not completely crushed by the news of her sister's death. Good night."

Pete left. Polly shut the door after him. Willy stood up reluctantly. He had questions, more of them coming at him with every second he stood there. "Polly, I have to talk to Pete about this."

She nodded, not exactly disappointed, not exactly relieved. In other words, the usual.

Willy caught up with Pete in his kitchen. The rest of the house was quiet and dark, making Willy feel like an intruder. Or maybe it was because Pete avoided settling into the chairs, opting to lean against the kitchen counter instead. Willy went for a chair anyway.

"What?" said Pete.

There were so many whats that Willy didn't know where to start. "Susan grew up in Weams Point."

"Apparently."

"But when she met you she said she had no family or friends in the area."

"Her parents were dead. She wasn't speaking to her sister."

"Why not?"

"I don't know. She never told me she had a sister."

65

"Or friends."

Pete didn't answer.

"This didn't strike you as strange. A woman down on her luck, an hour away from her hometown, and the best she can come up with is you."

"Thanks."

"I'm not arguing she didn't make out okay."

"She made out dead, that's how she made out."

Willy rubbed his face with his hand. "Let's back up, shall we? We're talking about the initial contact. A woman from Weams Point—"

"I didn't know she was from Weams Point. She said she had no family, no friends. She obviously didn't feel there was anyone she could go back to. What do you want? She said she was in trouble. I didn't give her the third degree, I gave her a job."

"And a room. And a few other comforts. All of which she accepted without the bat of an eye until she decided out of the blue to go stay with these friends she said she had none of."

"So?"

"So your answer to my question is that none of this struck you as strange until last Saturday when you fished her out of the—"

Pete pushed away from the counter. "Yeah, that was strange. I'll give you that was very strange. Kiss a woman good-bye and the next time you see her you mistake her for a volleyball. Are you through?"

Willy pushed back his chair. He felt old. Tired. "I'll be through when I know who killed Susan Jameson. In the interim I would like you to consider the importance of those friends of Susan Jameson's.

66

I don't think I need to spell it out for you. As it now stands, they were the last people to see her alive. I would like to talk to them. I will go door-to-door in Weams Point if I have to. But I would like you to try to remember if she mentioned any names in the five weeks that she lived here. You know where to find me if you do."

Willy said good-bye. Pete didn't. When Willy got outside, he looked up at Polly's windows.

Black all around.

Connie got undressed, but before she slid into bed she thought better of it. If she got into bed she'd go to sleep, and she didn't want to go to sleep until Pete got back from seeing the chief. She pulled on Pete's threadbare corduroy robe, bunched up the pillows to keep her upright, plopped down on top of the quilt, flicked on the television, and saw, not Cary Grant and Joan Fontaine, but Pete and Susan Jameson.

So they walked the beach. So they talked about things. Well, so did Pete and Connie. Or they used to, anyway. Now they read Winnie-the-Pooh and said eat-your-carrots and don't-jump-off-the-porch-rail and I-thought-you-bought-the-cookies. And when was the last time they'd walked the beach, just the two of them? Connie couldn't remember. But she could sure remember the last time she'd seen Pete "walking" it with Susan Jameson. Connie had arrived back at Factotum after a long, hot day that had ended with a long, hot ride to the airport to pick up Eva Maxwell's cousin. Everyone else had gone home, except for the people who lived there, but she'd found no sign around the house of either Pete or Susan, which had suited her just fine. She'd decided to cool off with a nice, solitary beach walk before she went home herself . . .

Or not so solitary.

She caught the flash of the red hair the minute she hit the sand. They were maybe fifty feet to the left of her, standing on the lip of dune between beach and marsh. She was sure they didn't see her. She saw Pete raise an arm and point backward, tracing the line of the creek, saw him raise the other arm and pull the woman in close, still pointing.

Oh, puke.

Connie tucked her head and pushed on down the beach in the opposite direction, but the voices floated after her from upwind. That figured. Well, she didn't have to listen. She waded into the water calf-deep and splashed loudly, but she couldn't help catching a few words now and then. "Did it? . . . such a drastic . . . how many years . . . boats here . . . this creek? Rumrunners? . . . *how* interesting . . ."

Blah blah blah. Puke, puke, puke. Like Susan Jameson was real interested in rumrunning. Connie clambered out of the water and pushed eastward along the sand, making a concerted effort to empty her mind of everything, but especially Peter Bartholomew and Susan Jameson. She'd actually done it, too, until she turned back and rounded the point and there they were, Susan Jameson on her back in the sand, Pete on his knees, Susan pulling at his belt buckle.

Connie had to hand it to the man—even in the heat of passion he managed to hang onto his peripheral vision.

There was a sudden check in the descent, followed by a drop-and-roll onto the right hip that instantly and effectively shielded Susan from her view.

Or vice versa.

"What are you doing?"

Connie snapped into focus to find Pete in the door and a bunch of fuzz on the television. "I don't know. I must have leaned on the remote." She switched off.

"Lucy's still asleep?"

"Lucy's still asleep. And even more strange, I'm still awake. I figured if I waited up we could have a whole conversation."

He paused halfway out of his shirt. "Conversation?"

"You know. One of those things where you tell me about your visit to Weams Point and I tell you about my visit to Alice Rose."

Pete sat on the edge of the bed and pulled off his sneakers. "She has a sister. But the sister wouldn't talk to me. So I sicced Willy on her. You saw Alice Rose?"

"Yeah, but she wouldn't talk, either. She called me a geek and told me to get out of there."

Pete turned to her. "So that's Weams Point and Alice Rose. Now what?"

"How about discussing your penchant for hiring every crazy redhead that comes through town?"

"What do you mean, 'crazy'?"

"Didn't you hear her? All that *yikes, zowie, kerblam*, like a Warner Brothers cartoon. And that stuff about Parcheesi and poker. And the impromptu dance recital. She's *nuts*."

"Are you kidding? She'll be perfect for Factotum." Pete elaborated. The puzzles meant she was handy. The ballet meant she was coordinated. The poker meant she was no quitter, and the Parcheesi, for some reason that eluded Connie, meant she had a heart of gold. And last, but far from least, she'd made Lucy laugh. There was only one thing he didn't mention, but as he stood up and unbuckled his pants, Connie saw it, as plainly as if it were still in front of her.

That red hair.

Not today's, but fifteen years ago . . .

Connie plowed away from them as fast as she could through the soft sand, but she had her own pretty nifty peripherals. And that red hair kept flashing in them. So okay. So she looked. And saw that old Susan hadn't given up on that belt buckle. Connie charged down the beach without turning again, crossed the marsh in record time, and arrived at the cottage just as Baby Hughie and Tim were coming out. It hadn't been a long walk, but it had been a hot one, and she felt oddly flustered.

"Anyone for a beer?" she asked.

"Yeah!" said Baby Hughie.

"Sounds good," said Tim. "Shall we see if Pete—"

"Pete's not through yet," said Connie. "Who wants to drive? My car's blocked in."

"I'm not pedaling you on my bicycle," said Hughie.

So Tim drove. They'd just settled into the car, all three in the front seat, when Connie remembered something. "Hold it, Hughie. You're not legal."

"That's okay. I'll hide in a booth and you can buy me one."

"I'll buy you a Coke."

Hughie snapped open the door. "Forget it. I'll go home and get one."

He stomped off across the lawn.

"And then there were two," said Connie.

The car didn't move.

She looked over at Tim St. George. "What's the matter, you're legal, aren't you?"

"I . . . yes. Of course I am." He reached for the key. "Where to?"

She looked at Tim St. George a second time. Not bad if you were into Marlboro commercials. A wild, Susan-Jameson-type urge to say "My place" almost overwhelmed her.

Now be fair, Connie scolded herself. Susan Jameson wouldn't say that. She'd just jump him in the driveway.

"Lupo's," said Connie.

"Hey," said Pete. "What happened to the big conversation?"

"It's coming," said Connie. They should talk about Lucy. For one thing, she wanted to get it straight once and for all about lollipops. And they'd gotten this thing from Lucy's teacher requesting a conference about her verbal skills. And they still hadn't settled the booster seat issue. But Connie needed something first. A drink of water, she decided. She slid off the bed and stood up. She took a step toward the door, but by now Pete's pants were on the floor. Their eyes ran into each other and stalled.

Pete said it first. "Or we could talk later."

"I don't know. I'm not sure I'm in the mood." It was that damned beach image that was bugging her. It was the right person on top, the problem was, it was the wrong person under him.

"Want help deciding?"

What the hell. She might as well give him a shot. But if he handed her a red wig, she'd kill him.

There was no red wig, but the specters from the past didn't exactly leave the bed the minute Pete and Connie toppled onto it. For one thing, as soon as conversation resumed, Connie found herself bringing up not lollipops but rumrunners. So Susan Jameson was interested in Pete's field of endeavor. Like Connie wasn't, or something? But as soon as Connie realized what she was doing, she was disgusted with herself. She wasn't going to lie here competing with a dead slut. She tried to change tack, but it was too late. Once Pete heard that one little word, he was off and running.

Connie managed to stay awake through most of the local stuff—it appeared that during Prohibition, when the only decent liquor was smuggled in from overseas, Nashtoba had been busy. The supply ship would load up in a foreign port and anchor just outside the point where U.S. jurisdiction came to a legal end—originally a three-mile limit, later extended to twelve, but either way, it had barely slowed the flow of liquor. The local fishermen would run out to the mother ship, hand over a large bundle of cash, load up with liquor, return to land, this time collect the cash, and unload into waiting trucks.

Pete rambled on about the various types of liquor. The good stuff, imported by a fellow named McCoy, hence the expression "the real McCoy," and the forgeries, actually funneled out of huge tanks and labelled on demand right on board.

Connie drifted off. She came to again at the words "run, geek."

She opened her eyes. "What? Alice?"

"What, Alice?"

"You said, 'run, geek.' "

"I said Rum Creek. This creek. Our creek. The place was ideal—deserted beach, lonely dirt road, it was such a thoroughfare for bootleg traffic they called the creek out here Rum Creek."

"Oh." She closed her eyes again.

And opened them again.

Rum Creek.

✖8✖

"**I** TOLD YOU," said Connie for the third time. "I asked Alice Rose if she knew where Manny was and she said 'Run, geek.' Or I thought she said 'run, geek.' But now I'm thinking maybe what she meant to say was Rum Creek. That's exactly where he was, right? Dead and buried on Rum Creek. At least it was Rum Creek back then, back when he disappeared in the early thirties, right?"

"Right," said Pete, but he sounded skeptical. "What else did she say?"

"Nothing much. Something about glem. She said 'won't talk, glem. Geep money,' something like that. But she hasn't talked in years. It's not too surprising it didn't come out just right. Run, geek. Rum Creek. Geep . . . no, wait. *Keep* money. What about 'keep money'?"

"I don't know," said Pete. "And who or what is 'glem'?"

"I don't know," said Connie.

"If—"

74

Connie covered Pete's mouth. Had she heard—?
Yes, there it was. The soft pad of tiny feet. She
reached over and switched on the light. The
cracked door widened, and Lucy appeared at the
foot of the bed.

"I'm hungry."

Connie looked at the clock. "It'll be time for
breakfast before you know it."

"I'm *hungry*," said Lucy.

Pete tossed back the covers. "Come on, Lucy, I'll
find you something to eat." He scooped her up and
carried her out.

Connie could hear him on the stairs. "A-rig-a-jig-
jig, three-men-and-a-pig—"

That wasn't how it went. Or was it? They should
teach these things in school, thought Connie.

Lucy's chirp carried up the stairwell. "Do
Leerie."

"In a minute. Now let's see what we've got
here."

Connie lay awake listening to the sounds of the
midnight raid. Refrigerator opening and shutting.
Milk, she hoped. Cupboard door. Cookies? She
hoped not. More tooth rot. She heard the clatter of
cups, plates, chairs sliding into place, and finally,
over it all, the deep rhythm of Pete's voice.

" '*My tea is nearly ready and the sun has left
the sky;
It's time to take the window to see Leerie going
by . . .*' "

Connie fell asleep.

* * *

Polly woke up the way she usually woke up these days—feeling cold, alone, down. It was like she was here and life was over there and all she had to do was to jump across, but she couldn't, somehow. But something had wakened her. Yes, there it was again. The phone. She looked at the clock. It was a lot later than it should have been. Rita was going to kill her. As a matter of fact, that was probably Rita now. She reached with trepidation for the receiver. "Hello?"

"Good morning."

Willy. She smiled into the phone. "Good morning."

"I've got a busy day ahead of me, so I thought I'd better call now. We said something about dinner, but I might not be back till late. I wouldn't want you waiting around."

"What's up today?"

"Joel Crawford, handwriting specialist, first. Then over to Weams Point to talk to this Rosella Jameson. Then the other man in her life."

"Tim St. George?"

If Polly didn't know better she could have sworn she detected annoyance. "I've already talked to the sainted George. It's the other one I've yet to track down. Your temporary conquest. Susan Jameson's ex."

"Roger Coolidge?"

"That's him. My only lead so far is yours. Gull Island. That's another reason I'm calling. Did he say he was definitely going there?"

"Let me think. I know he'd been there before. He

said he knew a nice, quiet inn that served terrific Mexican omelets at breakfast."

"Did he, now? That might help."

A brief silence fell. So, *jump*. Polly took a breath and plunged. She could do this. "Why don't I come along?"

"No can do, Polly. As much as I'd like you to."

And she heard how much he'd like her to. Polly thought furiously. She was supposed to be working. For Pete. But so far, all she'd done was clean up a few yards after Hurricane Charlotte, quit early, sleep late. It was a wonder her brother hadn't already fired her. But as far as she knew, Pete had never fired anybody. She bet Rita had, though. "You'd better do Gull Island before you do Weams Point," she said. "That ferry leaves at eleven."

"Nope," said Joel Crawford.

"Nope?" repeated Willy.

"Not the same woman. No way. Nada."

Nada? The man looked about as un-Spanish as a man could look, thought Willy. Straw blonde hair, blue eyes, the red-veined skin that came from either too much sun or too much booze. He pointed to Susan Jameson's W-2 signature and resumed. In English.

"Here you've got a light, even pressure, circular stroke, good rhythm, gentle forward slant, easy, full loops on the S and the J, nothing fancy. Light, happy, easy. Got me?"

And just what did he mean by *"easy"*? wondered Willy. But he supposed almost any variation on the definition would fit the Susan Jameson Willy was coming to know.

Joel Crawford now pulled Pete's precious postcard closer. "But this one's got problems. First off, you've got this inconsistent slant in the printed body of the message. Look here. Backward. But here, see how the upstroke creeps forward? Second, look at the actual stroking itself. Thick, heavy. Digs in on the downstrokes. And the *t*-crosses. Straight and strong. Look up here at the *J*-cross in the W-2. See how it drifts skyward? She's not too worried where life takes her. This one down here, she's much more deliberate." He paused. "Or he is."

Willy looked up. "He?"

"Sorry. I thought I made it clear. This second one, this postcard, is a forgery."

"How do you know it isn't the W-2 that's a forgery?"

"Don't get me wrong. I have no way of knowing if that signature on that form is in actual fact the signature of the real-live Susan Jameson. All I can tell you is that it's the undisguised, comfortable, natural, mark of the person who made it, while this postcard, despite the fact that it's obviously been printed very slowly and meticulously, is a poor attempt to camouflage the natural hand of the writer. Or to imitate another one."

Willy picked up the W-2. "To imitate this one?"

But here Joel Crawford exhibited his first signs of confusion. "If it is, it's an extremely clumsy attempt. Yes, you have that *S* in the Susan, but then again, you have that slant. And unless there has been a marked physical or emotional upheaval, there are things that generally don't change. The thickness or thinness of the actual stroking. Spacing. General arrangement on paper. T-crosses. I-dots. Unless, of course—" He examined the two samples again. "I don't know." He waved the papers at Willy. "May I keep these?"

"I'll get you copies."

"Good ones?"

"Good ones," said Willy.

When he got back to the station he put in a call to the Weams Point Police. He wanted any background he could get on the Jamesons before he went to see Rosella, but the chief wasn't available and no one else seemed to want to talk to him. The desk sergeant promised to have the chief call him the minute he got free. Willy hung up the phone and thought. Rosella was key. But so was this old boyfriend, Coolidge. And what about the new boyfriend, Pete? Something fishy there, but not that. Not Pete. Willy looked at the clock. Last ferry at eleven. He grabbed his jacket and left for Gull Island.

Pete came downstairs that morning about as tired as he got, which was as tired as he'd been a lot, lately. He was in no mood for the face that greeted him as he rounded the kitchen doorway. Or the words.

"See?" said Connie, pointing to Lucy's soggy cereal bowl. "Again. She's not eating. And why should she if you keep feeding her in the middle of the night?"

"You want her to starve? Lucy, eat your cereal."

Lucy picked her spoon out of the cereal and threw it on the table. From there it bounced to the floor, splattering milk and a half-dozen semidissolved Cheerios onto Pete's ankle.

"Hey," he said.

"Brilliant," said Connie.

"Look," said Pete.

"I want *donuts*," said Lucy.

"We don't have donuts," said Connie.

Pete opened the freezer and took out a bagel. It had a hole in it, anyway. He popped it in the toaster and poured himself a cup of coffee. So they'd reached the testing phase. They'd been warned about this, that sooner or later Lucy would want to test out her new boundaries, that it would come as soon as she began to feel at home. So this was a *good* sign?

"So who does what today?" asked Connie.

It was a new code that Pete was just beginning to decipher. What it meant was, *who's got Lucy?*

"I want to take a look at what they did to the marsh," said Pete. "Lucy can come with me."

"And find more treasure!" shouted Lucy.

"Oh, please," said Connie. But Pete saw her eyes narrow suspiciously. What did she think he was doing, hoarding all his old girlfriends' bones out there, digging them up one at a time just to torture her?

The bagel popped up. Pete slathered it with cream cheese and set it down in front of Lucy.

"What's that?" asked Lucy.

"A flat donut," said Pete. He turned to Connie. "So you do Sarah."

"Yuck," said Lucy, and threw the bagel, cream-cheese-side down, on the floor.

"I'll do Sarah," said Connie and shot out the door.

Pete picked his way along the driest marsh route, keeping one eye and one hand on Lucy as she jigged along beside him. The marsh was at its best in October—gold-tipped grass dotted with sea lavender, asters and sea goldenrod. He stopped a good safe distance from the creek and surveyed its winding outline. Rum Creek? Hard to imagine. But give it another fifty years and it would widen again, as it had already begun to widen in that last big storm that had helped to churn up Susan's bones. A few more cave-ins at the sharpest turns and the creek would break through to itself, straighten itself out again, start over back where they'd begun.

Back where they'd begun.

"Come on." Pete gripped Lucy firmly by the hand, found Susan's makeshift graveyard, and gazed down morosely. The investigators had turned that part of the marsh into mud soup, a vat the size of a small quarry. Some final resting place. But now that Pete thought about it, the marsh wasn't such a rotten grave site for Susan. She'd loved it here. They'd taken many a walk here. She'd been fascinated by the ever-evolving ecosystem . . .

"It's so desolate out here," said Susan, waving a hand across the marsh. "You have this all to yourself. Is there no one else around here?"

81

"One house over that way. You can't see it from here. A pair of elderly sisters live there."

"And this marsh. It looks like it's been here forever, will stay forever. Like nothing will ever change."

"Oh, it changes."

"Changes how?"

"Let's see." Pete looked around. *"The creek's gotten narrower, for one thing. They used to be able to run boats right up to my door. You should see the old pictures."*

Susan stopped walking. *"You have old pictures?"*

"Not me, Sarah Abrew."

"So how did they get to the beach from the cottage? They couldn't have done what we just did—hopped it."

"Nope. There used to be a plank walk out here."

"Right here?"

Pete looked around. *"I'm not sure just where. I think it was over there. Or maybe back that way. I know I've seen it in the pictures."*

"I'd love to see those pictures sometime."

Pete smiled at her. *"I think I can arrange that."*

"But not right this minute."

The next thing he knew it was full court press—wet mouth, hot hands, whole body . . .

Damn. There she was again. The other one. Coming their way over the marsh.

Suddenly Pete was no longer in the mood.

But wait a minute. It was his marsh. It was his living fantasy. Who was she to barge into the middle of it and wreck everything?

He turned his back and tried to empty his mind of that tall, gold apparition, but it was no good. He was

*no exhibitionist. He caught Susan's hands and stood her
away from him.*

"Let's look at those pictures."

"All right," she said brightly.

There was just no disappointing her.

So this had to be a fantasy.

"Hey!" said Lucy tugging at his hand. "I *said*
why can't we?"

"Why can't we what?"

"Why can't we go swimming?"

"Because it's fifty degrees in there. You'll freeze."

"It's not fifty degrees. I'm *boiling*."

Pete looked down. She did look awfully pink. He
knelt down and put a hand to her forehead.

Boiling.

❖9❖

RITA PECK'S DAY began like Captain Bligh's probably ended. First there were the parting words from her gentleman friend, Evan Spender, as he dropped her off.

"I'm not planning to stay single forever, Rita."

But before she could decide whether his words were threat or optimism, she spied the note from Polly, lurking on the far edge of her desk. "Off to finish up Beggs yard, then on official errand with police chief. Catch you tomorrow. Polly."

And before Rita could complete the thought that began, "I'll catch *you*," there was Phoebe Small's flaming hair, absorbing most of the sun that would normally at that hour have been streaming through the open doorway. Oh, Lord. What to do with her? There were no poker games or ballet lessons or puzzles on today's agenda.

But before Rita could decide what to do with Phoebe, there was Connie, announcing that she was off to read Sarah Abrew the morning paper, a job that traditionally fell to Pete.

"Where's Pete?" asked Rita.

Connie didn't seem to hear her. She was staring at Phoebe. Again.

So Phoebe answered her. "I saw him out on the marsh with his daughter."

"No, you didn't," said Connie. "At least not as far as I know. But he is out there with Lucy."

"Lucy has no family," explained Rita. "Pete and Connie are taking care of her. All right, Connie, why don't you take Phoebe with you to Sarah's?"

Connie silently contorted her features in an ill-defined but definitely negative response to Rita's suggestion. Well, too bad. That was another tradition, established long ago, when Connie had been first hired, as a matter of fact. Sarah got to pass on all new-hires. There were, of course, a few exceptions. Susan Jameson, for example.

And speaking of Susan Jameson . . .

Pete blasted through the office door looking frantic, Lucy cradled in his arms, her smaller ones encircling his neck, her head on his shoulder. "Do we have a thermometer?"

"How should I know?" said Connie.

"Well, dammit, we should have a thermometer."

Phoebe reached out and placed a hand on Lucy's forehead as Rita opened her desk drawer and withdrew an old-fashioned mercury-filled thermometer, a leftover from her own days as anxious mother.

Pete sat Lucy on the edge of the desk. "Come on, pal. Open up." The thermometer went in. Pete checked his watch. Lucy spit out the thermometer, which Phoebe somehow caught. She replaced it in Lucy's mouth and held up a finger. "Bet you can't keep your mouth shut till I finish this picture." She picked a blank piece of paper off Rita's desk and began to draw.

Lucy watched, eyes wide, mouth closed. So did Rita. A little girl with a thermometer in her mouth took shape. The thermometer turned into a bubble-blower, bubbles issuing from the end of it and circling the little girl's head. Phoebe connected the bubbles, added petals, made a daisy chain.

Pete took out the thermometer, looked at it, handed it to Phoebe. "I can never read these things."

Phoebe looked. "Everything okey-dokey. You were just hot from all the hop, skip, and jumping, weren't you, Lucy? You're a good hopper, I saw you."

Lucy beamed proudly.

General movement toward the door alerted Rita to the fact that if she wanted to avoid further mutiny, it was now or never. "All right," she barked, "Connie, Phoebe, you're off to Sarah's. Pete, you're supposed to drive out to Bennington's and price out that fence for him, but—" She looked doubtfully at Lucy.

"Lucy and I can ride out there as long as we're back in time for that bus. Can't we, Lucy?"

"Yay!" shouted Lucy.

Pete left hand in hand with Lucy. As Rita watched the two diverse shapes go through the door, an eerie sense of déjà vu overtook her. She'd heard all this before. Seen this before. Same man, different child . . .

"I go with Pete," said Maxine.

Rita peered at her small daughter. "You're going with your father."

"Hey," said Nicky Peck. "Let her go with Pete. I've got to be in Bradford in a half hour."

Rita glared at her husband. "And Pete has nothing to do, I suppose?"

"He damned well doesn't have to be in Bradford in a half hour. What do you want from me?"

"I want a little help. I want a little consideration. I would also like—"

Pete caught Maxine by the hand and moved toward the door. "We'll take a little walk on the beach."

"Yay!" shouted Maxine.

"When you see Susan . . ." began Pete, but there she was.

Not that Rita needed to actually look at the door to know she'd arrived. All she needed to do was to look at her husband, drooling.

Honestly.

Rita began introductions. "Susan, this is my husband—"

"Why yes, hello, Nick," said Susan.

Hello, Nick???

When Pete and Susan and Maxine left, Rita turned on her husband. "And just how do you happen to know Susan Jameson?"

"Is that her name?"

"Yes, that's her name. And how—"

"How do you think? She came in looking for a car.

*Got real interested in one of those new RVs I was trying
to tell you about."*

"And you got real interested in her."

*"Grow up, Rita. Good-looking women occasionally do
buy cars."*

*But not good-looking women without two cents to
their name, thought Rita.*

So Evan wanted to get married. Well, Rita had
been there once already, and all she'd ever gotten
out of it was more work for no pay and more
scenes for *Who's Afraid of Virginia Woolf*, which, as
far as she was concerned, was already a few scenes
too long.

So no thank you, Mr. Spender.

Connie led Phoebe to her new vehicle, a used and
abused Jeep Wagoneer. They'd discovered early on
that families of three didn't do well in Triumph
convertibles. Connie shot a surreptitious glance at
Phoebe's left-hand ring finger. No ring, but nowadays that didn't mean anything. She'd learned to
take a kid's temperature somewhere. "Do you have
kids?" she asked her.

"Nope." Phoebe paused. "But I've worked with
kids a lot this past year. And I know kids like Lucy.
I don't have much family, either. What happened
to hers?"

"Her mother's dead."

"And her father?"

"Doesn't seem to know what one is." Connie
looked sideways. "And you?"

"Pretty much the same, actually. I was raised by

my grandparents. I don't know how they did it."
After a minute Phoebe added, "This can't be easy
for you two, either."

"Like Chinese water torture. And all the time I
keep thinking, What if they don't let us keep her?"

"There's some danger of that?"

"We're trying to make it official, but it gets tricky
with the mother dead. They have to make sure
there's no next of kin who might lay claim later
on." And what the hell made her come out with
that? wondered Connie. She didn't trust this
woman as far as she could throw her, which was
probably not far. In the first place, she wasn't used
to women who were taller than she was, and it
made her nervous In the second place, there was
that hair. Association of ideas. Neither of these
things were Phoebe's fault, of course, but there you
were. So why was Connie suddenly blabbing her
innermost fears, two minutes after she'd met this
woman? Connie clamped her jaws and kept them
clamped till they reached Sarah's.

They found Sarah perched in her huge chair,
white hair ruffled into spikes around parchment
skin, blue eyes twinkling.

"And who do we have here?" she asked.

"Phoebe Small," said Connie. "Phoebe, Sarah
Abrew. Phoebe's our newest employee. She's come
to read you the paper."

"Oh, bother the paper." Sarah held out a gnarled,
brown hand. Phoebe shook it. "My, my, my, look
at the size of you. You'll be handy for the kitchen
cupboards, I see. I've met you before?"

"No, I don't think so," said Phoebe.

"Your mother, perhaps? Or a sister? Where are you from?"

"The Hook. Elder Bay."

"No, then, I don't think so. Ah well, enough of this chitchatting. So are you going to clean my cupboards or aren't you?"

"Welcome to Factotum," said Connie.

Polly lurked on the top deck behind a lone couple holding hands. She saw him on the dock, first, talking to the harbormaster, watched him go into the office of the steamship authority and come out a few minutes later. He approached the loading ramp, talked to first one deckhand, then the other. Showed the older one a picture. Climbed the ramp. Polly ducked into the rest room until she felt they were in motion, then came up behind him where he stood at the forward rail and said, "Boo."

He turned without flinching, as if he knew she was there. Or knew someone was there. When he saw her his eyes narrowed with concern, but Polly wasn't worried. She'd seen them widen with delight first.

"Polly, this is not a good idea."

"Sometimes you sound just like my brother. It's a free country. I can spend a nice fall day on Gull Island if I want to."

"Now who sounds like your brother?" But he seemed to consider her point, which was more than Pete would have done. And besides, there wasn't much he could do about it now, was there? They pulled into open water, and Polly shivered. The chief removed his leather jacket and folded it around her. He was like that. "Since you're here, why don't you tell me about this Coolidge."

"I told you. He ran into me when he was leaving. I heard him arguing with Pete. I remember it because you never heard Pete arguing. Not before Connie, anyway. Doesn't that figure? She's on the scene two whole minutes and there he is, practicing." Polly felt a foolish thrill when Willy smiled at her. "Anyway, there they were, glaring at each other and not saying anything. Then all of a sudden . . ."

"I think I've made it pretty clear," said Pete. "Susan doesn't want to see you. Neither do I, as a matter of fact. If you'll excuse me."

Pete turned away. The stranger grabbed his shoulder Polly sucked in her breath. Pete was one forehead taller, but the stranger was a few barbells wider. Still, Polly should have known her brother better. He came around with open hands raised, not fists.

"Look, we've got two choices. We punch each other and you go, or we don't punch each other and you go. Personally I prefer option two, but if you choose option one, I warn you, I go a little crazy when people try to move my nose around."

And you couldn't say much fairer than that, could you? Apparently the stranger must have thought the same. He about-faced so smoothly that Polly almost got caught staring. The reason she was staring was that he was smiling. She would never understand men. Was this all just a game to them? But here he came. She ducked behind Pete's truck, which was dumb, because the stranger's van was parked next to it. So she dropped her bag so she'd have an excuse for the posture when he came around the corner.

He smiled again when he saw her, as if he'd been selling Fuller brushes, not contemplating pummeling her brother.

"Hello," he said. "And who might you be?"

"Polly," said Polly. And only because she was curious how he'd react, she added, "Pete's sister."

The smile only got wider. He had big teeth and thin lips. "You live here?"

"Not anymore. Now I'm just a visitor."

"So we have something in common. Or had. I'm afraid I'm just leaving this fair isle." He held out a hand. "Roger. Roger Coolidge."

Polly gave him her hand, which he didn't shake so much as hold, and all the time his eyes stayed fixed on her.

"He was not very attractive," said Polly. "Dark. Thick. But he had this mesmerizing quality. I remember I stood there like a deer in the headlights. Or maybe it was me. I used to respond like that to any hint of male authority. It was easier."

"You didn't respond to Coolidge that way. He wanted you to go to Gull Island and you said no."

Polly laughed. "Don't give me too much credit. I had Pete to deal with. He would have had a fit if I went off with Roger. So I responded to Pete's authority."

"And Coolidge went to Gull Island without you."

"I'm not sure he went at all."

"He went, according to the ferry reservation records. Brought a van over. But the van never came back the other way. And the registration was never renewed thereafter."

"You mean—" After a minute Polly said, "You don't actually think he did it, do you?"

"Why not?"

"Well, I don't know. The jealous boyfriend. It's just too . . . *ordinary.*"

"And Susan wasn't, is that it?"

"No. *No.* It's just that—" Just what? Just that it was never that easy in the movies.

Willy reached for her. Or she thought he was reaching for her. She couldn't help it. She backed up. But all he did was to slip a hand into the pocket of the jacket she was now wearing, pull out a photograph, and hand it to her.

"That's him! Where'd you get it?"

"Registry of Motor Vehicles."

"He looks the same as he did fifteen years ago."

"That's because it was taken fifteen years ago. It's the last known record we've found."

"Maybe he's dead, too."

"I hope not," said Willy.

Polly stared at him. "You really think he did it. You've decided already."

Willy remained silent, but by now Polly had learned that sometimes Willy's silence was as informative as the Encyclopedia Brittanica. She turned her back to the chief and looked out over the water. The sun bouncing back at her off the tops of the waves nearly blinded her, but between the hot metal glare she could see the deep, dark troughs. She shivered again, and Willy pulled her backward until she was against him. She could feel his heart beating through the leather. Life. Here. But she couldn't help it. She pushed at the arms that were crossed over her chest, fighting a sudden, odd sensation that she was sinking. Going down. "Look," she said brightly, pointing to the flat, brown pancake on the horizon. "Gull Island."

Gull Island was as small as a populated island could get, and that was using the term *populated* lightly. Eight boats at the dock, two cars. One small cluster of buildings around an ancient, cobbled street, a few muddy side roads, a handful of hardy year-round souls going back and forth about their business paying them no attention.

Until they walked up the steps of the police station.

Gull Island had one policeman, Nelson Parks, or Nelly, as he admitted to being called, and Gull Island had had Nelly for going on forty years. He was so excited to talk to a fellow officer that it was all Willy could do to get them out of there. He began by showing Nelly the picture of Roger Coolidge, which Nelly turned over and upside down and sideways and finally handed back reluctantly.

"Can't say as I've ever laid eyes on this man. Roger Coolidge you say his name is. What's he done?"

"We're looking for him in connection with a fifteen-year-old murder."

"Which isn't to say he did it," said Polly.

Nelly looked at Polly. "This fellow a friend of yours?"

"No," said Willy. He pointed to the picture. "Try

removing some of the hair, changing the color, adding fifteen years."

Nelly shook his head. "Sorry. I've about memorized everyone there is to know around here. Nothing like this fellow."

"What about any newcomers over the past fifteen years?"

"Newcomers. Thing is, see, we've been in pretty much of an economic downturn since the boat company cut down the run out here. Most people been going the other way the past fifteen years. We've got Joey Blossom's nephew, signed on over at the garage a couple years ago, but we've all known him since the day he was born. He's not this fellow here. Let's see, there's the Baxters, elderly couple from Bradford who refurbished the old Sawyer place. And those nice lesbians who live behind town hall. And that crazy Gilligan family, come here ten years ago to get back to nature, never seen 'em set foot out of doors. But every one of them Gilligans is blonde-haired, blue-eyed, freckled. Not this fellow here."

"Thanks," said Willy. He handed Nelly his card, asked if there was someplace he could get a good Mexican omelet, and got five minutes of intricate directions that boiled down to walk-out-the-door-and-turn-left-at-the-corner.

They walked out the door and turned left at the corner, and there was the Gull Island Inn. White clapboards, green window boxes, brick walk. They walked through the door into a cheery, pine-panelled room. The proprietor's seamed face opened brightly when he saw them, closed again the minute he learned they weren't there to book a room. But when Willy handed him the picture of Roger Coolidge, he brightened again.

"You're looking for him, too?"

"I'm looking for him," said Willy cautiously. "Why, are you?"

"I've been looking for fifteen years."

"And why is that?"

"Because he owes me money, why else would I want him? I don't usually get fooled, but this one fooled me. He paid cash for night one. When he decided to stay over another one I trusted him for it. He disappeared the next morning with the second half of the bill outstanding."

"Do you have a guest register?"

"Yes, of course, I have a guest register. But if you're looking for the one with his name on it, I can't help you. It disappeared with him. Same morning he did."

"How do you know it disappeared with him?" asked Polly. "Anyone could have—"

"Did he leave anything behind?" Willy cut in.

"No. Nothing."

"Fifteen years is a long time," Polly tried again. "Are you sure this is the right—"

The innkeeper pointed to the picture. "This is the man. And he left nothing. If he had, I'd have remembered. He was the first guest to stiff me. I even went through the trash, looking for credit card receipts, anything. There was nothing. He obviously knew what he was doing. Why are you looking for him?"

"He may have stiffed someone else," said Willy.

He thanked the man and escorted Polly out the door.

"He stiffed someone else?" asked Polly.

"Stiffed as in made into a stiff. Maybe you'd rather wait outside from now on."

"No," said Polly, "I wouldn't." This one-track mind on Willy made her nervous. She had a gut feeling she was behind some of his convictions about this Coolidge, partly because of what she'd told him, partly because of her own past experience. So it was up to her to even things out where possible, keep at least one of their minds open to other possibilities.

They checked the remaining establishments in town and found no one who remembered Coolidge by name or picture until the coffee shop. A middle-aged, dyed blonde, worn-down woman whose name tag said Sondra took one look at the picture and shot it back across the counter and onto the floor.

Willy calmly picked it up and held it up where she could see it again. "You know this man?"

"Coolidge. Roger. Sure, I remember him. First summer I started working here."

"Which was when?"

"Fifteen years ago July. But it was August when he came in."

"And you last saw him when?"

"Two days after I first saw him."

"I'd like you to be sure, ma'am. This was fifteen years ago. It must be difficult to remember one customer out of—"

"I don't remember him because he was a customer. I wish that was why I remember him. I wish I'd given him his coffee and left him alone."

"But instead you—?"

"Instead I what-do-you-think?" Sondra looked from Polly to Willy and back again. "Ah, what do I care? I took him home with me. Next morning he left town. He said he'd come back. And I believed him. Drove him to the ferry and that was the last I saw of him."

"You drove him to the ferry? What happened to his van?"

"What van?"

Polly opened her mouth, but Willy laid a hand on her arm. "You saw him get on the ferry?"

Sondra shook her head. "I saw him to the dock. I was late for work. He blew me a kiss and that was it for old Roger. Story of my life. But who wants to hear that same old song?"

Willy did, apparently. He listened, he asked, he listened more. Quiet, patient, without judgment. Polly knew the routine. She'd been there.

From the coffee shop they went to Archie's Garage, a building that looked like the town dump on the outside, the local bank on the inside. The owner, a man as old as the police chief but a lot less grizzled, heard what they were after and led them proudly to an office full of file cabinets. But none of the files had any records that helped them. No work jobs on vans, no records of any abandoned vans during the fifteen years in question. And the one van known to be currently on the island was too new to have helped them.

"If you wanted to get rid of a car on Gull Island, how would you do it?" asked Willy finally.

Archie looked at Willy like he was out of his mind. He pointed a thumb at the floor. "Deep six. Pick a dark night. Pick a dock. We've got dozens of 'em out there."

As they walked to the ferry, Willy said, "End of trail on Mr. Ordinary."

"You might pick up the trail on the mainland."

"I've already covered that end. Since the ferry reservation there's nothing. He hasn't renewed a license, registered a car, bought a house, voted, installed a phone, used insurance, sued or been sued, subscribed to a magazine, given job references, used a credit card, cashed a check—"

"So you decided he was holed up on Gull Island, using an assumed name?"

"Murderers do tend to like to disappear."

"So do dead people," said Polly.

❖10❖

SARAH ABREW SAT back in her chair and listened with one ear as Connie read the paper, keeping her other ear tuned to the kitchen. The hollow clatter was the wooden salad bowl. The *tink, tink, tink* was the Waterford. Let that long, red firecracker make it through those in one piece and she'd let her loose on Grandmother's wedding china.

"Do you?" said Connie.

Oops. Must have lost track of the first ear, there. "Do I what?"

"Do you remember Susan Jameson?"

Ah. The other redhead. Maybe that's why this one seemed so familiar. One such remarkable feature, and it was easy to forget about the others. Susan Jameson. "Yes, certainly I remember her. One of those fluttery types. Never managed to do a thing but distract that damn-fool husband of yours." Still and all, Sarah could recall certain pleasing aspects of Susan Jameson. For one thing, she'd expressed an interest in Sarah's worn-out old tales, and even back then good listeners were getting hard to come by, Peter Bartholomew excepted, of course. But she did recall that sinking sensation when he'd first brought her around . . .

They came through the door like a pair of Siamese twins, all twined together in the middle. The girl saw Sarah and broke away, hanging back, but Pete pushed her forward, his hands on her hips as if they were part of his own body.

Now here's trouble, thought Sarah.

"This is Susan Jameson," he told her.

And what was she supposed to say to that, Hallelujah?

But the girl came forward nice as you please and took Sarah's hand between both of hers. "Oh," she said "Mrs. Abreu. I feel like I know you. Pete's told me how much he—"

"I want you to show her your old pictures," Pete interrupted. "She can look while I'm reading the paper."

But they did no reading. They sat three on the couch, Susan in the middle, Pete pointing at pictures and explaining the general scene, Sarah filling in the details. The girl was interested in all Sarah's old snaps of Nashtoba, but she really came to life over the one that featured Pete's small corner of it—cottage, beach, marsh. Susan sat with her hand on Pete's thigh and beamed up at him as he answered her questions, turning deferentially to Sarah when she'd expound, but obviously eager to get her eyes back on Pete. Polite, affectionate, lovely.

And all wrong for him, thought Sarah.

* * *

"What he needed was a nice, stiff, crosscurrent," said Sarah. "Something to keep him flailing. That girl would have lulled him to sleep."

"Eventually," said Connie.

Sarah chuckled, but as the silence grew, she got serious. "Don't tell me you're troubled by a little past history. That's all dead and gone."

"It was until he found out she was actually dead. Now we seem to have resurrected her."

So that was it, thought Sarah. She knew there was something. Then again, there usually was.

"But that's not really what I came to ask you," said Connie finally. "What do you remember about rumrunners?"

"Rumrunners?" asked Sarah, surprised. Leastways, she was surprised until she thought a minute. "Ah, yes. You're thinking about Manny Rose."

"So was he a rumrunner?"

"Lord, yes. He and Clem Rogers. Aldo Fox, Ed Sears, Paul Dillingham. You knew who they were by what they bought at the grocery. Some poor, struggling fisherman suddenly buying roasts every Sunday. And the boats. Out every dark of the moon, and yet there was the fishing gear, rusting to its hinges."

"You said 'Clem'?"

"Clem Rogers. Those two were like brothers. You didn't see one without the other, ever, work or play. 'Course which they considered running rum, work or play, I'm sure I couldn't say. Certainly nobody seemed to think of it as evil. That was the peculiar thing about Prohibition. For some dang-fool reason nobody considered it the kind of law it made you a crook to break. Oh, when they brought in Clem's young nephew there were a few who had something to say. Corrupting a minor, they'd call it now. But those two were no gangsters, just two honest, hardworking fishermen. Or so most people believed." Sarah chuckled. "There were some interesting moments during those years. I was seeing something of young Sanford Bell around that time. He used to take me sparking down the old Point road. One night Aldo pulled us over and suggested to San that he choose another location. That was where the liquor was coming in." She chuckled again, but this time she grew sober faster. "Still and all, you live by the sword, you die by the sword. I see how Manny Rose might have ended up in that marsh with a bullet in him. But how does that young woman fit in?"

"I don't know. What happened to Clem Rogers?"

"Oh, he and his wife and daughter moved away long ago. But Alice Rose is vegetating over in that nursing home."

"I know."

Oh did she, now? Yes, it appeared she did. Out came the story of the visit. Rum Creek. Clem Rogers. Keeping quiet and keeping the money.

So old Alice Rose could still make sense.

1930s sense, leastways.

Pack snack. Change clothes. Wash up. Run for bus. He was getting this down. Finally.

"I don't want red, I want a blue one."

Pete removed the strawberry granola bar from Lucy's pack and replaced it with blueberry. "Okay.

Time to change." He surveyed what had been a clean jersey not ten minutes ago. He'd have to remember to go with apple juice in future instead of grape. You could get away with an apple juice stain, but grape? He opened Lucy's bureau drawer and pulled out a purple sweatshirt. Grape color. Good.

"I want the pink one," said Lucy.

"You're wearing the pink one. Which is now a purple one. Arms up."

Instead of raising her arms Lucy plunged them into the drawer and withdrew a blue-and-white polka dot jersey. Okay, so the blue dots would camouflage any disastrous effects of the blueberry. He next hustled her into the bathroom and learned lesson number two of the morning—the smaller the face and hands, the longer it took to wash them. In the end there was nothing for it but to scoop her up, take the stairs two at a time, leap out the door, jog to the corner.

"Why are we always *running?*" asked Lucy.

Good question. He went over the revised list on the walk back. Start earlier. Pack snack. Change clothes. Wash up. Walk to bus in leisurely fashion.

This time he was almost to the driveway before that queer twist began in his gut and time went haywire on him . . .

Pete pulled on the parking brake and looked over the vehicles in his driveway. Something was wrong with this picture. The hired crew should have left long ago. So why was Baby Hughie's bicycle still here? And who belonged to that van?

He opened the cottage door, called, got no answer. Well, he was back earlier than expected. He'd found what he needed at Beston's, hadn't had to go all the way to Bradford. And he knew where to look for Susan. Especially at sunset. He went out the door and had just rounded the corner when he saw them on the marsh.

Susan. And another man. Susan's arm in the air, pointing out a few scenic highlights. The stranger's arm on her shoulder. Suddenly he gripped her, turned her, pulled her close. Susan motionless for what seemed like more time than was probable, then a flash of the red hair, the white face. She jumped back. And Pete was already moving long before the pale arm lashed out, before her hand made contact with the man's face. The man took off in a direct line for the van in Pete's driveway. By the time Pete reached Susan she was sitting down on a mound of salt hay, trembling.

"You okay?"

"Oh, Pete! You saw that, didn't you? What melodrama. That's my old boyfriend, Roger. I don't know how he found me here. He said he'd had a change of heart. I told him I had, too, but in the other direction. He seemed to take it okay. I thought we would part friendly. I brought him out here to show him around the place and the next thing I knew, he grabbed me."

"You think he got the message?"

"I don't know. I don't think so. I don't know what to do."

Pete stood up. "I'll handle it."

And he had, too. Caught up with the guy on the lawn and told him where to go. Returned to Susan on the marsh, collected every perfect inch of her into his arms, and held her till she'd stopped shaking.

And that was the last they'd seen of Roger Coolidge.

That was the last Pete had seen of him, anyway.

Willy pulled into Factotum's driveway behind Polly. He was here, he reminded himself, because he had to talk to Pete, had to get Rita's ex-husband's address, had to collect some handwriting samples. Might as well follow Polly home and do it now. That's what he'd told her at the dock. It had nothing to do with the fact that the momentum had shifted dramatically today. She'd actually taken some initiative, invited herself along to Gull Island. Skittered away once or twice, sure, but that didn't mean . . .

Damn. Pete. He intercepted Willy between his car and Polly's, and by the time Willy got clear of him Polly had disappeared. But he should talk to Pete anyway. And alone, preferably. How would Pete take what he was about to say? He supposed there was only one way to find out. He caught up with Pete on the stoop and gave it to him unadorned. "Susan didn't write that postcard."

And what would you call that expression? wondered Willy. Or *expressions*, plural. As Willy watched, Pete was already moving through a second and into a third.

"How—?"

"Handwriting analyst. The person who filled out

that W-2 is not the same person who wrote that postcard. Which means—"

But Pete was there already. "Which means she never left here. Which means she was murdered and her belongings were removed and the postcard was sent from Weams Point to convince me not to look for her."

"Did you?"

"Did I what?"

"Did you look for her?"

Expression number four. "There was no return address."

Willy waited.

"It wasn't . . . I didn't—" Pete stopped. "Did you talk to her sister?"

"Not yet. I have a few things to do here, first."

Which he did. Legitimate things. So why was he standing on Pete's doorstep explaining them so painstakingly? He had to collect handwriting samples as a process of elimination for the handwriting on the postcard. He had to collect Rita's ex-husband's address because, according to Rita, he also knew Susan Jameson.

"Susan Jameson, Susan Jameson," said Connie behind them. "Does anyone here even vaguely recall the second body that was found out on that marsh? Because if you do, I've got news for you. He was a rumrunner."

"Who, Manny?" asked Pete.

"Yes, Manny. And I found out who Glem was."

"Glem who?" asked Willy.

As Connie reported on her visit to Alice Rose, Willy felt his ears get hot. Was he losing his edge?

He should have been able to get that much himself.
But he hadn't, and Connie had. She recounted some
further details she'd gleaned from Sarah Abrew
until finally Pete cut in.

"Yeah, but Manny Rose had nothing to do with
Susan Jameson."

"Who says?" asked Connie. "She was in the same
hole, wasn't she? And you two were always talking
about it."

"Talking about what?"

"Rumrunners," said Connie.

Willy gestured toward the door. "May we?"

❖11❖

PETE WENT IN. Connie didn't. Pete wasn't sure it was a nod from the chief that made Connie bolt, but he suspected it. The two men settled across the kitchen table from each other, and Pete tensed, waiting for the police chief to start.

"You and Susan were always talking about rumrunners?"

"No, we were not. I don't know where Connie gets these things. Susan and I talked about island history some, I remember brushing on the rumrunners once or twice—"

"So brush them again."

Pete ran a nervous hand through his hair. There was a vague, uneasy memory drifting around out there somewhere, but all he could pull in clearly was more of the same . . .

Christ, she was going to kill him.

He'd only just plunged into a pitch-black, sated sleep when he surfaced again, smack in the middle of another

109

real-life dream—Susan Jameson's naked body silhouetted against the moon.

He slipped out of bed and came up behind her. "Can't sleep?"

She started, sighed, leaned back against him. "I think it's the moon. It's lit up the whole room. And the beach, see? Even the creek glows. No wonder the rumrunners cussed it. But I don't see how they found their way without it. That tiny little creek, that long black shore."

"They knew this stretch of shore the way you know the main street in your own hometown. And they also used signals. A flick of car lights, a lantern in a box that would shine out to sea but not down the beach, I've even heard tales of them hanging lanterns off kites. And don't forget the creek itself was wider then."

"That's right. You told me. I even saw the pictures at Sarah's. It didn't look anything like this, did it? No wonder you couldn't pick out that old plank walk."

"I could now, I bet." He looked out over the marsh. It was true that in the moonlight the creek seemed to glow. And he'd just seen the old pictures. It should be easy enough . . . "There," he said finally. "You see that little pool? Where the loop got cut off? To the left. That's where it was."

Susan twisted in his arms and looked up at him. "How can you tell for sure?"

"It stands to reason. It's the shortest route from house to beach. And I remember in the old picture it was almost exactly halfway across."

First she leaned forward, pulling away as she looked out. Then she leaned back, reaching for him.

Oh, he'd be dead by morning, for sure.

*　　*　　*

Much more of this, thought Willy, and this go-slow rule with Polly was going to go straight out the window. It wasn't hard to imagine what was going on between the lines of Pete's nature lessons. The trouble was, in the middle of this latest trip down memory lane, a nagging suspicion had begun to form that was going to require further mining.

But first things first. The handwriting samples. Not that he thought any of his friends killed Susan Jameson and forged that postcard, but on paper, at least, a case could be made for a couple of them, and Willy wanted enough paper on file to clear them.

So he collected the handwriting samples.

The reactions were mixed. Pete, agitated, distracted. Still back in that bedroom? Probably. Connie, distant and cool. If he was going to act like a policeman, she was going to treat him accordingly. Polly seemed to think the whole thing was funny. Either that, or she was amused by his demeanor, which he supposed could best be described as teetering precariously between the forces of law and the forces of nature. Rita was plain old furious, but she cheered up when he asked for her ex-husband's address.

Willy stopped at the station and found that he'd of course missed the call from Weams Point. He rang them again, got put off again. This time the chief was in a meeting. So it was time to see a man about a car.

As Willy approached the highway exit he pulled out the address Rita had given him for her ex-husband, but as it turned out, he didn't need it.

The first sign off the exit was Peck Auto Sales, and he would have picked Nicky Peck from a lineup in five seconds, thanks to Rita's description. *Mick Jagger on the eighteenth green,* she'd told him.

And there he was, standing in front of his desk in his office, gesturing wildly with one arm while he held a portable phone with the other. Long, coiffured hair, ravaged face, knit shirt, yellow pants. So trim that the very effort to remain so must have aged him. He swung around as Willy walked in and stopped talking.

"Call you back," Peck said into the phone and clicked off. "What can I do for you?"

"Not a car, thank you. Your ex-wife suggested I talk to you. She thought you might be able to help with an investigation. It's about Susan Jameson."

The thick lips tightened. In irritation? Confusion? General tension? "I'm trying, but I'm not getting there. What could Rita possibly have said to you to make you think I could help you? No, wait. I think I've got it."

"You know Susan's dead?"

"I wouldn't know if she were dead *or* alive. I don't know the woman. I never did. Biblically or otherwise. Despite what Rita may have told you."

"But you obviously know who I'm talking about."

"Sure I do. I met her when she came by looking for a car. Then I ran into her at Pete's place once or twice."

"She seems to have made a lasting impression."

Peck eyed Willy curiously. "You've never seen her."

112

"Not in the flesh."

"Well, if you had, you'd remember her."

"Tell me about when she came in to look for a car."

"What's to tell? She came in, she looked, she didn't buy."

"Can you tell the lookers from the buyers, as a rule?"

"Most of the time. The ones who come right out and tell you they're just looking? They're the ones who buy. It's the ones who walk around trying to look like they've got twenty grand burning a hole in their pocket that turn out to be the waste of time. But this one, she said she was just looking and that's what she did. Never did come back to buy."

"What was she looking for? New? Used?"

"Back then I was strictly in used. But she went straight for the high end. All terrain. Sporty. Lots of extras. AC. Sun roof. The works."

"You seem to have excellent recall."

Suddenly Peck looked uncomfortable. "I know what you're thinking and the truth's more the opposite. I remember all this because of the grief it caused me, not the pleasure. So I looked. You would have too, if you'd seen her. Rita saw me looking and that was it. Back then she was into making lists of my character flaws. She decided Susan gave her cause to add one more. Adulterer."

"Which you weren't."

"Look, if Susan Jameson were standing here and you asked her about Nicky Peck, she'd say, 'Nicky who?'"

Which didn't necessarily answer the question.

But long after it might have occurred to somebody else, it finally occurred to Nicky Peck to ask
a question of his own. "You say she's dead?"

"Murdered."

That set him back a second or two, but not
longer. Willy heard the click of heels on linoleum and barely had time to turn before a
woman probably half Peck's age, clad in trendy
exercise garb, came up to him and kissed his
cheek. "Eeeee," she squealed when she saw Willy's official paraphernalia. "The fuzz. What did
the bad boy do?"

A pained expression crossed Peck's face.

"Depends who you ask," said Willy.

"Joanne," said Nicky, "be a love and wait outside. We're almost done."

After Joanne tripped out he added, "Aren't we?"

Willy flipped open his pad and handed it across.
"I need a sample of your writing and I'll be off. I'll
dictate." He repeated what he had gotten down by
heart some hours ago and watched Nicky Peck
closely as he laboriously printed the words in large
block capitals across the page. Any curiosity seemed
curiously lacking, but then again, he seemed distracted
by the sound of Joanne's voice from outside the office,
discoursing at length with someone about the best
procedure for tightening the lats, wherever those
were. Peck finished his printing and looked up.
"Now sign the name Susan," said Willy.

And there it was at last, not curiosity, but some
good old-fashioned anger.

*　　*　　*

Connie had gone halfway toward the boat barn when she changed tack and headed for the marsh. She told herself she needed a short breather from work, but what she really needed was a long breather, from the color red. Phoebe Small's Volkswagen Cabriolet was still in the driveway, so that meant Phoebe's red hair would most likely be in the boat barn. It wasn't that she had anything against this Phoebe Small personally. It was just that at this particular point in time the last thing she felt like looking at was red hair. Was she that small and petty?

Yes.

Connie strode across the marsh, keeping a careful eye on the wet spots, but the typical October day, sixty degrees, dead calm, bright sun, wasn't doing it for her. She about-faced. What she really needed, she decided, was Pete.

When she reached the kitchen Pete wasn't in it, but—just her luck—Phoebe Small was. Phoebe stood with her back to the door, Connie's phone in her hand. "Cute as ever? I can't speak to the *ever*, but other than that I'd confirm the diagnosis . . . nope. No chance. Eat your heart out . . . no, nothing earth-shattering as yet . . . yowie . . . yes, I met her . . . Seven-thirty? . . . No, you pick me up. Okay. Bye." She replaced the phone, turned, and yelped.

"Sorry," said Connie, "but I do live here."

"Oh, yikes, *I'm* sorry. I asked to use the phone, and Rita sent me in here. I'll get out of your hair."

Hair. That goddamned hair. It was the same flaming red as Susan's, even the same electrified mass, not cascading down her back, maybe, but crunched up in a leather thong that left a few wisps spilling over.

"Is something the matter?" asked Phoebe.

"I . . . no. We're a little crazy around here right now."

"No wonder. I heard about the body."

"Bodies, plural. An old rumrunner and—"

"And you've got Lucy on top of all that. I've been thinking about her since we talked. If you two need a break I'd be happy to baby-sit for you."

"Thanks, but she's still gun-shy around strangers." Connie might have elaborated if her right eye hadn't happened to catch the kitchen clock. "Bus time. Gotta run."

To her annoyance, Phoebe came with her.

Polly was on her way to the Whiteaker Hotel to help Jack Whiteaker price the furniture he'd decided to sell. This was item number one on the list Rita had given her. Starred and underlined. But as she drove by Nashtoba Ladies Library, she found her mind taking a U-turn, her wheels following soon after. It had been an interesting talk with Willy about rumrunners, but what were they, exactly? She remembered reading about Prohibition in school. Or, rather, she remembered she was supposed to read about it. Well, it was never too late.

Nashtoba Ladies Library had been founded in the mid-1800s by the wives of the island's most prominent sea captains—that was where the name came from, not from some exclusive and exclusionary finishing school—but Polly always walked in on her best behavior all the same. Yes, please. No, thank you. Oh, excuse me. She walked sedately to the reference shelf, began with the first encyclopedia she found, looked under Prohibition, and found enough information to have satisfied even her history teacher. After the Eighteenth Amendment was passed in 1920, making the transport and sale of all alcohol illegal, special prohibition agents were charged with enforcing the rule. But there were more runners than there were agents—before its 1933 repeal, U.S. Treasury agents, customs officials, FBI, local law enforcement, the Coast Guard, and the U.S. Navy had been drafted to stem the flow. Coast Guard, thought Polly, and a dim, childhood memory took hold. Beston's store, an old man, a tall tale.

Beston's store wasn't one of Polly's favorite places on Nashtoba. She'd always dreaded the gauntlet run past the three old men who had appropriated the porch bench—Bert Barker's lascivious stare, Ed Healey's sickly-sweet whiskey breath, Evan Spender's long, silent contemplation before he could answer a simple "Hi, how are you?" And it hadn't changed much since she'd been back. But then again, what had changed around this place?

Polly armed herself with a Coke out of the rusted machine, settled onto the bench next to Evan Spender, and waited.

Naturally Bert was the first to let go.

"So, young lady. No need to ask what's new with you. Matter of fact, we're thinking of putting a meter in your driveway, get back some of the tax money the chief's wasting over there."

"Wasting? By investigating two murders?"

"Hah! Like he's got a prayer of solving one. You ask me—"

"No I don't," said Polly curtly. It was one thing for her to have her own doubts about the chief's course. It was entirely another when every Tom, Dick, and Harry felt they could jump in criticizing. But the reason she was here at all was because of those doubts of hers, she supposed. So get down to it. "Maybe you could tell me something. Do any of you remember an old man who used to be in the Coast Guard? I can't remember his name, but he used to hang around here telling stories about rumrunners."

"Ben Fox," said Evan.

Ben Fox. That was it.

Evan cocked an eye at her. "Manny Rose, I take it?"

"Ah, ha," said Ed. "Old Manny with a bullet in him."

"That was no Coast Guard bullet," said Evan.

"How do you know?" asked Polly.

"Because Ben wouldn't allow it."

"Ben was the man in charge," said Ed. "That was his rule. No taking shots at any rumrunners."

"He didn't go for Prohibition?"

Bert snorted. "He didn't go for anybody shooting his cousin Aldo."

"His cousin was a rumrunner?"

"That's it," said Evan. "They set up a sort of a code. Aldo Fox would say, 'High tide in the creek

118

two A.M.' That meant he had a load coming in. That meant Ben patrolled elsewhere that morning."

"Do you know where I could find this Ben Fox?" asked Polly.

"What's it worth to you?" asked Bert.

"Try Field House," said Evan.

"And better hurry," said Ed.

12

TIM ST. GEORGE'S private office was nicer than
his office at the hospital, and without the commo-
tion outside the door. He was on the phone when
Willy was ushered in, but disengaged rapidly.
"Seven-thirty. See you then." He saw Willy examin-
ing one of several diplomas on the wall and smiled.
"I assure you, it's not a forgery."

"I'm relieved to hear it. Not that I plan on need-
ing your services any time soon."

The smile faded into more serious contemplation.
"Am I allowed to ask why you are here, then?"

"Same old thing. Murder of Susan Jameson. I've
come to collect a sample." Comedic pause. "Of
your handwriting."

No smile on that one, and Willy thought it was
as good as the forgery line. St. George flipped a
prescription pad out of his coat pocket and wrote,
tore off the top sheet, and handed it across the desk.
Take two aspirin and call me in the morning. Okay,
enough with the funny stuff. Willy handed across

120

a pad of his own. "Print, please. I'll dictate." He slowly recited the contents of Susan Jameson's postcard, watching Tim St. George's features carefully as he went. A mild flush, but other than that, less agitation than he'd seen in, say, Pete. "Now sign it, please. Susan."

St. George looked up.

"Sound familiar?"

"Yes. Once you mentioned the name. This was the postcard she sent him."

"Pete showed it to you?"

Tim St. George nodded.

"I guess you two were real buddy-buddy."

Eyes met eyes. "It was a postcard, not a sealed letter. I saw it when I brought in the mail."

"So he didn't exactly show it to you."

St. George sighed. "I only meant to indicate by the shortest possible route that, yes, I had seen the postcard."

Willy closed and pocketed the notebook. "Thanks. That's all for now." He walked to the door, paused, pointed to the dates on the diplomas, one from medical school, one from his residency. "You were out and done fifteen years ago."

"Out and done? You mean . . . I see. Yes, fifteen years ago I suppose I was."

"You suppose so? You don't know if you were a fully licensed physician when you went to work for Pete?"

Tim St. George closed his eyes and heaved a classic, aggrieved sigh. "I was a fully licensed physician. Yes."

"Which means that instead of hanging out your

121

shingle and collecting a neat, what—Six-figure annual salary—you opted to work for Pete for an hourly wage of—"

"I stopped by to see Pete. He was looking for help. I decided to give him a hand."

"Now that's what I call a friend."

St. George said nothing.

"One last question," said Willy. "You're a doctor. If you wanted to kill someone with a blow to the head, how would you go about it?"

"I'd ask a policeman."

Even better than the two aspirin, thought Willy.

Polly followed Ed Healey's directions to the letter and ended up at the bakery. She walked in and smelled bread baking. And cinnamon. And something chocolate. She should have eaten first. She asked at the counter for Field House and was sent around back, where she found a long, low, shedlike el extending off the back of the building with a separate exterior door that was fronted by a ramp. Polly skated up the ramp and knocked. A woman in a bright blue smock opened it and smiled at her. Maybe it was that smile. Or maybe it was the bright blue. Or maybe it was all the travel posters on the walls. Whatever it was, suddenly Polly felt cheerier. She introduced herself and asked for Ben Fox.

"Oh good," said the blue woman. "We're running behind today. Maybe you could read the next chapter." Somewhere to Polly's left the soft incoherent mumbling that had been present since her arrival changed to an angry shriek. The blue woman thrust a weather-beaten old volume of *The Three*

Musketeers into Polly's hands and said, "Third door down, chapter twenty."

Polly crept down the hall with some trepidation. What was this place? In the first room she passed, an old woman with a spine so buckled that she stared permanently at the floor was shuffling over a path of yellow bricks that had been painted on the linoleum. Maybe it was some sort of loony bin for the elderly, thought Polly. But in the second room she passed, an old woman in a wheelchair sat hunched over a pile of flyers, which she was meticulously folding and passing across the table, where another woman, younger by a decade, maybe, sat in a regular chair and stuffed the flyers into envelopes. So it was some sort of sweatshop where the old and alone were exploited and robbed. At the third door it began to look more like a good, old-fashioned nursing home. A very old, very bald man lay propped in a hospital bed, but from there, the nursing home image faded again. These walls, too, were covered with travel posters. Next to the bed was what looked like an old leather armchair, but on closer inspection it turned out to be upholstered in vinyl. Next to the chair was a table, a goose-necked reading lamp, a pitcher of water, a small vase of chrysanthemums, an apparently much-read letter. The old man's eyes were open and fixed on Polly, so she said, "Hello, I'm Polly Bartholomew."

A hand like a claw crept out from under the covers and hovered. Polly approached the bed and grasped the hand, at first lightly, then in response to the answering grip, more firmly.

"Can Fox," he said. Or that's what it sounded like. Polly was able to make the translation when she noticed the address on the frayed envelope of the letter. *Captain Benjamin Fox.*

"How do you do, Captain Fox?"

He beamed. Waved at the chair.

Polly sat down and held up the book in her hand. "I've come to read you chapter twenty."

The captain nodded to her. Permission to proceed. Polly opened the book. "At two o'clock in the morning, our four adventurers left Paris . . ."

It didn't take long to read the twelve pages, and Ben Fox seemed to cling to every word. She would have gone on, but something told her that the idea was to string it out, give him something to look forward to. As she drew to a close with D'Artagnan in full gallop for London, Ben Fox pointed at the wall. London. The poster next to it was Paris. Do they change them with every book? wondered Polly.

She laid *The Three Musketeers* on the table and smiled at the captain. He smiled back at once. "I came to see you because I remembered you told good stories," she began. "About the rumrunners."

The captain uncovered his hand and waved it at her. "No stories. True."

"Do you remember Manny Rose?"

His face crinkled. Or, rather, it crinkled more. He nodded. He said a word that Polly didn't catch at first. She asked him to repeat.

"Rapscallion," he said more clearly.

"Do you know what happened to Manny?"

"Drowned."

So much for the big Ben Fox solution, thought Polly. But she seemed to have primed the pump, and there was no stopping it. Not that she wanted to. The stories were fascinating. It took a long time, and most of it came out piecemeal, disjointed, halting, with spots of some confusion that Polly tried to straighten out as politely as possible.

"You said the rumrunners sank their boats. You meant the Coast Guard sank them, didn't you?"

Ben Fox shook his head vigorously. "Built smuggling boats special. Sea cocks in the bilge. See us coming, open the hatch, swing levers, go down in minutes."

"But why?"

"Keep us from the boats. Faster than ours."

"You mean if you actually captured a rumrunner's boat you used it to chase them?"

Ben Fox nodded, his face crinkling again.

"So you arrested the men and sat and watched the boat go down."

Another head shake. "Not arrested. *Rescued*. Picked 'em out of the water. Our job."

"And then you arrested them?"

Another head shake. "No boat. No liquor. No proof."

Polly pondered that in silence for a minute. "Was there ever, well, a battle? With guns and everything?"

"Once. Fired across the bow. Warning. Fellow zigzagged. Running black. Thought I killed him."

"Running black?"

"No lights. Black ships, we called 'em."

"But you didn't hit anyone?"

Ben Fox shook his head firmly. "Saw fellow downtown. No holes in him." The face crinkled again, the chest heaved. It took Polly a second to realize the wheeze meant he was laughing.

"But how did you know who it was?"

"Knew all of 'em. Look at the boat. Paint marks."

"Paint marks?"

"Tie up against the mother ship to load. Paint rubs off. Different paint on gunwales? Rumrunner. Riding low, no fish? False bottom. Full of liquor."

Polly decided not to mention the additional method of detection—the fact that he was related to one of them.

But eventually, and simultaneously, the captain ran down, and a red-smocked young man poked his head in. Polly stood, shook the captain's hand, thanked him.

He bowed his head with old-world courtesy and said, "Come 'gain."

"I will," said Polly. For one thing, she needed to find out what happened to D'Artagnan. For another, she liked old Ben Fox.

As the red man walked her to the door she asked, "How old is Captain Fox?"

"One-oh-five next Tuesday."

"And what is this place?"

"Field House? The alternative to being put out to pasture. We haven't been here long, but we've already got a waiting list."

"Put me on it," said Polly.

Connie settled Lucy at the kitchen table and opened the refrigerator. The first order of business after school was always the snack. Connie might not know much about five-year-olds, but she did know that if you wanted them to see six with all their parts in working order, they had to eat something besides cookies. Fruit, she and Pete had decided, would be the after school snack of choice.

After the apple ended up in the geranium and the banana ended up mushed into the treads of her sneaker, Connie gave up and got out the cookies.

Ten minutes later, when Pete walked in and saw the sticky residue, she raised an ominous finger. "One word and I'll sue."

"For what, my half of the Sunday paper?"

Lucy picked up the empty cookie box and threw it on the floor.

"Hey," said Connie.

"Brilliant," said Pete. "Lucy, you'd better pick up that box."

Lucy slid out of her chair and ran out of the room.

Pete picked up the box. "I think it's time we set up some rules. Number one, no throwing."

"And if she disobeys?"

"Then we do what regular people do. Send her to her room."

"Her mother's *dead*."

"I don't think they have separate rule books for the kids with dead mothers."

Connie looked doubtful.

"What we really need is some sort of wedge. Something she likes that we can take away without stunting her growth."

Connie brightened. "Cookies."

"Cookies. Right. So if she doesn't finish dinner, no cookies for dessert. But we have to stop giving her cookies all the other hours of the day. There are plenty of other things she likes to eat. Cookies are the reward at the end of the day."

"Cookies are our wedge."

"Right," said Pete.

They sat silent. Is this how Patton felt on the eve of a big battle? wondered Connie.

Finally Pete stood and squared his shoulders. "I'll get her."

So he got her. Sat her at the table and explained to her. There were going to be some rules. There were going to be rewards, and there were going to be consequences.

"What's cottondishes?"

Pete started again. He gave examples of some rules. No throwing. No hitting. No running off and hiding, a recent favorite. No calling names. He gave examples of rewards (cookies) and consequences (time alone in her room). "Do you understand?" he asked.

"You're mean and I hate you!" Lucy shouted. She ran out of the kitchen.

"She understands," said Connie glumly.

When Pete got back in the truck he was sweating. It had seemed so much easier when he was a kid. Clean up your room or no TV. One more crack like that and you're grounded for the week. And had he thought his parents were mean? Probably, but he'd gotten over it eventually. Lucy would get over it. If she didn't learn about rules from them at home, she'd be learning about them later at the police station.

Police station.

He was supposed to be on his way to Mrs. Pond's to remove the red squirrel from her attic, but as he drove down Main Street thinking about police he happened to spy Budge Lorimer's house on the corner of Main and Wood Road. If Manny Rose had been a rumrunner, that could easily have been a lawful bullet in his skull, and old Budge Lorimer, who had once been chief of police on Nashtoba, had certainly been on the force during the Prohibition era.

Pete turned off Main onto Wood and into Budge's driveway.

In response to Pete's knock he heard a noise not indigenous to Nashtoba—the sound of a dead bolt being drawn. The door was opened by an elderly, bald man in glasses, flannel shirt, and jeans.

"Chief Lorimer?"

The man turned without a word and pushed open a door to his immediate left. "Dad!" he called.

He pointed through the door.

Pete went in.

Budge Lorimer. He should have known. The bald man at the door was probably in his mid-seventies, but the bald man in the chair near the window had to be close to the century mark. He splayed knotted fingers across the arms of the chair and pushed, struggling to his feet.

Pete held out a hand. "Please. Sit down."

"Yeh," said the old man. "Sit down." His speech was slow, raspy, deliberate, but clear.

Pete sat on the couch, close to the chair, so he could be heard. "I'm Pete Bartholomew," he began. "You knew my grandfather, Ray Bartholomew."

"Sure. Knew Ray. How is he?"

"Well, he's dead."

The old man raised a hand and let it drop. "Yeh. Knew that. Meant your dad. How is your dad?"

"Well, good. They live in Florida now."

"Your mother?"

"She's good, too."

Out in the street a car backfired, and Budge Lorimer's head swung around. The dry, stringy flesh on his neck creased into a fine web of ravines as he craned to see out. "Sounded like a gunshot."

"I think it was a car."

"Yeh. Knew that. Sounded like a gunshot, though. What can I do for you?"

"I was interested in anything you could tell me about Manny Rose. Speaking of gunshots. They just found his skull on my marsh, complete with bullet hole. I hear he used to run bootleg liquor."

Budge chuckled, a dry, stringy chuckle. "You heard true. Wasn't a shot fired on this island till the syndicate came in."

"And when was that?"

"Oh, they had a good grip by twenty-nine or so. Still used the locals—men who knew how to run a boat, knew the water—they'd lay down cash for the fellow's boat, buy him a new engine, take the money out of the first few runs."

A dark brown United Parcel truck rattled past the window, and Budge craned again. "Slow down!" he shouted and began to cough.

In a flash the younger Lorimer was in the room. "Settle down, Dad, will you?" He rolled his eyes at Pete and left. Budge took up where he'd left off, or thereabouts.

"Came on the force in twenty-one. Came across young Manny Rose a few years after that. And his partner, Clem Rogers. Wore out four sets of tires chasing those two."

"Why was that?"

"*Why?* 'Cause they were breaking the law, that's why. Chased them all over hell and gone, never caught 'em with the goods. 'Course my jurisdiction ended at the dock. Did pick up Ed Sears once, though. Ran him in. Lot of good it did me. By the time I got back from filling out the papers he was waiting on the dock."

"How did he work that?"

"Same way they all did. Money changing hands. Offered me a dollar a case to turn my back. When I said no they upped it to two."

"And you still said no?"

"It was against the law." Budge spat out each word as if he'd spelled them.

Pete cleared his throat. "I'm getting the idea this was big business."

"Big as it got around here. The higher up the chain the better you did, but even Manny could have made enough to retire on if he played his cards right. Most of them didn't though."

"Didn't what?"

"Play the right cards. Look what happened to Manny."

"What did happen to Manny?"

"Went down with the boat, that's what we were told. Clem was supposed to go out with him. Last minute come down with the grippe. Blamed himself high and low. Said Manny had no business going out alone, must have got caught up in the rig, gone overboard, boat foundered, went down."

"What happened to Clem Rogers after that, do you know?"

"Left here soon after Manny went. Heard he died himself, must be at least ten years ago, now. Nephew Reese Rogers might still be around, who knows? Not my problem anymore."

If Pete didn't know any better, he'd have thought the man sounded disappointed. Somewhere outside a small child screeched. This time Budge struggled all the way out of his chair. "Where'd that come from?"

Pete went to the window and looked. "At the corner. Somebody fell off her bike."

"Yeh. See 'em now. Fool, mother! Get her out of the road, will you?"

The voice was loud enough to ring Pete's right ear and bring young Lorimer back into the room.

Something in the younger man's eye told Pete it was time to go. He thanked Budge Lorimer and shook his hand. He felt nothing but papery skin and overgrown bone.

"Back anytime," said Budge. "Best to your grandfather."

"Will do," said Pete and followed the son out of the room.

As he pulled out of the driveway Pete looked

back toward the window. The old man was just settling back into his chair, but where were those sharp old eyes trained?

Pete made sure he camc to a full stop at the cor ner just in case.

⊱13⊰

Hᴜɢʜ Pᴇʟᴇᴛɪᴇʀ seemed a hair less cocky the second time around. Maybe it was because he didn't have the fishing gaff with him. He went through a one-two-three nervous motion of checking a shirt cuff, scratching his elbow, turning over the notebook he now held in his hand. "You want me to do what with this?"

"Write something down. Print, please."

Willy had to recite it three times before the words sank in, but finally Hugh printed the message and handed Willy the pad. "I'd like to know where you think you're going with this."

Willy handed the pad back. "Sign the name Susan, please."

Hugh stared at him. Did the cuff routine again. Signed.

"Thanks," said Willy. "We'll be in touch."

"Hold it. Hold it one goddamned minute. What do you think you're playing at, here?"

Willy smiled again and left him there.

This time Willy decided to head straight for Weams Point and barge in on the police chief in person. He had a foot large enough that anyone who tried would have some trouble slamming it in the door.

And nobody tried.

Weams Point police station was bigger than Nashtoba's but not as busy, which meant it was near comatose. The sergeant at the front desk, a tired-looking man who seemed held upright by a bristling gray crew cut, appeared to be in the middle of a personal phone call when Willy walked in.

"I said hall closet . . . behind the vacuum cleaner . . . don't touch those clubs . . . so look again." The sergeant hung up and looked sheepishly at the police chief, but Willy only got five words into his introduction before he was cut off.

"You'll want to talk to the chief." He dragged himself out of the chair, ambled down the hall, and returned with a long, gangly fellow in a navy suit jacket and gray pants, who held out a hand and smiled. There were two types of police chiefs in the world—the policemen and the politicians. Willy made a point of remaining in uniform to remind everyone which type he was. But suit or no, right from the good-old-boy smile, Willy knew this one was type two.

"Granville Foster. How'd you do. This way. No calls. Meeting at half-past?" Willy assumed some of that was for the sergeant, but the sergeant didn't seem to catch on.

The chief stopped walking. "Sergeant? Meeting at half-past?"

The sergeant came to. "Yes, sir. Meeting at half-past."

Willy knew that code. What it meant was, get this clown out of here in half an hour. The two men continued down a hall that contained more doors than there were in the entire Nashtoba station, counting closets and rest rooms. They passed through the door at the far end, and Willy found himself in a room that made his own office look like a closet. Or a rest room. Foster sat behind a desk that served as a nice, sturdy barrier and smiled again.

"I know what you're after. I've got the file right here and was just about to call." Sure, thought Willy. He knew that code, too. When in doubt, stall. "And what file might that be?"

Foster raised a lanky eyebrow. "Rosella Jameson. That's what you wanted to know, wasn't it? About the Rosella Jameson episode?"

"She had an episode?"

The other eyebrow rose. "What exactly are you looking for?"

"Anything you know about the Jamesons. It was Susan we found dead. You heard about it, I'm sure. Skull with a frontal fracture. Man-made. Ten years old or more."

Both eyebrows dropped, and the eyes underneath locked on Willy's. Finally Foster pushed the file across the desk. Willy opened it and leafed through. One look at the date and the first eerie vibe took hold.

Less than a month before Susan Jameson had dropped out of the sky onto Pete's beach, the

Weams Point police had received an anonymous call to check on 104 Back Street. On arrival at the house they'd found a note on the hall table. and the note was enclosed in the file. written in a distinctive, backward slanting hand. *Susan, It's not because of what happened. It's because of what I feel like. Good-bye. Good luck.*

Willy knew what that note must have done to the officers on the scene, knew the foreboding they must have felt as they proceeded down the hall and eventually into the bath where they'd found Rosella Jameson with her wrists cut. Willy read on. The paramedics had been summoned, Rosella had been saved, she'd been admitted for medical and psychiatric evaluation, had confessed to the suicide attempt, and the case had been closed.

Willy looked up, Rosella's note in hand. "Can I get a copy of this?"

Foster got up, left the room, returned with copy in hand. Willy slipped the paper carefully into his notebook. "What else can you tell me?"

"What else is there? She was kept in Penbrook for a couple of weeks, apparently saw the error of her ways, and was discharged."

"And the reason for attempting suicide?"

Another big smile. "Penbrook tends to treat information like that as confidential. As I'm sure you know."

"And in a town this size you never heard a rumor?"

"Ah. Unofficially, now." He picked up the phone, spoke into it in a mumble, and in the space of time it would take a long-legged healthy police officer to traverse the length of the hall, one appeared. "This is Lieutenant James. The lieutenant used to know one of the parties involved. Lieutenant, Chief McOwat here would like a little more information on Rosella Jameson than we seem to have in the file. Reason for attempted suicide and so on."

Lieutenant James looked from one chief to the other.

"Go on, Lieutenant," snapped Foster. "You're aiding a murder investigation, here."

The lieutenant didn't seem to need to ask whose. "The Jameson girls' parents died in a plane crash four or five years before the suicide attempt," he began. "The sisters were of age. No other family around. They lived on together in the house. They got along all right until they ran into some man trouble."

"Anyone you know?"

"Somebody from out of town, but he had a connection here. Coolidge. Roger Coolidge. He came to visit his grandfather, met Rosella, got engaged, at least according to Rosella. He wasn't seen around much. He ran off with Susan later on. Since then nobody's seen him at all."

Of course, thought Willy, feeling dumb. Roger Coolidge dumped Rosella for Susan. Rosella tried to kill herself and failed. Then changed her mind and tried to kill her sister and succeeded? And possibly Roger Coolidge as well? Dead people do tend to disappear, as Polly had said.

"Is this grandfather still around?"

"None of them are. All gone. Clement Rogers, the grandfather, he died about fifteen years ago. He had a daughter, Coolidge's mother, but she died of breast cancer a year or two before that."

"And what's Rosella up to now?"

"About two hundred and fifty pounds," cut in Foster, and laughed.

Budge Lorimer was right. Clem Rogers's nephew Reese *was* still around, if the phone book didn't lie. Reese Rogers, 19 East Court in Arapo, just over the causeway on Cape Hook. Pete looked at his watch. Almost four. Plenty of time to stop in on Reese Rogers and still be back for the witching hour. He and Connie had made a solemn pact to join forces by five-thirty wherever possible. It had to be alien airwaves, Pete decided, that juiced up Lucy every day around that time, but whatever it was, it was a time of day that definitely required double-teaming. And besides, it seemed the best way to convey a sense of family, a sense of security for the recently orphaned Lucy, to have them both front and center at mealtime.

East Court was an apartment complex, or half of an apartment complex. West Court was the other half. But if you put the grass from both halves on either one or the other lawn, it still wouldn't have covered the bare spots, and the same could be said for the paint. Pete found number nineteen on the top southerly corner of East Court and knocked. The door was thrown open with gusto, and a wiry little man with shaggy white hair and less than the full complement of teeth beamed at him.

"Hello!"

"Hello," said Pete warily. This wasn't the kind

of greeting a stranger usually got in these parts, not if the screws were tight all around.

"Come in!"

Pete went in.

The little man shoved out a brown hand. "Reese Rogers!"

"Pete Bartholomew."

They shook, and for a minute they seemed to be done.

"Well!" said Reese, still beaming. "Always glad to get a little company, but am I s'posed to know who you is?"

Pete laughed. So much for missing screws. "No, you're not supposed to know me. I came to pester you with questions. I'm told you used to run bootleg liquor with a fellow whose bones just turned up in my front yard."

The teeth disappeared, and most of the old man's high spirits with it. "Manny," he whispered.

"You heard?"

"I should of. Been listening long enough. You with the police?"

"No. I'd just like to know how he got there." When Reese said nothing, he added, "Wouldn't you, if it were your yard?"

Reese seemed to consider. "Come in," he said finally. "Let me get you a little something to warm your cockles."

"No, that's all—"

Too late. Reese Rogers had reached behind the nearest cabinet and withdrawn two shot glasses and a bottle of something pale brown whose label Pete had never seen before. Reese poured two fingers in each glass and handed one to Pete. "Here's mud in your eye."

Reese tossed his down.

Pete took an unmanly sip and suppressed a grimace. Mud was definitely the word. He braced himself to ward off the inevitable refill and was surprised to see the bottle and Reese's glass go back into the cupboard.

"Almost never touch the stuff," said Reese. "Wouldn't believe me if I told you how long that bottle's been around." He dropped into a sagging canvas chair.

Pete sat opposite on a sprung couch, set the shot glass as inconspicuously as he could on the floor, and looked around. Whatever money Reese might have made bootlegging, it hadn't taken him this far into his old age. What little there was in the room looked like it had come from the town dump. Pete waited for Reese to start talking, but after a few seconds in which nothing happened but some eye-glazing, Pete began. "It seems the tale of Manny's watery demise has sprung a few leaks."

The eyes snapped into focus. "That it has, boy. That it has. Ah, well, s'pose it's time to come clean."

Was it going to be that easy?

Almost.

"Yessir, we was bootlegging," Reese began. "Me and my Uncle Clem and Manny. And we had a pretty good system down. Used three different sites. Rotated 'em random, like. No set pattern, see? Some fellows, they'd go every night, same place same time. Not us. We'd change it every three trips.

Only went out dark of the moon. There was plenty of money to be made without taking chances. Unneedful chances, I mean. That place along Rum Creek was situated just about ideal. Summer cottage back of the creek empty most of the year, two miles of dark beach, creek itself, handy road, what else did we need? You say that's where you live?"

"In that summer cottage. Since winterized."

"My-oh-my." Rogers stalled briefly. "Well, then, let me see. Things went along kinda nice for a spell. But let me tell you something. It weren't no long arm of the law that troubled us. Was all these new fellows come to town, cocked and ready to roll, looking to make a fast buck off some other poor slob's sweat. No honor among thieves. And the rules was skewed up some, see? There was some figured if you stole illegal liquor it weren't stealing, see?" Reese paused. "I weren't much more than a kid at the time, mind. Weren't in on the whys and wheretofores. All's I remember is we'd just finished unloading a mess of liquor into the cottage and was all three inside the house when we see this car pull up with lights blazing, plowing right over the grass, smack up to the door. I can't see much against the headlights, just a big fellow in a long coat and hat, yells out, 'Feds!' top of his lungs and I tell you I near piss my pants. I'm nearest the door, see? Manny's behind me, Clem's behind Manny, but good old Manny, he knows the asses from the elbows. He says, 'That ain't no Feds,' and the minute he says it the man in the door whips out a gun and fires and right then I knows, it's one a them hijackers."

"Hijackers?"

"Hijackers. Pirates. Only on land instead of sea. The lips was loose around town, see? I remember one night I'm hanging out at the old diner when Aldo Fox comes in in hip boots with a coil of rope over his shoulder. 'Load coming in,' he hollers, 'need two more men,' free as you please. So it ain't hard for these thugs to get wind of a liquor drop. They show up at the landing site, wait till we get it unloaded, try to take it off our hands, see?"

"So this hijacker shot Manny."

Reese paused. "I'm wondering if I'm doing right by telling you this," he said finally. "But I can't see there's anybody left here to hurt 'cepting me. And I'm too old to care. Three squares and a nice warm cell don't sound half bad about now, see?"

"*You* shot Manny?"

Rogers shook his head. "Not me. But I seen it clear as day. That hijacker, he don't shoot anywhere but straight up. I hear it, see? That slug going *thwap*, into the roof right over my head. But let me back up a mite, tell you something about how it is with us three. Manny Rose, he's captain of the boat, it kind of follows natural-like he takes charge on land, too, see? So Manny runs things. Manny makes the rules. And rule number one is no guns. To him it's good, clean sport. You get caught, you give up nice and peaceful, no matter if it's Feds, cops, hijackers. And why not? If it's the law gets you, the worst you get's a little inconvenience and a fine you make up in one good run. If it's hijackers, all they want is your liquor, and there's plenty more where that come from. There's only one trouble with Manny's rule—Clem's got a rule of his own, which is every man look out for himself."

"Clem has a gun?"

"Clem has a gun. But Manny, he don't know that, see? So as soon as this hijacker fires his warning, Manny steps out sideways from behind the pile of cases where he's took cover, waving his hands in the air. Going by the rule. Giving up peaceful. Not expecting any gunshot from *behind* him, see? But poor old Clem, he's never caught on that first shot ain't meant for nothing but noise. He hears it, he pulls out his gun, he fires. Just the split second Manny steps sideways right into it and *blam*. Manny takes Clem's bullet in the back of his head."

Reese closed his eyes. When he opened them there were tears on his cheeks, but he didn't seem to notice. He pushed on. "The hijackers see Manny hit the dirt and take off. Hell, I would of too, I s'pose. Clem and me, we rush over to Manny, but he's gone. Nowadays you read in the papers just because somebody ain't got no heartbeat, ain't breathing, you don't give up on him, but back then, for fellows like me and Clem, gone is gone. I don't remember just what we done next. I do remember at some point Clem sitting me down, shining the lantern in my face, talking to me real low down. This here is a terrible accident, he says. But what's done is done. We can't help Manny no more. Manny's gone. But we can help each other and we can help Manny's widow. What do you think happens to us, to all the money, hers and ours, if we call the law in here now? Even if they believe the shooting's an accident, there's all this liquor sitting here, see? Even if we get rid of the liquor, how do we explain Manny being dead in this broke-into house we don't own? And won't they just love an excuse to go poking around what we do own, poking around Manny's house, finding all that money he keeps hid? What's Manny's widow gonna live on then, and her with her man being gone? If we don't owe it to ourselves, we owe it to Alice Rose, says Clem."

Reese looked up at Pete. "What do you s'pose you'd of done if you was there and you was fifteen and you seen with your own eyes how it was an accident and it was your uncle you'd looked up to since practically before you was born?"

"So you buried him."

Reese let go with an old, old sigh. "Guess you're there ahead of me. Yes, we buried Manny. Out on the marsh, next the old plank walk where there's plenty of soft mud. We clean up the floor, get rid of the liquor, Clem runs Manny's boat offshore, scuttles it, rows back in the skiff he's towed along."

"Why didn't he just leave Manny on board when he scuttled the boat?"

"And let him wash in with that bullet hole in him? You oughta know how the sea works, living where you do. Half of what it swallows it spits back out, either on shore or pulled up in somebody's net. Couldn't take a chance like that, now, could we?"

"And everyone believed Manny went down with the boat?"

"Believed or pretended to. But Clem told it to Alice true. He told her what he told me. She could talk and lose the money or keep quiet and live easy.

She chose to keep quiet. Done a damned fine job of it, too. When the boat don't come in she goes straight to the Coast Guard, plays it up real good. They make a nice search, but it ain't long before some of the gear washes up and that's the end of it. Later I go see Alice Rose. Pour out my heart. Never forget it to my dying day. She lets me say my piece, thanks me for coming, tells me she don't hold nothing against me. Then she looks me in the eye and says, 'This is the last we'll speak of this,' and it were." Reese paused again. "Till now."

Pete decided there was no point in passing on what he knew about Connie's recent conversation with Alice Rose. "And your Uncle Clem? What did he do?"

"Clem, I'm not so sure he trusts old Alice to keep mum. Packs up his wife and daughter and moves to Rockwell. You know Rockwell?"

"A little. Wasn't it a mill town back then?"

"Sure was. Clem figures he'll try a whole new kind of life, far away from the water as he can get, just in case anybody comes looking for him, but he don't last long. He ends up over in Weams Point, running rum in a boat of his own for a year or so, outrunning everything in town before Prohibition winds down. Finally goes back to fishing." Reese chuckled. "Outruns the fish, too. Never spoke of Manny to me again, but it were clear enough it preyed on him till the end. I were there when he died fifty years later. It were the last words he spoke. Haunted him all his life. Same as it haunted me."

Till now, maybe, thought Pete. It didn't take a

licensed psychiatrist to see that Reese Rogers had been waiting to unburden himself of this one.

Reese reached into his pocket and pulled out a battered pocket watch, not gold, not working. Engraved on the cover was a four-masted schooner, and engraved on the back was the name *Clement B. Rogers*. "That were his," said Reese. "He come to me and give it to me on the day he left town. Said it were lucky. Maybe it were. I could've done worse in life, I s'ppose." He looked up at Pete, and his face cracked in a painful grin. "Could've been Manny, you know?"

❊14❊

As Willy McOwat knocked on Rosella Jameson's door he recognized the old, familiar adrenaline surge that had been with him since his first days as a cop. It was weight-on-the-balls-of-the-feet time. Who knew what he'd find behind that door? Any door?

But what he found behind this door was a woman who looked like she'd gotten her last adrenaline rush when Elvis was still king. Willy had talked to people like this before. He knew that his badge would get him in the door, but it would take what was behind it to get him anywhere further. He decided to keep her standing face to face rather than let her sink into a chair, but either way it would be easy to lose her, to let her run down, dry up, go back into that dark place where she appeared to have been living for some time now. It took everything he had to get his questions through to her. It seemed to take everything she had to give him an answering nod, yes and no. Yes, she was

Rosella Jameson. Yes, she'd had a sister Susan. Yes, she knew she was dead. No, she hadn't seen her since she'd run off.

None of Willy's questions raised a flicker in the eye until he asked about Roger Coolidge. Had she seen Roger Coolidge since he'd left with her sister? It wasn't much of a flicker, but it was something. Willy probed gently, patiently, persistently. It took a long time, but eventually the nods were replaced with single words, then two together, then three. She had seen Roger, once, two months after he'd first left with Susan. He'd come back asking for Susan. He'd said Susan had left him, had said she was going home to patch things up with Rosella.

But Susan had never come.

And Roger had left.

Again.

There was more life in Rosella's face when Willy left her than there had been when he'd found her, but he knew that wasn't necessarily a good sign. Willy considered the possibilities as he drove along. At the very least, he was a knife that had opened old wounds. At the most, if she had indeed killed her sister and her ex-boyfriend, he was her Armageddon come to call. Either way, with her history, he wasn't too happy about driving away and leaving her alone. He decided he'd better make a short detour on his way back to Nashtoba.

This time the sergeant waved him down the hall without bothering to hang up the phone, and, as a result, Willy walked in on Foster as he was attempting to hustle a current issue of *Sports Illustrated* into a drawer. But when he saw Willy he abandoned the subterfuge, shooting him that good-old-boy grin once more.

This time Willy didn't bother to grin back. "You might want to run a patrolman out to the Jameson house. See if you can get the social services in."

"Why, what's she done now?"

"As far as I know, nothing. But she's just been dragged over some painful old ground and she's got a history. Right now it looks like the fog's beginning to lift. That can be a dangerous time. She might just remember why it was she wanted to kill herself before. She might just do it this time."

Foster continued to smile complacently. "I'm not running a Miss Lonely Hearts Club, Chief McOwat. My men are on more important duty elsewhere."

Willy remained unperturbed. He knew his politicians. He leaned over the desk till its function as barrier was annulled. "Then it looks like you've got two choices, Chief Foster. You can get off your ass and stroll down there yourself, or I can take care of it and you can read about it in tomorrow's paper."

It took four seconds, maybe five. Foster picked up the phone and barked into it.

Willy walked out the door, and, as he passed the front desk, he could hear the sergeant on the radio, dispatching a cruiser to 104 Back Street.

Willy swung by on his way home, just to be sure, and not only had the cruiser beaten him there but so had Lieutenant James. Willy cut down Governor Bradford onto Front Street, and his mind was on so many things that the man opening the mailbox almost slipped past him unnoticed.

Almost.

Willy slowed and watched through his rearview mirror as Dr. St. George proceeded up the walk, mail in hand, inserted key in door, and disappeared. Willy circled the block and drove by again, curious, more or less. Nothing remarkable about the house—white Greek Revival, standard porch, standard small yard, standard motorboat under that god-awful blue shrink-wrap parked along the fence. Polly liked boats, he recalled. Every time Willy set foot in a boat his gorge rose. And he was about as far from the Tim St. George type as a man could get. Was he wasting his time with this dogged pursuit of Polly? And what about Coolidge? Maybe he was wasting time, there, too?

No.

And no.

At least not yet.

The witching hour was in full swing when Pete walked through the door, and by the looks of things, it had gone into overtime. The first thing that greeted him was the sight of Connie's rear end projecting from the open refrigerator, ominous muttering echoing from within. The second thing was a horizontal glass on the kitchen table next to a plate of macaroni and cheese, green beans, and tomatoes, all swimming in a pool of milk. The third thing was Lucy, balanced precariously on the kitchen chair, reaching for the cupboard over her head. Pete sidestepped Connie and completed a timely interception of the cookie box with his right hand while, with the left arm, he returned Lucy protesting to earth.

Connie backed up, whipped around, saw him with the cookie box, and aimed a forefinger at him. "You give that kid a cookie and I'll tell you where you'll find the rest of them."

Pete set down the box. "Okay. Don't shoot."

"*Shoot?* You are very close to being drawn and quartered. *And* disemboweled. Do you have any idea what time it is?"

"Yeah, but I found out what happened to Manny Rose."

That stopped her, but not for long. Lucy had picked up the mangled plate and was calmly pouring the milk off her dinner and onto the table, from which point it was slowly working its way to the floor. "*Yuck*," she said.

Connie appeared to be contemplating a word that rhymed with it. She grabbed the plate as Pete grabbed the sponge. It didn't seem right that it should take two adults to feed one small child. "Is there more macaroni?"

"*No*, there is not more macaroni. And there's not more anything else, either."

Pete opened the refrigerator and found eggs, milk, an orange. He set about assembling a quick meal that contained at least three of the essential food groups. To his surprise, Lucy ate two-thirds of a scrambled egg, most of a piece of toast, and half the orange before she pushed her plate away and said, "*Now* cookies!"

Pete reached into the box and extracted two cookies.

"After you finish the orange," said Connie.

"Cookies!" shrieked Lucy.

There was a familiar halloo at the door. Pete took his eye off the ball, and one cookie disappeared.

Connie opened her mouth, but seemed to have run out of usable words.

Pete decided the best course of action was to separate the overexposed parties. He crossed Willy in the hall as he carted Lucy upstairs and set to with the nightly routine. Wash. Pajamas. Bed. Leerie. It must have been a long afternoon. By the time Pete got to papa-the-rich-banker, Lucy was asleep.

When Pete came back downstairs the conversation at the kitchen table came to a suspicious halt.

"I assume at some point you did plan to tell me about Manny Rose?" asked Willy.

Pete sat down and laid out Reese Rogers's tale. "Which answers all the Manny Rose questions," he finished, "but still leaves all the Susan Jameson ones untouched."

A weird look went back and forth between Connie and the chief.

"Okay, what?"

"Manny Rose's murderer was Roger Coolidge's grandfather," said Willy.

It took a minute to sink in. The minute it did, Pete began to feel like he'd tripped down that Wonderland rabbit hole. "I take it you've decided this means something?"

"He's decided this means Susan Jameson didn't exactly drop into your lap by accident," said Connie, "which, when you think about it—"

"Which, when you think about it is a bunch of baloney," said Pete.

Connie opened her mouth. Willy held up a hand.

"If we could go back to Susan Jameson. Or Tim St. George. Were you aware that he was a fully licensed physician when he worked for you?"

Pete thought. "I knew he'd done some medical school."

"And graduated. And completed a three-year residency."

"So?"

"It never struck you as funny that he decided to help you out instead of launching his own medical career?"

"Well, I don't know. I guess I didn't think of it like that. I didn't think of him as a doctor."

"What did you think of him as?"

"A friend of Bob Fleet's. Bob was my freshman year roommate. I ran into Bob end of senior year at a basketball game. He had Tim with him, we went out for a few beers, Tim had some Celts tickets and Bob couldn't go, so I went. We hit a couple of other games together, met up for beers once or twice, talked a lot of sports. I guess that's how I thought of him. A fellow sports enthusiast."

Willy didn't look too happy with that answer. "Okay, back to this tale you got from Reese. You're saying this all happened right here in this house."

"It was no tale, I'd bet money on that. But yeah, it was probably right out there in the living room. It was only a summer cottage back then, four rooms and a porch. No ceiling, just rafters. I've seen the old pictures. Lots of pine—" Pete stopped cold, pushed back his chair, stood up. "Come on."

* * *

The attic door creaked. "You're going to wake up Lucy," said Connie.

"No I won't, she's dead to the world." Pete ducked through the door, dropped onto all fours, and disappeared from sight. The chief dropped down and followed. Connie was damned if she was going to stand there and wait for Pete to tell her what he was trying to prove. She scrambled after them, and when she caught up with them they were squatting on their heels, training a flashlight on the roof overhead.

"This is what they would have looked up at," Pete was saying. "The sheathing, the exposed struts. This section here is directly over that main room. Reese said he heard the hijacker's warning shot slap into the wood over his head. It could have hit one of those struts or it could have hit the —"

"There," said Willy. He took the flashlight from Pete. He stood up as far as he could, which wasn't far. He pulled a jackknife out of his pocket, steadied the light, dug into the wood like one of those carpenter bees that kept drilling holes in the eaves at the front of the house. When he finished he held out his hand, redirected the light.

All these years, thought Connie, as she looked down at the small, dark piece of metal. All the years, off and on, that she'd lived in this house, there'd been a bullet overhead, blood underfoot?

"Yuck," she said.

All the ghosts were keeping Connie awake. The ghost of Manny Rose, who'd been shot dead a few yards below her. The ghost of Clem Rogers, who'd been tormented by one false move that had followed him all his life. The ghost of Reese Rogers, the fifteen-year-old boy who over half a century ago had been forced into a man overnight.

And those weren't the only ghosts. Despite his efforts to pooh-pooh it, Willy's news of the Rose-Jameson connection had rattled Pete all the way down to his toes. Or halfway down, at least. Connie drew closer to the sleeping body that lay curled with its back to her, letting her own flesh find and fill the nooks and crannies in his, and right away she could tell by the lack of give in him that he was awake. Awake and faking sleep. Not a good sign. What was the deal, here? There was something about this whole Susan Jameson thing that was making Pete feel rotten, but it wasn't just the kind of rotten that came with shock, or even grief. Connie had known Pete a long time now. She'd gotten to know that set to the spinal column and usually it had something to do with how he felt about himself, not how he felt about someone else. Connie laid a palm against the curve of muscle just above Pete's shoulder blade. It was clenched like the withers of a hopped-up thoroughbred before a race. She'd felt that before, long ago.

But not so far away . . .

He hadn't heard her come into the room. He stood with the drill in one hand, the drawer pull in the other, neither of them anywhere near the drawer itself. Which was just as well, considering his eyes were trained out the window. But there was something about the stance that suggested inner, not outer, visions, something about the jaw that suggested whatever he was seeing wasn't all sweetness and light. She'd been about to ask him where he'd been for the last few weeks. Been about to tell him that the bureau had been sitting there for so long it was getting dry rot. Instead she walked up behind him and laid a hand on his shoulder. Even before he jumped she could feel the knots in his flesh through his shirt.

"Jesus Christ," he said. "What are you trying to do, kill me?"

"No, just trying to wake you as gently as I could. Next time I'll wear hobnail boots."

"Thank you, I'd appreciate that." And suddenly, surprisingly, he smiled at her. It was maybe the second time she'd seen him do it, aimed in her direction, at least, and she was mortified to find it worked on her the same way Clark Gable's had been rumored to have worked on Margaret Mitchell—everything she'd been about to say went clean out of her head.

Suddenly Peter Bartholomew didn't seem to have much in the way of snappy comebacks himself. "Well," he said finally. "I guess I'd better stop daydreaming and get back to work."

"I'd say that depends on what you're dreaming about."

For a second it actually looked like he might tell her. And for that same second she could have sworn he was talking nightmares, not dreams. Then she realized he wasn't looking at her, he was looking behind her, and with good enough reason, she supposed, as Susan Jameson came bouncing past and twined herself around every piece of him she could get.

Connie beat a hasty retreat but found herself pausing

at the door, looking back. She caught Pete's eye over Susan's head, and for the second time in a short period, she found herself taken aback. The look she'd caught wasn't the usual man-in-paradise thing she'd come to expect. This one was more like man-caught-in-serpent's-mouth.

Connie barreled out the door so fast that she crashed into Baby Hughie. He caught her by the hips, first, but actually worked the handhold well aft before she could assemble the will to break them apart.

I've got to get out more, she thought.

"Did I know he was a *what?*" asked Polly.

"A doctor," said Willy. "Has a nice big practice in Bradford now, but back then he was working for your brother."

"*What?* I mean, like, *no.* A doctor. I don't remember him saying one single solitary—" Polly held up a finger. "Hey, wait. I do remember something. I ran into him one day in Smith's liquor store. Well, I didn't exactly run into him. I was driving by . . ."

Now isn't this my lucky day, thought Polly. There he was, in all his splendor, getting out of his car in front of Smith's Liquors. Polly pulled her car in beside his and went inside. She found him standing in front of the beer cooler, chiseled features wrinkled in thought. "Hello," she said.

He turned and beamed at her so brightly that Polly's knees almost buckled. "Polly! Hello! Just the person I need. I thought I'd buy your brother some beer. He's offered me a few at the end of the day, I feel I should help him restock. What do you suggest?"

"Budweiser."

"Something he'd pull out for special use."

"Budweiser."

"What about this?" Tim pulled out a bottle whose contents looked like brown shoe polish. "This is an intriguing little newcomer."

"He'd pour it down the sink. You know a lot about beer?"

"I know a lot about everything in here. My great-uncle owns a liquor store. I worked it for twelve years. Every summer since freshman year high school." He replaced the bottle of ale. "Oh, well, if you insist." He pulled out a case of Budweiser bottles, giving Polly a brief glimpse of rippling musculature. She followed him to the register.

"May I help you find something?"

Polly plucked a bag of chips off the rack. "This is it. Thanks." If she walked outside with him she could say something like, "Care for a drink?" No, that was a guy line. How about "I'm off for a swim, care to join me?" That way he'd get to see her in her suit. But wait, with her luck, Susan Jameson would be down there in her brand-new string bikini, and that kind of comparison shopping she needed like she needed a third foot. Think, Polly girl, think.

Tim opened the door for her and stepped back. She walked through it with her tongue glued to her teeth.

"See you back at the ranch," he said in the parking lot.

She decided to take that as an opening, go with what she'd got. "Are you going back there? So am I. I thought I'd run down to the beach for a swim. Want to come?"

"I don't have a suit with me. Maybe some other time."

Before she could offer the list of solutions that immedi-

ately sprang to mind—borrow-Pete's, or who-cares-about-suits—he was dust.

Polly resurfaced to the sound of a voice and found the police chief watching her gravely.

"And?"

Polly lifted her shoulders. "That was it. Strike one."

"I'm referring to his being a doctor."

"Oh! Well, that was it on that, too. That part about him working twelve summers since freshman year high school. Nobody works just summers unless they're in school, do they? And if he was in school for eight years after high school that would include four years of medical school. But we never really talked much. I think I was too busy ogling." She giggled, paused, peered up at Willy. He looked less than his usual rocklike self, and it gave her a shock.

"I've always been able to talk to you," she said.

"Thanks." But for some reason it didn't seem to perk him up much.

It must be the case, Polly decided. "You're not thinking Tim St. George did something to Susan?"

"I'd like to know what he was doing here."

"I can tell you what he wasn't doing. Fooling around with Susan. They hardly spoke to each other."

"Some people talk. Some don't."

Polly peered at the chief. And what did he mean by that? Or wasn't it obvious enough? Given the choice between this new Polly Bartholomew and that old Susan Jameson, Polly knew which one

Willy would want on the other end of the couch.
So what was her big problem? Why was Willy, the
perfect gentleman, scaring her so much? No reason.
None that she could think of, at least.

So *jump*.

She slid along the couch toward him. She'd been
going the other way for so long that she wondered
if he'd get the hint, but she needn't have worried.
She closed her eyes, felt a large, warm hand on her
neck. She leaned into it and tipped her face. She
felt a warm mouth. A warm body. She felt those
rusty old defenses begin to melt.

And she panicked.

Jumped back.

❖ 15 ❖

WILLY STRUGGLED OUT of his Explorer the next morning and yawned his way up the walk to Joel Crawford's door. He'd lain awake most of the night in unaccustomed self-doubt. He'd badly misread Polly the night before. Was it was possible he was misreading this case as well? No. But he knew it was the damned case, that damned Susan Jameson, that had caused him to blow his cool on Polly's couch. It hadn't taken him long to see what was going on in Polly's head, but he didn't want her by the force of her will, he wanted her by the force of her natural ardor. So now what? Willy didn't have a clue.

But whereas he now had no clue where to go with Polly, the instinct that had been honed to a fine edge through years in law enforcement told him he was still on track with the case. Follow the threads and they'd lead him to Coolidge, he was sure of that.

He tried to focus as Joel Crawford lined up the

two pieces of paper—the supposed Susan Jameson postcard and the Rosella Jameson suicide note. "Where's the other one?" said Crawford.

Willy had collected a few pieces of paper since they'd last met. "Which other one?"

"The W-2."

Oh, that one.

He removed the W-2 from the file and set it next to the two papers on the desk. After a minute he said, "Well?"

"If you're looking for instant answers, I'd say maybe yes, maybe no. Give me a day on it."

"In that case," said Willy, and he brought out the whole collection. Handwriting samples from the old Factotum employees, from Willy's old friends, and the fifteen-year-old signature from Roger Coolidge's driver's license.

Joel Crawford's face turned into an interesting mix. "Two days."

He was already pouring over the top piece of paper. Willy couldn't ask for more than that.

Reese Rogers started visibly when he saw the chief, but he settled down soon enough when Willy assured him he was not under arrest as accessory after the fact. Reese told a tale that varied in inconsequentials from the Pete version just enough. A story that came out verbatim twice was likely memorized. One that missed some small details, added others, was likely on the mark. Willy next spent some time going over the Rogers family tree. There wasn't much of it to start with, and now there was less of it left.

"I'm all that's left of the Rogers crowd," said Reese. "My folks only had me. I never did get around to getting married. Clem only had the one girl. That's why Clem's girl, my cousin, named her boy what she did. Roger. See? Keeping the name around. After me, young Roger's all that's left. Assuming he's around someplace. Ain't seen or heard from him since Clem died. Fifteen years. But why should I? Once removed cousin, that's all he is."

"But you saw him when his grandfather died."

"I seen him. Stuck around long enough to collect his take, that were it. Not that it come to much. Clem didn't own a house—died in a rented apartment on Back Street. Weams Point, that is. Left me a thousand dollars outright. Must of thought there'd be more left over, but there weren't. Roger took some exception to that, but he didn't take it far as court. It could be why I ain't seen him, though, now that I give it some thought."

Or it could be that he was dead, as Polly seemed to think, but Willy couldn't afford to subscribe to that theory right now.

So, next stop, the banks. There were two of them on Cape Hook, each with a branch in all five mainland towns, one with a branch on Nashtoba. In the only account Willy could find for Reese Rogers there was the vast sum of ninety-two dollars and eighty-six cents. But after the third of the month there would be a little more—the man had automatic deposit of Social Security and public assistance checks. There was no record of any Roger Coolidge accounts, but Willy learned Alice Rose had a sizable trust fund, managed by the bank. Willy was unsuccessful in tracking down its source. The current law requiring banks to report large cash deposits hadn't been in place in Alice's day. That didn't mean there weren't those who might remember where the money had come from, and Willy knew just where he wanted to ask first.

Sarah Abrew peered at the police chief. He was all the way across the room, squatting on her love seat, and still he seemed to loom. Either he was still growing or she was still shrinking. "You want something, I assume?"

"The way I look at it, you owe me one."

True, thought Sarah. She'd impeded his last murder investigation a mite. "Always happy to oblige the forces of law and order," she said primly and was delighted to hear him choke down a laugh. "What might I do for you, Chief?"

"You might tell me where Alice Rose got her money."

"Where do you think?"

"Rum?"

"Funny about that. Seemed it was anything but. Plenty of whiskey and gin. I seem to recall brandy was mighty high on the list."

"And Manny Rose just stashed the money in the bank?"

"S'pose he could have. Things were that easy back then. But rumor around town was he stashed it under the floorboards in the barn. Later on, after things had quieted down, old Alice shuffled it into the bank. They set up a trust when she went off her rocker."

"Any idea how much there was?"

"Enough to keep her. That woman never did a lick of work in her life."

The police chief fell silent. He was a man who never let a little quiet bother him, and Sarah had to admire that. If more people took good, sensible stock of what they had to offer, they'd shut their yaps, too, now and then. But after a good piece of quiet had slipped by, Sarah got the notion the police chief had something more to say that wouldn't quite come. Well, she'd skinned a few cats in her day. She cast around for likely sources of difficulty. If it was more about Manny Rose, he'd come out and say so. So it had to be about that other one, Susan. And what about her could make him sit here chomping down on his tongue like that?

Peter, thought Sarah, and the ends of her fingers went numb.

"Don't suppose you've got any idea what happened to that young woman yet?"

"No," said Willy, sounding glum.

" 'Spect you're casting a wide net. She was the type of woman who'd attract trouble from miles around."

"And why was that?"

"Don't play coy with me, young fellow. I imagine you've come across the type a time or two yourself. But she wasn't all window dressing. She liked to settle down with me from time to time for a nice, long chat. Seemed partial to my foolish yarns. Never did seem to get around to the job she'd come to do. I'm thinking they'll do better with this new one. Phoebe-what's-her-name. Have you seen her? Striking, wouldn't you say? And more your size than that little elf you're fussing with." Sarah said it by way of a gentle warning. She knew Polly. But the chief seemed determined to miss the point.

"If we could get back to Susan Jameson," he said. "In these yarns of yours, did she seem partial to a particular subject? Rumrunners, by chance?"

"You think I'm an elephant? How do you expect me to recall—"

But suddenly Sarah did recall. The last time Susan had come. Pete had dropped her off on his way to meet someone at the train. She was supposed to have waxed the floor. She'd actually gone down on her knees with the cloth and the can . . .

"I didn't know they still made this kind of wax," said Susan.

"Been around a long time. Longer than I have, even."

Susan sat back on her heels. "Were you born on Nashtoba, Mrs. Abrew?"

"Born and bred. Or as bred as they could get me. I was a mite troublesome when I was a tyke."

"Well, there was the depression. That was hard on the children, too."

"Thank you, child, but I was twenty years old when Hoover was elected."

"Still, it must have been hard on someone who was twenty. I understand no one had money except the bootleggers."

Sarah chuckled. "Oh, my, yes, there were a few mattresses stuffed with something other than straw around this place."

"That's what they did with the money, stuffed it in mattresses?"

"Oh, they got cleverer than that. I heard one fellow stuffed a horse collar with thousand dollar bills. Another sunk it in a lobster trap."

"Did some bury it?"

"They buried liquor, I can tell you that. Fred Smollett's still plowing up bottles in his cornfield now and then."

"Some relative of this Smollett person must have been a rumrunner, then?"

Sarah opened her mouth to tell her about Hugo Smollett, but just then something in the window caught her eye. Sarah's eyesight was poor. Getting poorer. But she knew that foolish boy's head when she saw it. She stepped around Susan and rapped on the glass. "You there!"

Susan leaped up. "What is it?"

"The Peletier boy. Peeking in here. Dashed off on a bicycle. Any Peeping Tom comes to this house has got to be the dumbest boy in town."

Sarah chuckled. "But he wasn't, of course. Somebody like Susan, crawling around on all fours, I'd say that was worth a look. I told Pete about it when he came back and he hardly seemed surprised."

"How did he seem?" asked the chief.

"How the blazes should I know? It was fifteen years—"

"Let me rephrase the question. Over the course

of the several visits he made with Susan, was it your impression that there was ever any downturn in the relationship? Any mention of a third party?"

Sarah peered at the chief. Damn her eyes. What the devil was he up to? He couldn't be such a fool. "If you're asking did the course of true love run smooth—" but she was interrupted again by the sound of voices in the hall.

Lucy. And Pete. She felt that old lurch in her chest cavity that came with pleasure.

And fear.

Willy watched in silence as Lucy dug out Sarah's checkerboard, settled on the other side of the table from Sarah, moved her first piece out into the no-man's-land in the center of the board. The little girl had lived with Sarah for a short time, but obviously it had been long enough to establish a rapport. Willy caught Pete's eye over the two bent heads, nodded toward the door.

"Sarah?" said Pete. "All okay here?"

Sarah looked up, not at Pete but at Willy. She seemed tense, but Willy had seen her more tense. She nodded, and the two men stepped out the back door.

"What?" said Pete.

"I want to throw something at you. I want you to think about it rationally. That means unemotionally. Understood?"

"When have I—" began Pete, but he seemed to think better of continuing the thought. "What now?"

"Let me lay out a scenario. Starting back some sixty-odd years. You already know the beginning of the script, so I'll summarize that part. A couple of rumrunners. An accidental shooting. A body buried on a marsh. Now, fast-forward fifty years. A beautiful young woman gets wind of this fellow buried on the marsh via her boyfriend, the grandson of the shooter. For reasons unknown to us, she wants to find this buried fellow, but she doesn't know just where he's buried. She has some information, but there are pieces missing. She begins to poke around, she lands on said marsh, but she finds she's not as alone as she'd hoped. Here comes this red-blooded young man in the prime of life, who appears to be living almost on top of the spot in question. He seems extremely familiar with the area. He's not exactly repulsive. He appears to live alone. She decides she can make use of him. She waits till late one afternoon when he's on the beach by himself. She does a little striptease to make sure she's got his attention—" Willy paused and looked at Pete curiously. He'd expected to be interrupted by now. "Stop me if this starts to sound familiar."

"I take it you've based this on something?"

"I've based it on something, yes. Number one, the fact that Susan Jameson's boyfriend happens to be the grandson of the fellow who killed and buried Manny Rose. Number two, the fact that sooner or later every conversation with Susan Jameson came around to the subject of running rum. And number three, the odds of someone like her dropping down on an inaccessible stretch of beach for no other apparent reason than to make all your hot little dreams come true."

Now that should do it, thought Willy.

"Aren't you forgetting number four?" asked Pete. "The fact that she ended up in the same hole with Manny?"

"Right," said Willy, nonplused.

❖16❖

"**I** DON'T GET IT," said Connie.

Willy got up and helped himself to a second cup of coffee. "What makes you think I do? I tell him the love of his life—"

"Excuse me?"

"In the context of the time in question."

"I told you. It wasn't . . . oh, forget it. You told him—"

"I told him this woman's arrival was not exactly a random act of kindness, and he went on his way as if I'd told him I wanted to borrow his lawn mower. Which I do, by the way. I thought you told me last time I wouldn't have to mow anymore."

"El Niño. Or the greenhouse thing, take your pick. So now what?"

Connie heard the door click, saw Willy's big body go on alert as he heard it, too. The door opened, and Phoebe Small came into the kitchen. This time she was wearing a black leotard under the overalls, which seemed to have miraculously turned her from *Plow and Hearth* to *Victoria's Secret*.

"Yikes," she said. "I keep walking in on people. Rita said Pete was in here."

"He isn't," said Connie. "Willy, this is our newest employee, Phoebe Small. Phoebe, this is our illustrious police chief."

Willy stood up and dipped his head with old-world courtesy. He said something inane about Pete always collecting an interesting group.

An interesting group of redheads, thought Connie darkly.

But unlike her predecessor, this one was no femme fatale. She stood in front of the chief and blushed and stammered like a twelve-year-old. By now, Susan Jameson would have had the chief halfway out of his pants.

Or would she? Now that Connie thought about it, Susan had never been one for the scatter-gun approach. It had been Pete she'd been after, but Connie had never imagined there'd been any motive other than the obvious one, even though, considering how idiotically they'd all acted, Susan could probably have had her pick of the lot . . .

There were four of them out there on the marsh, dark shapes against the late-day sun. No, five, thought Connie, as it dawned on her that one of them was carrying someone. And once she recognized the babe in arms she supposed she could have named the rest of the pack with her eyes shut—Pete, Tim, Baby Hughie, and, carrying Susan, Nicky Peck. Nicky and Susan were covered in mud. The remaining three hounds were only mud to the calves, as any blind fool might be who chose to walk straight through the low spots instead of around them.

"What happened?" asked Connie as they came within range.

Nicky Peck barged past in stalwart silence, bearing his precious cargo. Hughie and Pete respectively grabbed the door and emptied the nearest chairs of debris.

Tim was the only one who had the decency to lag behind to answer her. "Some sort of accident. Susan fell in the creek. The Peck gentleman pulled her out. Eventually the rest of us saw them and ran to offer assistance, but there was no need."

What was Nicky Peck doing out on the marsh with Susan Jameson? wondered Connie. As Connie stepped through the door, one look at Rita's face told her Rita was wondering the same thing. By the evidence of the mud alone, it looked like the two of them had done some rolling in it. But it was Pete who hovered close, who kept repeating, "Are you all right?" until Connie wanted to rap him upside the head.

"I'm fine," said Susan at last. "Nothing's hurt. It was so silly of me." So why don't you just bat your eyes at him? thought Connie. The tremor in the voice was done to perfection. And the female mud-wrestler look didn't appear to be hurting her standings with the crowd. Baby Hughie's eyes were about to escape their sockets. She supposed Nicky Peck's heavy breathing could still be attributed to the unaccustomed physical activity, but if he didn't turn around soon, he was going to end up with one of Rita's freshly sharpened pencils in his ear. Or somewhere else.

Pete finally put an end to the sideshow by a firm

hand under Susan's arm. "Come on, let's get you into the shower."

Connie could almost see the imaginations around her sliding into overtime. They all watched as Pete and Susan made their way down the hall, Susan doing her best to muddy the rest of Pete by leaning all over him.

"I'd better get to a shower myself," said Nicky.

"Make it a cold one," said Rita behind him.

Connie resurfaced to the sound of wailing. This wasn't the I-want-a-cookie thing, this was real. This was pain. Connie felt all the blood leave her extremities. She rushed toward the door just as Pete came through it carrying Lucy, one small, bloody finger held high. He perched her on the kitchen counter, and, as Connie stood frozen, Phoebe took over.

"This isn't too bad," Phoebe told them, dabbing the wound with a wet towel. "No stitches required. Do you have a gauze pad, tape, some sort of antiseptic?"

Connie doubted it. Miraculously, now that she thought about it, this was their first bloodletting. She retreated to the bathroom and rummaged around, managed to unearth close facsimiles to the necessary items. When she returned to the kitchen, Phoebe again took charge, washing, drying, taping, talking to Lucy the whole time.

"What happened, did a bear bite you?"

"I cut my *finger*," said Lucy.

"On a razor clam?"

"On a *glasses*."

Connie listened hard, but already she could tell

the small voice was more filled with outrage than pain. She exhaled. Breathed in.

"Yikes. And here I thought it was a silly old clam."

"Or a *bear*," Lucy threw in. She hiccoughed twice and giggled.

"What glasses?" asked Connie.

Pete rolled his eyes at her. He looked like he'd lost a little blood himself. "My sunglasses. Nabbed them off the dash. They broke, and she cut her finger."

"There," said Phoebe. "All done." She held a professional-looking bandage aloft.

Connie pushed Pete aside and picked Lucy up in her arms. "You were very brave. How about a cookie?"

"Yay!" said Lucy.

Connie shot Pete a sheepish look. "Special circumstances."

"Special circledances," said Lucy.

Pete backed around as he and Phoebe carried the table up the cellar stairs so he could take the lion's share of the weight, but he suspected Phoebe could have handled it. She'd already hefted a solid oak end table up the stairs all by herself.

"Do you remember where this stuff goes?" she asked him.

"Sort of." He'd moved it down here in the first place so he could sand and varnish the floors per the McAllisters' instructions. Now it was just a matter of putting the house back together more or less as he'd found it. Which wouldn't have been such a problem if he could just keep his mind on it. He kept seeing all the blood on Lucy's hand. And it had been hardly more than a scratch, he'd seen it plain enough once Phoebe had cleaned it off. Good old Phoebe. To the rescue again.

"Hello?" said Phoebe above him.

"What?"

"I said left or right? I wasn't here when you took it apart."

"Sorry. Left. Dining room."

They planted the table, made individual trips with the eight matching chairs, picked up the china closet in tandem. But when Pete nearly pushed her through the far door and into the kitchen, Phoebe set down her end.

"Look," she said. "Why don't we take a break? I could use a glass of water."

Pete set down his end. They went into the kitchen. Phoebe filled two cut glasses with ice and topped them off with the famous Nashtoba well water. They sat, Pete on the kitchen stool, Phoebe on the kitchen counter.

"Thanks," said Pete. "And also for before. With Lucy."

"Cripes, that wasn't anything. Actually, I've been meaning to thank you."

"What for?"

"For hiring me. You had no reason to."

"Sure I did."

Phoebe laughed. "I'd like to know what it was. But I'll tell you why I'm glad you did."

Someone knocked on the front door. Pete and Phoebe looked at each other. Someone knocked again, louder. Pete got up and went to answer it. A man wearing abused denims and a tough-guy squint stood on the steps.

"Pete," he said and thrust a hand at him.

When Pete's own hand came out slowly, the man grinned. "You don't recognize me. Not surprised. Hugh. Hugh Peletier. Baby Hughie, you used to call me."

Pete's eyes widened in amazement. This was Baby Hughie? "What are you doing here? How did you find me?"

"Easy enough. Went to the source and Rita sent me. Told her it was urgent. Kinda urgent, anyway." He peered around Pete. "You alone?"

"No."

"Then we better talk out here."

"Hang on," said Pete. He went back to the kitchen where he found Phoebe, one hand on the counter, one hand on an ankle that was up around her ear somewhere. Well, she did say she loved ballet.

"Can you carry on without me for a few minutes?"

Phoebe returned her leg to the floor. "Sure. I'll do the china." She didn't ask any questions, for which Pete was grateful, since he was short on answers as yet. He returned to where Hughie was now seated on the front stoop and sat down beside him.

"So how've you been?" he asked lamely.

"Hard to be better. I own the marina in Bradford now. Far cry from when you last knew me, huh? But look, I don't have all day, here. I've had a couple of enforced chats with that police chief of yours and there's something I want you to know. I didn't tell him anything, okay? I want you to know that. After all, I figure I owe you one. I take it you're in some trouble here."

Pete decided not to ask him what he meant. "I'm not in any trouble."

"You sure?"

"Why? What's going on?"

"Well, you know. Susan and that other guy."

Pete's face must have looked like it felt.

"Come on," said Hughie. "Don't tell me you didn't know."

"Know what, Hughie?"

"Jeez, Pete. Come on. Nobody'd blame you. You were good and stuck on her. Jeez, she was something. I couldn't keep my eyes off her. Which is how come I kept catching her and that guy."

"What guy?"

"What do you mean, 'What guy?' That dark one, built like a fireplug. You almost went at it with him one day in the yard. That guy. Don't try to tell me you didn't know."

"Sure, I knew. I saw it, too. That's what prompted that little discussion. There was a linguistics problem. He didn't seem to understand the word no. I persuaded him Susan was no longer interested, and he left."

But Hughie was shaking his head vigorously. "It wasn't just that day. There were plenty of them. You got to get the picture. The things I saw, nobody was saying the word no."

"Oh, really?" said Pete calmly. "And when was this?"

"When? You name it. Every chance they could get. She'd stroll off down the beach, he'd pop up out of the woods. But only that once right on the marsh. No, hold it. There was one other time, the night she took off. I remember because when I heard she was staying with friends I figured I knew what 'friend,' get me? I tell you, the way those two were slobbering down each other's throats—"

"And you didn't tell the police chief about this because you assumed I'd finally caught them and killed Susan in a jealous rage, is that it?"

"Like I told you," said Baby Hughie magnanimously, "I figure I owe you one."

"Thanks," said Pete.

✦ 17 ✦

WILLY MCOWAT was at his desk, making a futile attempt to form logical piles out of the illogical information he'd collected thus far. When the phone rang he was almost relieved. When he heard Joel Crawford's voice on the other end he found that he was curiously unrelieved. "You're early."

"That's because I have nothing to give you. Or almost nothing. I've certainly got no matches here."

"It's the postcard I need matched."

"Then you're out of luck. As we discussed before, that postcard's a mess. But I called in part to ask you a question. Assuming the postcard's a forgery, would you also assume the hand the forger is trying to copy is one of the hands in the samples you've given me?"

"It could be. It doesn't have to be."

"Because if I had to pick one of them for the purpose, it would appear that the hand our forger was attempting to copy was either that of this Rosella person, or Susan Jameson herself."

"Why not Rosella herself as the forger?"

"Unlikely. Too many discrepancies."

"Even if the personality underwent a marked emotional change as you mentioned before?"

Lengthy silence. "I'd need something more convincing."

"If you had to match the postcard to any of the others—"

"I told you. The postcard's a mess. Now I can tell you that the W-2, the Rosella note, none of these match up to any of the numerous samples that you gave me."

And I could have told you that, thought Willy. "The postcard," he said again. "If you had to pick one and declare it a match—"

"How many different ways do you want to hear it? There are no definitive matches. There are innumerable possibilities. I would tend to eliminate only two of the Bartholomews, but after that—"

"Which two?"

He could hear the papers shuffling. "Let's see. I've got a PO and a C and a PE. I would eliminate the PO and the C. Oh, and the R. Peck."

"The women."

"I'll leave in the Rosella if it makes you happy."

It didn't.

After Hughie left, Pete sat on the McAllisters' step without moving. Susan Jameson and Roger Coolidge. Together again. Or all along? The more Pete thought about it, the more likely the all-along scenario seemed. Especially if he took Willy's theory as a given, that Susan had come to Pete's beach not by accident but by design. And all the time there was old Roger, waiting in the wings. He'd taken a chance the day he'd come so close, the day Pete had seen them on the marsh. True, Pete hadn't been expected back so soon. But as soon as Susan had seen Pete, realized Pete had probably seen them, she'd slapped Coolidge, sending Pete straight into his Dudley Do-Right routine.

But what had Susan been looking for out on that marsh? Unless Willy found Roger Coolidge, they'd never know. Susan was dead. Manny was dead. Clem Rogers was dead. But before Clem had died, he must have told someone something to . . .

Before Clem had died.

Pete shot off the step, opened the door, hollered to Phoebe. He must have hollered kind of loud. From the other room, he heard a dish crash. She flew through the dining room door like a red Roman candle.

"What happened?"

"Nothing. Sorry. I have to go. We'll finish tomorrow. Gotta run."

And he ran.

Reese Rogers seemed just as glad to see Pete the second time around. When Pete announced that he had a few more questions, Reese nodded brightly and waved him into the room. This time, though, he left the bottle alone.

"Last time I was here you told me you were present at your uncle's death," Pete began. "You told me he said something to you about Manny."

Reese shook his head sheepishly. "Not to me. He

don't say nothing to me. It's his grandson he's talking to. I kinda overhear the two, see? I ain't no eavesdropper, but considering what I'm listening to—"

"Sure," said Pete. "I bet I'd have listened, too."

Reese nodded eagerly. "I know old Clem don't have much left on the old shot clock, see? I run over to Weams Point to see him. I don't know young Coolidge is going to be there. I find Clem and Roger talking. I back out the door, hang in the hall, wait for them to get through so I can say my farewells. But there I is in the hall, and there they is in the room, and there's the door wide open. And when I hear what they's on about, I can't help but stand there and listen. Old Clem ain't too clear in the head by this time, see? But there it is, laid out so plain, every sorry detail. I tell you, it almost stops my heart cold. He starts in about Rum Creek, see? About that plank walk. I hear him plain as day tell young Roger that what's buried there is worth more than his own life."

"What is?"

"What do you mean, *what*? Manny's what. That's what's buried there, see? That's what's worth more than Clem's life. To Clem, anyways."

"But there must have been something else. Something to—" Pete stopped.

"Something to what, young fellow? There's nothing but Manny."

"Nothing was buried with him? No money, no personal possessions?"

"Bury money? You think we's crazy? There ain't nothing in that hole but Manny and the clothes on his back. Clem emptied his pockets and give the junk to Alice. A little change, a penknife, a licorice. Manny were partial to licorice. That's all. We never collected no money for that last load of liquor, see? What are you driving at, here?"

Pete thought. "But Clem never said right out that what he'd buried was Manny?"

"No he don't, thank the sweet lord. Young Roger keeps pestering him, just the same 'What, Gramp? What, Gramp? What's out there?' Just like you, only more so, see? Then he goes on about that old creek. 'What creek? What plank?' By this time I don't think Clem hears one single solitary thing Roger's saying. Finally I've had enough. I come 'round the corner and Clem looks up at me and says, 'Lord, oh, Lord. Manny.' And that's it."

"He died?"

"A few hours later. Never says another blessed word after 'Manny.' Roger hangs close. I hang, too. Don't want him getting too many answers to his questions, see? After Clem's gone Roger asks me. What's he mean? I says I ain't got the foggiest. Let the whole sorry tale die with Clem, that's what I figure, see?"

"So Roger went his merry way."

"Yes and no. First thing he does, he starts asking around about this Rum Creek all over the Hook. A couple of the fellows tell me. Then after a while Roger disappears. Ain't seen hide nor hair of him since."

Pete paused, thinking. "You said the other day there was no honor among thieves," he began, but

Reese interrupted before he could take the thought where he wanted to go.

"Maybe I phrased that kind of poor. Me and Manny and Clem, we was no thieves. We was doing an honest day's work, same as the rest."

"An honest day's work that happened to be against the law."

"And what kinda law, I ask you? A law's gotta be something you can count on. Who's going to lose sleep over a law that gets ignored more than it gets kept? Besides, I ain't the one drinking it. If we land it, we get paid. Ain't my business what happens to it after that."

"And if you got caught?"

"Five hundred dollar fine. Make that up in one trip. Don't lose no sleep over that, either. Now you got what you call your unsavory element, same as everywhere else. But most of us from around these parts, we're as undevious a bunch as you ever want to meet. Hardworking, too. Don't let anybody kid you. It's a lot of work and a lot of sacrifice. And plenty dangerous. Ain't no braver men than Manny and Clem, let me tell you."

"I take it all this hard work paid off, as a rule?" Pete tried not to let his eyes travel around the room as he said it, but Reese seemed to catch his drift.

"Keep in mind I'm fifteen years old at the time, in for maybe six weeks altogether. I get me pocket change, that's it."

"And Manny and Clem?"

"Done better," said Reese, and grinned.

* * *

Willy had just hung up the phone, but he was still staring at it blindly when Pete waltzed in. Willy reviewed the various reasons Pete might be here and decided on the usual. "If you found another body you can damn well keep it."

"I didn't find another body. I found Baby Hughie. Or Baby Hughie found me." Pete expounded.

"I see," said Willy. But did he? It explained the feeling he'd gotten at the marina that there was more to Hughie than met the eye, but it didn't explain other things. For example, if they were going to take this Baby Hughie's present word as his bond, it meant that the whole time Pete was in his Susan Jameson glory, he was being two-timed. So why was he looking so perky?

"You had no suspicion about any of this?" asked Willy finally.

"No. The one time I saw them together, she slapped him. If you'd asked me, I'd have said she was afraid of him. That's why I chased him off." After a minute Pete said, "There's more."

"More" was Clem Rogers's deathbed scene. The connection Willy had been looking for between grandfather and grandson. The catalyst that had put all these crazy wheels in motion.

"So your scenario's changed some," said Pete when he finished.

"Some. For one thing, it sounds like it was Coolidge who was behind it, not Susan, going after whatever he thought was buried on that marsh. Clem's rumrunner fortune, by the sound of it."

187

"What was he thinking, that Clem stuffed it in a coffee can and buried it on the marsh?"

"Either that, or that he'd find the key to it out there. He knew he needed to find that plank walk, at least. It sounds like he scouted around from afar, confirmed the location of this 'Rum Creek,' took in the general demographics—"

"Meaning me."

"Maybe. Then he returned with his secret weapon."

"Meaning Susan."

Willy studied Pete. Hardly a ripple. "Rosella must have posed some sort of problem. Either he asked her and got refused, or decided she wasn't enough firepower for a strapping young thing like you, so he dropped her and opted for Susan. Maybe seduced her into his plans by virtue of his endless charms, or made a hard, cold cash proposition. A hefty cut of the take, whatever the take might turn out to be."

"In other words, he pimps, she whores."

"You don't know what his instructions were," said Willy, trying to be kind even as he sensed his kindness wasn't needed. "Maybe all that was required was that she make contact, find out what you knew, get out of there. But once she came face to face, or whatever-it-was to whatever-it-was—"

"Why don't you skip on down to the point? Who killed her?"

Willy's eyes widened in surprise. "Coolidge, of course. A falling out among thieves. He decided he wanted the whole, not the half."

"So they found what they were looking for."

"They found Manny. That's all we know for sure. How else would Susan end up in the same hole? Now as to how they found Manny—"

"Not so hard. Between Sarah and me, we mapped out the route to the old plank walk. So he finds Manny, then he bashes in Susan's head. Probably with my shovel. Chucks her in the hole they just dug. Then what?"

"Then Coolidge goes back to the house, clears out her things, leaves you the note on the Kleenex, follows it up with that postcard to make sure you don't come looking for her. As long as you don't look, no one knows she's missing."

Now there was a ripple. After a moment of silence, Pete said, "What about that postcard?"

"No definitive answers there. A few eliminations. Not you, though. Did you write it, by the way? After you killed Susan? Cleared out her things, drove off to Weams Point, wrote out a postcard from the jilted sister's hometown, in the jilted sister's handwriting?"

"It was in the sister's handwriting?"

"Maybe. By the way, I could use an answer to my question. Just for the meticulous records I'm keeping."

Pete closed his eyes. "I did not kill Susan. I did not write the postcard. I didn't even know she had a sister, let alone a jilted one."

He opened his eyes. Willy could have wished he'd done it a little sooner. Open, Pete's eyes were like one of those billboards along the highway, but closed, he was inscrutable. Not that Willy actually thought Pete had killed Susan, but there was something he was keeping to himself. Willy decided it was time to find out what it was. Despite his recent lack of success with a few old ladies, he was supposed to be good at these things. "So you had no suspicion Susan was still involved with Coolidge?"

"None. If you'd asked me, I'd have said he was the type only a mother could love. But apparently Susan thought he was something."

"Polly called him mesmerizing."

"Yeah, well, Polly called Bobby Sherman mesmerizing."

Willy cleared his throat. It seemed he'd been doing it a lot, lately. "So at no time did you see this Coolidge as a serious threat?"

Pete shot back his chair and stood up. "What are you getting at here, Willy? If you mean did I kill her in a jealous rage, I already answered that. If you mean did I know Coolidge was going to kill her, the answer is no to that, too. And what makes you so sure he did kill her? What about Tim St. George? The more I think about it the weirder it gets. I hardly knew the guy. Then he shows up here and goes to work. Then Susan drops in out of the blue. What if all this grandfather-grandson-Manny-Rose-coffee-can crap is just exactly that?"

"Polly says St. George barely spoke to Susan Jameson."

"Polly says. Why don't you dial one of those 900 numbers for a psychic while you're at it? But there you go. Tim and Susan barely spoke. I'd say that's weird enough right there."

Pete strode out the door.

So Willy had hit another nerve. But where? He tried to replay the mental tape, but he didn't get far.

Bobby Sherman, mesmerizing.

Oh, he was in big trouble here.

❖18❖

PETE GOT HOME to an empty house. His first instinct was to revel in the unaccustomed peace, but after five minutes of reveling, he realized that in the long-short month since Lucy's arrival, he'd forgotten how to do peace. He began to feel lonely. Then abandoned. Then stir-crazy. By the time he'd worked his way up to just plain old crazy, he was out the door. And going where? He looked around and happened to notice the exterior stairway that led to Polly's door. *Polly says, Polly says.* Okay, so Pete had tossed out some unkind words back there. The truth of the matter was, he'd been so angry with the chief that he'd lashed out in all related directions along some convenient, well-worn paths. What did Willy think, anyway? That Pete should have known about Coolidge? That he should have foreseen this danger for Susan and beaten the crap out of Coolidge when he'd had the chance? And besides, who *said* it was Coolidge who'd killed her? If you asked Pete . . . but the chief didn't ask Pete.

Who did he ask? Polly. Christ. What did Polly know about Susan Jameson?

But as it turned out, what did Pete know?

Pete hung left and bolted up the stairs to his sister's apartment. Although Polly constantly walked into Pete's house without knocking, Pete was careful to knock and to wait for the magic word "enter." This was his sister. There were plenty of things she could be doing that he was quite sure he didn't want to witness.

But at least when she opened the door she could have made some attempt not to look so disappointed. "Oh, it's you."

Pete went in anyway.

"I thought you were Willy."

"People do tend to confuse us. But I'm happy to inform you that when I last saw him five minutes ago he was hunky-dory. Apart from the fact that he accused me of murdering Susan Jameson."

Polly's eyes grew round. "He didn't . . . you didn't—"

"He did. I didn't. But he seemed to think I had motive once I told him she'd been running a couple of us in tandem."

"Will you speak English? She was what?"

"Still hot and heavy with the supposedly old boyfriend."

"Pete."

Pete held up a hand. "I'm not in need of a sympathetic ear, I'm in need of an objective one. If yours is available."

In answer, Polly turned around and plopped onto one end of the couch with her feet tucked up under her. Pete sat on the other end. He repeated most of what he'd learned since Lucy had first found Susan Jameson's skull, culminating with the chief's Coolidge theory.

"He's stuck on this Roger thing," agreed Polly. "By the way, I must say you're taking this awfully well. If it were me, I'd be out in the garden eating worms, crying about how nobody loves me."

Pete remained silent. It was true, he was taking it well, but he wasn't at all sure he wanted to figure out the reason.

"So what's your theory?" asked Polly finally.

"I don't know. I have problems with this Coolidge thing. The main one being that they would have had to sneak around me. Susan and I were—"

"Obnoxious," said Polly. "Like glue. Siamese twins. I take your point. And you'd already run Roger off. If he'd showed himself again you'd have smelled trouble. Been on your guard."

"And when did they dig up Manny? It had to be at night. At night, if I wasn't out with Susan, I was home with Susan. And what about after he killed her? How could he sneak into my house, pack up Susan's belongings, and leave without me seeing or hearing anything?"

"So it was probably somebody you'd expect to see hanging around. Like that sneaky little Hughie."

"Or Tim."

"Oh, please."

"No, wait. Say Tim planted Susan. The chief says you discount him because he and Susan hardly spoke. Isn't that suspicious enough? At least Tim makes more sense than Baby Hughie."

"Oh, does he? How do you explain Hughie's sudden rise to fame and fortune? And if you want to talk suspicious, don't you find it a little suspicious his showing up out of the blue with this new information about Roger Coolidge? What if he's just trying to throw everyone off the track? What if he made all that up about Susan and Roger? How come he sees them all the time and no one else does? Tell me that."

"So what was the point in coming to tell me—"

"Look what happened when he did. You ran straight to Willy with the news, like anyone who knows you knows you would. And look what Willy did. He accused you of murdering Susan. He didn't give Hughie a second thought."

"If I'd really murdered Susan I wouldn't have gone running to Willy."

"But say Hughie murdered her. He'd know you didn't, right? And where did Hughie get all his money? What if Clem Rogers's secret hoard really was buried out there on the marsh and Hughie found it? Nobody else seems to have it."

"Who says there is a hoard?"

"There has to be. Otherwise none of this makes one bit of sense."

Pete stood up. "I don't know why we're talking about this. It's Willy's problem, not mine."

"Unless he really thinks you did it."

"He doesn't."

"You're sure?"

Pete paused at the door. "Why, did he say something to you?"

"No. But he wouldn't."

No, thought Pete, he wouldn't.

"And besides—" she stopped.

Uh-oh. Pete's first instinct was to hit the door. His second was to get the bad news over with. "Things okay with you two?"

"What's that supposed to mean?" said Polly hotly. "What did he say to you?"

"Nothing. I mean nothing about you."

"Too busy talking about Susan Jameson?"

Pete didn't answer.

"Tell me about her, Pete."

Oh, he should have kept going, for sure. "What do you mean?"

"Tell me what she was really like."

"I don't know what she was really like. Apparently I never did." He got up and went for the door, but once he was there, he hesitated. He'd vowed to keep out of it, but she was the one who'd started it. "About Willy."

"We're not talking about Willy, we're talking about Susan." But she couldn't seem to help herself, either. She looked up. "All right, what?"

"He's an okay guy, Pol. I don't see how you'd find one better."

"You mean considering my track record."

"I mean considering Willy."

"And you said the same thing to him about me, of course?"

Pete hesitated.

Polly burst out laughing, but not like anything was really funny.

But the minute Pete stepped outside onto the landing, Polly and Willy and Susan were forgotten as he heard an eerie echo coming from the direction of the beach. When he realized it was Connie calling Lucy's name, he took the stairs in fours. He intercepted Connie in the dune between beach and marsh. "What happened?"

"She's gone. *Missing*. Pete—"

"All right. Where was she last?"

"She was here, with me. We were combing the dune for driftwood to make a fort. She kept running off and I *told* her—stay where I can see you or we go straight home and you go to your room. I *told* her."

"All right," said Pete. "You keep going that way. I'll try the marsh."

They took off, yelling for Lucy.

In what was probably three minutes but what seemed like most of Pete's adult life, Lucy came running across the marsh from the west. Pete yelled for Connie and headed to meet the little girl. He was moving fast, but Connie beat him there. She grabbed the little girl by the shoulders and shook her.

"Don't you ever, *ever*—"

"Easy," said Pete.

"Easy, nothing," shouted Connie. "You know better than to run off that way. We've gone over it and over it. Do you know how scared you made me? Do you know how I would feel if something happened to you? You're going straight to your room when we get back." Suddenly the shaking turned to hugging.

Lucy burst into tears.

"Okay," said Pete, to no one in particular.

When they neared the house Lucy pulled away and ran in ahead of them.

"So she goes to her room," said Pete, trying not to sound like the wimp he felt.

Connie looked up at him, stricken. "We've never sent her to her room before. She won't understand."

"We explained it. And you just warned her, didn't you?"

Connie nodded. But the minute they walked into the kitchen she pointed to the clock. "Look. It's past time for dinner. She must be starving."

So they gave her dinner, and because she ate it all, a cookie after.

Rita Peck raised her glass to Evan's outstretched one and clinked. "Happy Anniversary," said Evan.

"Anniversary?"

"You think a night out in the big city in the middle of the week is for nothing? Anniversary of our first date. But now that we're discussing it, maybe it's as good a time as any to pick out a real date. For a real anniversary."

Anniversaries, thought Rita. Oh, how she hated them. The worst had been the tenth. No, she thought, the fifth, because that was when she'd first realized. She remembered it as if she'd lived through it fifty times. Which, in a way, she had.

He'd called her from work midmorning. About money, as usual . . .

"You're asking me for money?" said Rita. "You just got paid last night."

"That was last night. You got paid today. I want to know if the deposit's in already. I need operating expenses. And stop asking questions, darling."

Of course. It was their anniversary. And he wanted to surprise her.

"Are we going out? Shall I get a sitter?"

"Okay by me. The money's in?"

"The money's in," said Rita.

She called around with the usual non-luck in obtaining a sitter. At three Maxine had already achieved a certain reputation. In the end, in desperation, she called Pete. Sure, he said, he and Susan would be glad to.

Susan. And didn't that just figure. Even her anniversary wouldn't be free of the competition.

But as it turned out, it was.

Nicky came through the door ripping off his tie and griping as usual. "Goddamned people. Make up their minds, why don't they? Gonna buy a car or not? Don't waste my time. I've just about had it. Time to get out. Open up a place of my own."

"With what money?"

"What do you mean, what money? You're really something, you know that, Rita? What money. Like it matters what money. So we take out a loan like the rest of the world."

Like the rest of the loans they could barely pay already. But tonight was not the night for this particular conversation. Rita ducked between the tie and the flailing arm *and kissed him. Or she would have kissed him if he hadn't reeled backward as if she'd come at him with a hatchet. Which only went to show you how much they'd been kissing lately. And if he wasn't kissing her, who was he kissing—Susan Jameson? But this was not the night for this particular rumination, either. "So where are we going?"*

"I don't feel like going out. I'm so tired I need oxygen. Why don't you just cook something."

"On our anniversary?"

"Anniversary? What the . . . oh, hell, Rita. Didn't I just say I was tired?" He opened his wallet, peeled off a twenty. "Here. Go buy yourself something."

Rita took the twenty, ripped it into four pieces, and threw it at him. He was still yelling when she went into the kitchen to call Pete off, feigning a sick child. She was pretty sure he could tell she was crying, but all he said was he hoped Maxine would be better soon, and don't worry about work until she was. Rita assured him Maxine was already feeling better and she'd be there first thing.

In the morning there was a single rose on her desk with a note that said, "Better luck next year. How about lunch?"

From Pete, of course.

" 'Scuse me?" said Evan. "I'm trying to propose to you, here. For the fourth or fifth time, by my reckoning."

"Oh, Evan, I'm sorry. But I really do wish you'd stop asking. I don't do well with marriage."

"Not something you do alone, Rita."

No? It had certainly felt that way last time. Rita

looked away from Evan's penetrating gaze, but what she saw when she did so made her reach across the table and grip his hand. "Evan, look. Isn't that . . . but I forget. You didn't know him."

"Who?"

"Tim St. George. Good Lord, he's with my gynecologist! But now look who's coming in. And sitting down with them. Phoebe Small. I don't know the man with her. But isn't that curious, Phoebe Small and Tim St. George at the same table?"

But Evan didn't seem to be listening.

Before Willy left the office for an appointment in Weams Point, he called Polly. They'd made tentative plans for dinner at Polly's, but the way things were going, he knew he wouldn't be back until late. After he begged off the meal he expected the usual half-relief, or, considering recent events, the full-fledged variety. He was pleasantly surprised when Polly said, "Stop by later, anyway. Even if it's the dead of night."

As Willy drove to Weams Point he refused to speculate on Polly's meaning, using the time to plan out the meeting ahead. Ever since his little chat with Pete, Willy had felt an odd sense of urgency about this case. He needed to find Coolidge and he needed to find him fast, but he was running out of places to look. And when that happened, the only thing to do was to back up and go over the old ground, casting a wider net, as Sarah had said. So he'd made a call and arranged to meet Lieutenant James at his home tonight.

Lieutenant James's house was one of those cozy,

dormered Capes that Willy had always been partial to. The woman who answered the door was even better yet. Smile you'd hurry home to. Sensible conversation. Economical movement in the right direction. There was an affectionate but not sloppy springer spaniel at her heel, smells from the kitchen that set his stomach rumbling, a clean-faced teenaged girl doing homework at the table, and to top it all off, he was led into a room in which he'd gladly have spent the rest of his life. Dark, substantial furniture, just enough windows, thick rug, fireplace, lots of shelves full of books. Was Willy any closer to these things than he had been a year ago? Two days ago he'd have said yes. After last night, he had his doubts. And after tonight? Tonight he was going to pay better attention to the policeman's most reliable tool—his instinct.

Lieutenant James rose from his chair and waved him into another one, offering him a drink, which Willy refused.

"Just stopped by to see if you could add anything," said Willy.

"On the Jamesons?"

"Or Roger Coolidge."

"Ah," said the lieutenant. "Still missing?"

"Or dead."

By the expression on the lieutenant's face Willy could tell he understood why "dead" was not the preferred option. "I can't help you with Coolidge. Didn't know the man."

"And how well did you know Susan?"

"We went through twelve years of school side by side. James. Jameson."

"Nothing closer than that?"

The lieutenant grinned. "I see you're not going to let me skate over that one. We were friends. We might have been more if there had ever been a lag in the parade."

"She had a lot of boyfriends?"

"In a word, yes. Never let one go if there wasn't another waiting in the wings. She couldn't handle being alone. You know what she used to remind me of? An image in the mirror. She could only see herself reflected through someone else's eyes. If she was alone, she didn't exist. That was where I came in. If there was ever a lull, I could always be found at the next desk or on the other end of the phone. Now that I think about it, I guess I had my chances. I guess she just scared me."

"Scared you how?"

The lieutenant thought. "Susan liked to break the rules. No, belay that. It was more like she didn't understand there *were* rules. She couldn't comprehend why someone would object to her stealing their boyfriend. If the poor slob decided he liked Susan better, it wasn't her fault, it was fate."

"And that's what happened with the sisters?"

He nodded. "Susan was actually surprised when Rosella wouldn't speak to her after that. But the funny thing was, eventually Rosella seemed to see it Susan's way. You saw her suicide note?"

"I saw it. So you don't see Rosella as the type to take revenge?"

"I don't know. Maybe at first. You wouldn't have believed Rosella fifteen years ago. Not the show-stopper Susan was, but nice to look at. Nice to be around. Low-key. Restful. And despite what she may have thought, the one who really ran the show. By the way, we called in Social Services, got her back on track with Penbrook as an outpatient. They're treating her for depression."

"Good," said Willy. "Can you tell me anything else about this Coolidge?"

Lieutenant James paused. "I'll tell you what Rosella said about him when we hauled her to the hospital. When it first sunk in she wasn't going to die after all."

"What's that?"

"She said, 'I guess I'm stronger than I thought. He'll kill Susan, though, you watch.' So you figure this for Coolidge?"

Willy nodded.

He wasn't surprised when the lieutenant nodded back. He, too, knew the statistics.

Polly looked at the clock. Eight-twenty. Not that she was actually counting or anything. But she'd told Willy to stop by even if it was the "dead of night," and he could have no way of knowing that the minute she'd said the words she'd wanted to take them back. What was he going to think she meant?

Polly wandered into the kitchen, hungry, but not wanting to waste the meal she'd planned for Willy on herself. She ignored the stir-fry, the wine, the candles, and made herself a salad instead. When she was through, she looked at the clock again. Nine-thirty. What was he doing in Weams Point? she wondered. And what would she do when he got here? She knew what Susan Jameson would do. She knew what the old Polly would have done. Not that the old Polly had gotten anywhere with Tim St. George. Maybe there *had* been something with him and Susan Jameson. It would certainly explain why all her efforts had come to nothing, efforts the likes of which had rarely been seen on Nashtoba Island. She'd lurked. She'd lain in wait. She'd plotted and schemed . . .

It took her three whole weeks to maneuver them into a job alone together. She finally cornered him one afternoon, standing in the driveway, staring at a piece of paper.

"Hi," said Polly.

Tim looked up and smiled. "Oh, hi Polly."

He had only one dimple, but even that was just right. And so was that little scar above his right eyebrow that puckered when he frowned. Like now. "Is something the matter?" *she asked.*

"I'm not sure. I'm apparently supposed to find a cat belonging to a Mrs. Potts, but the directions to her house are somewhat confusing. Rita had to leave in a hurry to collect her daughter. Apparently her husband was unavailable for pickup as per previous arrangement."

"Yes, that would confuse her," *said Polly.* "I'll tell you what. I'll go with you. I know right where Mrs. Potts lives, and besides, her cat's a team effort."

More dimple.

Oh, somebody just shoot me, thought Polly.

"So you've had to find this cat before?"

"Not this cat. The previous one. And if you stick

around long enough, you'll be looking for the next one. All Fergy's cats learn to hide from her eventually."

Polly didn't mention that they always learned to hide under the bed. She got into Tim's car and gave him the lefts and rights to Mrs. Potts's house, throwing in a couple of extras for good measure. On the way they made a few breakthroughs—Polly found out, for example, that Tim was originally from the city. And more to the point, on the last but one unnecessary right-hand turn, he seemed to take an interest in her origins. "You and Pete grew up right here, didn't you?"

"Here on Nashtoba. Not here in that cottage. Pete's just renting."

"And he plans on staying?"

"God, yes. And pity the poor soul who tries to budge him. Not me, though. Here. Turn left here."

Tim turned. And drove in silence a little too long for Polly's liking. She hated it when people didn't do their half by the conversation.

"I couldn't wait to get off this island," said Polly finally.

"Oh? And you don't miss it?"

"A pile of sand in the middle of the water? No thank you."

"But the peace and quiet. The rich heritage. I find there's a certain independence, especially in the older people—"

"A certain stubbornness, you mean."

"That might be part of it. But they think for themselves here. No sheep syndrome. No mob rule. I believe it's no accident that so much of the renegade activity that spawned this nation came from this very region." And he began to quiz her on a bunch of examples of

*what he called innovativeness in the face of oppression
but what Polly called locals-run-amok. She might actually have known the answers to some of his questions if
she'd only listened to Pete for more than half a minute
when he got going. "There," she said finally, out of desperation. "That's Fergy's driveway."*

*And before it could dawn on Tim that he'd been by
it twice before, she hustled him out of the car and up to
the frantic Fergy Potts. He was so patient with the old
lady, even listening through the entire hiatal hernia saga,
that she decided to give him another chance. She took
him by the arm and led him off to cross-hatch the yard,
but when he let the third hint about showing him the
island splash dead in the water, she gave up, took him
back inside, and lo and behold, there was the cat, under
the bed.*

And there was strike two for Polly.

✦19✦

PETE FELL INTO bed near-comatose and landed smack in the middle of a bad dream. Stuck in quicksand. No, stuck in marsh mud. Susan Jameson's skull, tumbling along the creek. Skull turning into small, lifeless body.

Lucy.

Pete yanked himself out of the dream and lay there, sweating. When Lucy woke he was almost relieved. Connie had her feet already on the floor, but he stopped her with a hand on the shoulder. After that dream, he needed Lucy. He brought Lucy back to her bed, brought her a glass of milk, no cookie, and told her about the friendly cow all red and white until she drifted off again, clutching his finger.

Pete returned to his bed, but now he couldn't sleep. He lay there thinking about losing things. Lucy, first, of course, but somehow it worked around full circle, back to Susan Jameson again. It wasn't Pete's pride that objected to the chief's theory. He could take the news about Roger and Susan—why, he still wasn't sure, but he could take it okay. The thing that bothered him about the chief's theory was the thing he'd been talking about with Polly. Where the hell could Pete have been all the time Susan was out getting herself killed and buried on his marsh? Pete tried to think back, to remember the routines of his life back then, what routine there was that hadn't been shared with Susan. What could possibly have distracted him long enough to allow someone to kill Susan almost under his nose, bury her, clean out her room, hang around forging notes? Well, there was work, he supposed, and . . .

"Listen," said Connie.

Pete listened. And heard nothing. "What?"

"The church bells. Six o'clock. We're never going to finish this tonight. And didn't Susan say she was going home to take a shower so she'd be ready in time? Aren't you going out someplace?"

"She is, I'm not. Shopping in Bradford. She wanted to catch the six o'clock bus. But you might as well go. I'll keep at it for awhile longer. They want to open this trail before summer's over."

"Are you calling me a quitter?"

Pete straightened. He'd be glad when summer was over, when this pain in the neck went back to wherever they'd found her. "I'm not calling you anything. I don't care what you do. I just thought—"

"Will you lighten up? I was only kidding. And you do care what I do, or you ought to. If you continue by your lonesome you'll be pulling thorns out of your back-

*side till December. Besides, no offense, but we should
be able to make some tracks now that Susan's out of
the way.''*

*Pete had to admit she was right. They had gotten a
good two-man system down once Susan had left. But
whatever tracks they might make would run straight
through a quarter mile of bull-briar. Another job he'd
have to remember not to take on—clearing nature trails.
"Okay," said Pete. "One more load and I'll buy you
a pizza.''*

"And a beer?''

"And a beer.''

*Which turned into three beers, only because the
woman made him so crazy he gulped the first two. He
didn't know what her excuse was for keeping up with
him. And he had no excuse at all for the ice cream and
coffee, except for the fact that when the waitress dropped
off the dessert menu they were deep in the middle of an
extremely tense and personal discussion about Nancy
Drew versus Hardy Boys. And the second cup of coffee
was only because when the waitress came by with the
pot they were deep in the middle of an argument over
the check. When Pete reached for it Connie snatched it
out of his fingers and launched into some ridiculous song
and dance about how he'd contracted for one pizza and
beer and she wasn't going to let him pay for anything
else that might have accidentally gotten added onto it in
the heat of the moment.*

*"Look," said Pete finally. "You've been working like
a galley slave all summer. If you don't let me have this
check I'll have to give you a raise, and I can't afford to
give you a raise.''*

So she let him take the check. And when they got back

to Factotum those August meteors were flying all over the place. So they stretched out on the warm hood of the truck and watched until they heard the phone ringing inside the house. Pete might have let it ring. It wasn't every night you caught a meteor shower like this one. But Connie leaped off the hood, said good-bye and thanks and see you in the morning. So Pete said the same and ran. He got to the phone on the sixth ring.

"Pete?"

"Susan? What's the matter? Where are you?"

"Nothing's the matter. I missed the last bus. Will you pick me up?"

"Sure. Where are you?"

"I'll wait for you in Tap's Tavern."

"You better wait somewhere else."

But she'd already rung off.

Christ, thought Pete. Tap's Tavern?

Connie couldn't sleep. It was all this thrashing of Pete's. Until he settled down there would be no hope for her at all. "All right," she said finally. "What's eating you?"

He rolled onto an elbow. "I've been thinking about Susan." Surprise, surprise. "The night she supposedly took off. That had to be the night she got killed. I was trying to remember where I was, how it could have happened right under my nose. You were there, earlier. You probably don't remember. We went out for pizza. It could have happened then, I guess. Or later, when I went to Bradford."

So it was good old guilt time. Well, Pete would have to wait in line. Connie had been lying there for what seemed like hours, thinking about the nightmare afternoon with Lucy, how fast the best intentions could go wrong. She'd decided she was spending too much time telling Lucy not to do things. She'd decided it was time to work on a plus side to the ledger. She'd decided they should do something fun.

Fun. Like screaming at her. Shaking her. She wasn't cut out for this, Connie decided. What she needed was a kid to practice on. Preferably one with training wheels . . .

"What are you looking for, your training wheels?" asked Connie.

Baby Hughie jumped first, then stumbled, then crashed to the ground in a heap of ripped sneakers, dirty jeans, tubular steel, and rubber tires. "Jeez, look out willya?"

"I was invited here. You're the one who's trespassing." Which was and wasn't exactly true, thought Connie. Pete had already dashed off to pick up Susan while Connie was still sitting in her car with her head out the window, transfixed by the falling stars. And once Pete had left, she hadn't exactly stayed in the car, either. It was that sky. She was caught up in the glow, not only of the moon and the stars but of the events of the night itself. It had confused her. Had what she'd thought was happening really happened? She wasn't sure. So she'd gotten out of the car, figuring to watch a few more stars fall, figuring to think a few things through, when she'd heard something in the bushes on the side of the house.

Baby Hughie and his bicycle.

"What are you doing here, Hughie?"

"None of your business."

"Why don't you take off?"

"Why don't you?"

Obviously, this was going exactly nowhere. Connie decided to get devious. "That was just what I was planning to do." And she got in her car and drove off down the road. Not far, though. When she walked back, Baby Hughie was no longer on the side of the house, but she could see the small, dark shape against the sky, working its way over the marsh. Okay, anyone in their right mind would opt for a beach walk tonight. As long as he wasn't lurking around Pete's house with nobody home.

Still, Connie didn't leave. It was the sky. She lay on her back in the grass and watched the darkest part of the sky, away from the moon. Or, rather, she didn't watch. How had Pete told her to do it? "Let your eyes relax. Trust to your peripherals. You'll pick them up best when you're not trying." So Connie lay there trusting and not trying, and saw the meteors and a few other things, too. But when she heard the car on the road, she leaped to her feet and cut back through the woods the way she'd come. This had been a good night. No sense wrecking it by watching the lovebirds come home.

"You know," said Connie, "It couldn't have happened when you were in Bradford. You weren't there very long."

"Are you kidding? I was there for hours. Two or three. I was royally pissed off. Tap's Tavern. What a dumb place to wait. And it got worse. I got to Tap's and she was nowhere around. The place was a real dive. I asked the bartender if he'd seen anyone of her description and he made some crack. I tell you, I was in no mood. *Then* he said . . . ,"

"*Looks like she moved on. Too bad for you. But she called in a message. That's if your name's Pete and her name's Susan.*"

Pete nodded. The bartender pulled a disreputable pad of paper from his pocket. "*Took this message myself. Says she'll meet you at the dock.*"

"*What do you mean, dock? Which dock?*"

"*Hey, I don't compose 'em, I just take 'em down. Message is, she'll meet you at the dock. End of quote. I'll be seeing you. Like in apple blossom time.*" And he laughed.

So Pete went to the dock. The big one. He decided if she didn't say which dock she must have meant the big one, the one with the ferry, but there was no Susan at the big dock. Not out in plain sight, anyway. It took him a good forty-five minutes to comb the pier, and after he'd combed it he went to the little dock, the one attached to the marina, but there was no Susan lurking around that dock, either. He even drove to the three town landings. Still no Susan.

Finally, in desperation, he went back to Tap's, and by this time there was a second message, delivered by the bartender with real glee. "*Says she met friends and got a ride back.*" This time Pete was so POed he snatched the pad out of the bartender's pocket where he'd just replaced it, but that was all it said. "*For Pete. Susan met friends and got a ride back.*"

What *friends?* Pete ordered a beer, drank it slowly to cool himself off, went home. And there he found his third message of the evening, blocked out on a piece of Kleenex *with some sort of goopy black crayon. "Pete, Decided to stay with friends a few days. I'll be in touch. Susan."*

"I went to our room and her stuff was gone," said Pete. "I didn't think it meant anything—she didn't have much and most of it she'd take for a stay of a few days, anyway. But I remember thinking afterward, when I got the postcard and there was no return address, where should I send her stuff? And then I realized there wasn't any stuff. And I still didn't think it meant anything. But that very night, if we can believe Baby Hughie, he saw Susan with Coolidge on the marsh."

This time Connie sat upright. "What?"

Pete told her about the visit from Hugh Peletier. He included all the details, like a tongue poking a sore tooth. The only trouble was, the tooth still wasn't all that sore.

"I think we can believe Hughie," said Connie. "At least the part about him seeing them on the marsh that night, since I saw *him* on the marsh that night." And she told Pete her half of the tale.

Afterward Pete lay with his mind spinning. So the night Susan had died, Hughie had been there. Coolidge, too, but only if Hughie was to be believed. Only if Hughie wasn't working on some alternate agenda of his own. Which, according to Polly, he might have decided to do, might have decided it would be worth the gamble of admitting his presence at the scene, especially if he'd remembered that Connie had been there and seen him. And who else had been there? From the sound of things, the car Connie had heard had not been

Pete's. He'd have hardly been as far as the second dock by then. So Pete had been conveniently running around the Bradford docks while Susan was killed and buried, and her belongings removed from his home. Coincidence? Unlikely.

Connie seemed to have got there with him.

"Pete. Those messages from Susan—"

"All secondhand, from the bartender."

"Not the note she left you here at the house. Couldn't you tell whether that was in Susan's writing?"

"How was I supposed to know Susan's writing? It wasn't like we sat around writing each other little billet doux. And besides, it was blocked out on Kleenex in what looked like black crayon."

"Crayon? Since when did you have crayons lying around? What about eyeliner?"

"And since when did I have . . . oh. Susan's."

"Did she wear eyeliner?"

"How the hell do I know?"

"She probably did. Looks like hers aren't born, they're made."

"Okay, so he used her eyeliner. So what?"

"Don't you get it? If Susan was already dead—"

"Of course I get it. If Susan never left here, if she was already dead, someone else wrote the note."

"And if someone cleared out all her stuff he'd have taken her makeup, too. And if he wasn't confident about faking Susan's handwriting, easier to do it by using something that would write funny in the first place, like eyeliner. Where was the note left, by the way?"

"On the bed. It's not like I keep a bunch of pads and pencils on my nightstand."

"But there were pads and pencils on Rita's desk, which he'd have seen on his way in. I tell you, the last thing this guy wanted was a legible note. So he used her eyeliner."

Which was all well and good, thought Pete, but *who* used it? Hughie? Coolidge? Tim? It could have been Tim's car Connie heard. They were still in need of an explanation for Tim's presence on the job. And Hughie's presence on the marsh. As hellbent as Willy was on Coolidge, his presence at the scene was the only one that could be explained rationally—he was there because Susan was two-timing Pete.

Sore tooth?

Maybe a little, but still not enough.

Willy pulled into Polly's driveway and sat there. His visit to Lieutenant James had done nothing but reinforce a hunch that was a dead end, he was going backward, not forward, with Polly, and right now the only thing his precious instinct was telling him was that he was running out of time.

On both fronts.

He looked up at Polly's window and saw that the light was still on, but he was tired enough and frustrated enough to wonder if there was any point in going up. What could they have to say to each other now? What more did he need? She'd sent the message loud and clear. Still, she'd said to come even if it was the dead of night, and he'd said he would.

And here he was.

He got out of the car and climbed the stairs. She opened the door and he was right. They had nothing to say. Still, he stood there. Maybe he should say it. Make it easy on her. Steal Susan Jameson's supposed last words. *Guess we're a no go.* But while he stood there thinking it, something in Polly's face changed, and suddenly he was looking at a Polly he'd never seen before, the Polly he'd been waiting for, a Polly with a full-fledged *don't go* written all over her.

So he didn't go.

Willy didn't sleep much that night, either, but he woke up feeling better than he had in years.

20

PETE'S DAY BEGAN like a punch from an unseen third fist. He'd actually felt in control in the kitchen. He and Connie had mapped out the day in mutual accord—she'd take morning duty with Lucy, and Pete would take over from return bus on. Even breakfast had gone smoothly, right through the kid insisting on Cracker Jacks and Seven-Up, the grown-ups actually holding out for Cheerios and milk. And once outside, when he ran into a disheveled chief of police just leaving Polly's, he actually refrained from issuing the warning that bubbled to his lips.

It was only when he walked into the brand-new Factotum office that he caught that third fist. It was partly the chief's fault. If Pete hadn't been so busy trying to keep his big nose out of his sister's life, he'd have noticed the other car in the drive. And here was Rita Peck, gripping the edge of her desk as if it was all that was keeping her upright, and there was Nicky Peck with a finger in her face.

219

"That's it, Rita. You take it under advisement. You remember who crossed the line and who didn't. And you remember what happened to one of those parties when it got crossed."

Pete let the door slam behind him. Nicky barged past Pete with a barely civil nod, his face that same old brick red Pete remembered from a few other times he'd had the misfortune to walk in on these two.

"Long time no see," he said to Rita.

She didn't answer.

"You okay?"

One tear welled from each eye. Then two. Pete stood frozen as Rita pushed back her chair and left the room.

"Apparently not," said a voice behind him.

Pete turned around to find Phoebe Small gazing at him with concern. "Although I have learned from both professional and personal experience that tears do heal some wounds. What are you thinking? Follow or leave alone?"

"I think I'll follow."

"Good man. I'll cover the phone." Phoebe slid behind the desk. Pete jogged down the hall to the bathroom and knocked. "Rita? How about a cup of coffee in the kitchen?"

Pete heard some snuffling sounds, the water being run, and before he was quite ready for it, the doorknob being turned. "I'm all right."

"Sure you don't want to take a minute?"

"No, but thank you. As usual. I'd better get back to the phone."

She pushed past him into the room. Phoebe

Small attempted to abdicate the chair, but one long leg got caught in the knee hole. She stumbled, saved herself, kicked over the tote bag she'd set beside her on the floor, and spilled the contents in an elongated fan in front of her. Sunglasses. Wallet. Keys. Bottled water. Notebook. Real book. Stethoscope . . .

Stethoscope??

Phoebe hustled the objects back into the bag, cracking the usual joke about her two left feet, adding a twist about the two rights she'd left at home, but soon poise was regained all around. Rita began assigning her crew. Phoebe was to give Lenore French's dog a bath, assemble the Harringtons' new gas grill, decorate the Guild Hall for the Halloween party tonight. Pete was to read Sarah the paper, close up the Swans' cottage for winter, and tackle the leaves at the Nashtoba Ladies Library. Polly, assuming Polly ever appeared, was to pick up Myrtle Snow's slipcovers at the upholsterer's in Bradford, then help Phoebe at the Guild.

Pete added a mental note to his own list—check on Rita later—and he left for Sarah's.

It seemed to Polly that she'd just closed the door behind the chief when the ringing phone wakened her, but she opened her eyes and saw that three hours had already disappeared from her life. She should never have gotten back into bed after she'd seen Willy off, but once he'd gone and she'd had a minute to herself she'd felt so . . . so weird. She wasn't used to feeling coddled instead of trampled. She wasn't used to feeling so certain that if this wasn't

Willy on the phone right now, it would be soon. She wasn't used to feeling so . . . so *weird*. She realized the phone was still ringing and snapped to. "Hello?"

"Hi," said Pete. "I was starting to think you were dead."

"I was *asleep*. What do you want?"

"I want you to do me a favor. Go to the window and see if there's a black Pontiac out there."

"Why? What's wrong?"

"Just do it, will you? Rita's ex-husband was hanging around. I'm tied up here at the library. I tried to call Connie, but nobody's home."

"Hold on." Polly went to the window. "No Pontiac."

"Good. You planning to report in with Rita any time soon?"

"What's that supposed to mean?"

"It means I want somebody to check on Rita. It looked like he gave her a pretty good working over. And last time I checked the payroll—"

"All right, all right, all right. I'll go down now."

"Good." Pause. "So. Everything all right?"

"Why shouldn't it be?"

"No reason. Just checking. Leave a message at the library if anything's wrong."

"There is *not*—"

"With Rita. I'm talking about Rita. And . . . well, you know."

Sure, she knew. She'd seen him on the lawn with Willy. So welcome to life in the fishbowl.

Polly hung up, showered, dressed, ate an English

muffin, drank the rest of the coffee Willy had brewed.

And still felt weird.

Rita, however, seemed to have fully recovered, considering the fact that the minute Polly walked in, she pounced. Get Myrtle Snow's slipcovers from Bradford. Deliver slipcovers to Myrtle. Go to Guild Hall to decorate. Pow, pow, pow.

Okay, so she'd go to Bradford. It wasn't like she'd planned on sitting around waiting for the phone to ring, after all. Willy would catch up with her sooner or later. And what would he say? Something just right, she was sure. And what would she say? Something dumb, she was equally sure. And then what? She tried to imagine this new life of hers, but all she could picture was what had always gone on before—that slow, insidious process that always resulted in total loss of control over her own life. *Do this. Do that. Sit down. Stand up.* Well, that wouldn't be the case here. Willy had already made it clear in a million little ways. She'd retain her choices. She'd make her decisions. And didn't *that* feel weird?

So, decision number one, go to Bradford.

And what made her suddenly think of Hugh Peletier, Tim St. George? Bradford, of course. And her conversation with Pete, the day before. As far as Polly could determine, there were two questions that needed answers. The chief knew one of the questions, but Polly wasn't sure the second had even occurred to him yet. Maybe it never would occur to him, especially if all he could seem to think about was Roger Coolidge. Question one, why had Tim St. George gone to work for Pete fifteen years ago? And question two, where had Hugh Peletier acquired all that money to build that marina? Now there was something fun she could do, while she was off doing all this Factotum garbage.

But to prove a point to the absent Pete she did the slipcovers first.

And to prove another one to herself, she did Tim St. George second.

She had to kill a little time roaming around in the waiting room looking at all his boring boat pictures, but suddenly there he was, coming down the hall.

The years had been kind, Polly noticed with a sigh. There were two shallow grooves that ran from either side of nose to mouth, a hint of collapsibility at the corners of the eyes, maybe a touch of frost at the temple. But the jawline still held true, the shoulders still carried the coat, there was nothing convex above the belt. And he was still short one dimple. And one wedding ring. And he sandwiched her hand between his in a much warmer display than she'd ever gotten before.

"Polly, how nice to see you. How are you? How's . . . everyone?"

"Everyone's fine. Except for Susan Jameson. I guess you heard?"

The dimple disappeared. "I . . . yes. Is that why you're here? Is there something . . . more?"

"No. Not really. No more bodies, anyway. I just heard from Pete that you were in Bradford and since I was coming this way today I decided to stop by. I had no idea you were a doctor, even way back then. You never said anything."

"Didn't I? It was no secret, I assure you."

"But what were you doing at Factotum at all when you could have been off healing the sick?"

He laughed. He looked at his watch. "Which is what I should be doing now. Polly, I'm thrilled to see you, but I'm—"

"Not as thrilled as I am. I used to have this fantastic crush on you. Did you know?"

The dimple again. "Same old Polly. I do have to run, but please say hello to everyone."

And there it was.

Strike three at last.

By one-thirty Pete was done with the library leaves. He grabbed a quick sandwich at the deli and called Rita from the deli phone. She sounded better. More her usual exasperated self. At Polly, of course. She hadn't returned from Bradford. "And that leaves poor Phoebe all alone at the Guild Hall. She'll need help with those cobwebs."

Pete doubted it, but he hated to aggravate Rita any more than she'd been aggravated already today. He said he'd go to the Guild Hall. He hung up and called Connie. "Hi. Can you meet the bus? Rita wants me at the Guild Hall. She seems to think Phoebe's going to hang herself in the cobwebs."

"I guess I don't have a choice, now, do I?"

Did Pete detect a bit of a tone, there? "Everything all right?"

"No, everything isn't all right. I took her to the Natural History Museum. I figured after yesterday the message had sunk in, but I explained again anyway. She had to stay with me. If she didn't we'd go straight home. We got as far as the turtles before she disappeared from sight."

"What?"

"I found her in the Indian tepee."

Pete groaned. "So you came home."

Silence. Eventually Connie said, "I let her stay to watch them feed the fish. What cobwebs?"

"It's the annual haunted house at the Guild tonight. I'm sure Phoebe can handle it, but Rita's a little off-kilter today. I shouldn't be long."

"If you are, I'm the one you'll find hanging."

"I'll be back soon," Pete promised, and hung up.

Willy McOwat left Polly's with renewed faith in his old instincts. Things had gone well the night before. A little rust in the old pipes, but if he did say so himself, he'd held up his end and more. And right now his instinct told him it was time for some good old-fashioned courting. He stopped at Betty's Bud Boutique and ordered a dozen red roses, pondered over the card, settled for the simple initial W. Better to say the rest in person. He went home, showered, shaved, dressed, made himself a cup of coffee, sat down at the kitchen table, and with a discipline that had been with him for twenty-five years, put to one side the feelings that had been brought to life a mere few hours ago. Finding Roger Coolidge was the problem on the floor now.

And how did you find missing people? You did all the things he'd already done—checked the paper trail, the money trail. He'd struck out there. So now he could assume that if Coolidge was alive, he was living under an assumed identity, which made finding him a hell of a lot harder. Harder, but not impossible. There were things people didn't change even when they shed their names. These were the things that tripped them up over the course of the long haul. Families. Interests. Habits. So he'd start with family. And who was Coolidge's family?

As far as Willy knew, it was down to one now.

Reese Rogers was more than glad to talk about his once-removed cousin. The only trouble was, he didn't have much to say about him. He soon danced backward to the person he did have something to say about—the relative they had in common, Clem Rogers. From there it was only a half-skip sideways to the tales of their shared days as rumrunners.

"We could tell where they was by the sound. Could tell who they was by the sound. We'd cut the engine and listen. Coast Guard had a distinct kind of thrum to 'em. Manny got these pipes, connected with an elbow joint, fit that over his exhaust to quiet us down. So they can't hear us, but let me tell you, we can sure hear them—"

The chief looked at his watch.

Reese rumbled on. "And once we hear 'em, that's when we run. Manny's old boat weren't near as fast as Clem's new one. Old Clem had a couple of twin Fiats in her. Make thirty, thirty-five knots loaded, half again what they got out of those old Coast Guard cutters."

"And what happened to Clem's boat?" asked Willy.

"Well, let's see. Sat in his yard rotting for so long I near forgot about it till now. Guess that grandson musta got it with the rest of the real, personal and mixed. Wonder what he done with it. I can tell you it ain't sitting in that old yard, that's for sure. Don't suppose it'd be hard to patch her up, get her roaring again. Those old boats don't crumble apart like they do nowadays. You get a little caulk, engine overhaul, fresh paint—"

And you get a fresh lead, thought Willy.

And about time, too.

❖21❖

SO POLLY HAD bombed out on getting an answer to her first question. The second one would be harder, she was sure. How did you ask somebody you hadn't seen in fifteen years how he came by the money to buy up half the Bradford waterfront? And Polly wasn't at all sure Hugh Peletier would even remember her. But there was no point giving up without giving it a try.

She found him in the Ship to Shore Shop at the Bradford marina, and the first thing she noticed was his eyes. Over the years they'd gone hard. At first she thought he didn't remember her, but then she realized it was just that he didn't care if he had.

"I'm Polly Bartholomew," she said.

His answer was a cocked eyebrow. *So?*

"I don't know if you remember me—"

"I remember you." *So?*

Polly felt like congratulating him. In the space of five seconds he'd managed to make her feel as insignificant as a week-old weather report. But at

229

least it was a more familiar sensation than the one she'd awoken with a few hours ago. She began to feel more like herself. Less wierd. She launched straight into the story she'd worked up on her way over.

"I'm doing a story on the old rumrunners. I heard they used to run liquor into this harbor."

"Yeah."

She smiled archly. "You haven't been running in anything illegal yourself, have you? You seem to have done awfully well since your days on Nash-toba. What's your secret?"

Hughie's face went dark. "Try hard work."

"Working at what?"

"At what I could get. You want to know how many jobs I've had since I was fourteen? You want to know how many hours a week it took to get me here? I've bagged more leaves, dumped more garbage, washed more dishes, waited on more ta-bles—"

"And that added up to this?"

"No. I shoved that in the bank and went back and did it all over. *That* added up to this."

He stopped and waited, raking her with his eyes in a way that was also familiar. "You know," he said finally, "you look like your brother. I don't remember noticing that before. Guess I was too busy wishing him death and dismemberment."

"Why? What did Pete ever do to you?"

"Other than feed and clothe my entire family? Nothing. Nothing at all. It was his little piece of meat I wanted. They find who killed her yet?"

"No."

"Or who killed the other guy?"

"That was a man named Clement Rogers."

Hughie's eyes narrowed. "Clement Rogers? That's who they're looking for, somebody named Clement Rogers?"

"They know where he is. Dead and buried in Weams Point."

Hughie crossed behind the counter, opened a drawer, pulled out a notebook full of papers and began to riffle through. "Here. Knew it rang a bell. Weird name, Clement. Dead and buried my ass. He called here looking for a part a few days ago."

"It's obviously not the same Clement," said Polly, but she took the slip of paper Hughie held out to her. A credit card slip. Clement B. Rogers. Back Street, Weams Point. But there was another slip attached to it, with another address scribbled in near-illegible writing that must have been Hughie's, because when she asked him to read it he did. "This is where I sent the thing. Eastside Marine, over in Murray's Mills. Just this morning, as a matter of fact."

Polly stared at Hughie. It couldn't be their Clem Rogers. First of all, he was dead. Second of all, if he wasn't dead, he'd be a hundred years old. But it might be a son. No, wait, there wasn't a son. Polly remembered hearing about the only child, the daughter, the one grandson named Roger. She looked up to find Hughie watching her with that same old eyebrow cocked and ready to roll. "May I use your phone?"

Hughie pushed it across the counter. If this had been Willy he'd have made some excuse to leave

the room, let her phone in privacy. Hughie crossed
his arms and watched her some more. Polly picked
up the phone and dialed the Nashtoba police station. Jean Martell, the dispatcher, came on the line.
Was it Polly's imagination, or was there something
new in Jean's voice when she heard who it was?
Was it all over town already where the chief had
spent the night?

"Chief's not in," said Jean.

"Can you get in touch with him?"

"*No*, I cannot," said Jean. "Not unless it's an
emergency. And certainly not for any social type
assignations. This is what he told me. Stop cranking
up that radio every time somebody's dog craps on
the sidewalk. Those were his *exact*—"

"Thanks," said Polly.

She hung up and dialed Pete.

"Tell me more about this boat," said Willy. "How
big was she?"

"I'd say close to forty foot," said Reese. "I told
you about those engines. And lots of deck up front.
Could do two hundred and fifty cases a trip. Clear
a thousand a load. This is big money back then.
And Clem just a little guy. Those big guys up top,
they made millions. And guess what they paid
those treasury agents? Two thousand a year. Not
hard to figure why what happened happened."

"Did this boat have a name?"

"The *Rose*. Bet you can figure that out, too.
'Course most of the time he covered the name with
canvas. It was all fit up for its job special. But Clem
only run her for a year before it ended. Shame."

Reese suddenly seemed to realize who he was talking to, and he grinned sheepishly. "Don't get me wrong. Never done a dishonest thing before or since. But it sure were fun while it lasted."

"As long as you didn't get shot in the back by your partner," said Willy.

Manny's grin faded.

As Pete had suspected, Phoebe was moving along just fine. The black drapes were hung over the windows, the helium balloons festooned with cheesecloth bobbed ghostlike around the room, the buckets of slime, the skeletons, the snakes were all dispersed in the nooks and crannies. But Rita was right about one thing: the cobwebs were enough to hang anybody. It took the two of them to tack the clingy, sticky mess of filament to the rafters and doorways, but they were almost done when they were interrupted by a phone ringing somewhere in the unexplored recesses of the building.

When Pete fought his way through to the undraped back room he was surprised to see that it was almost dark. He picked up the phone, expecting it to be an irate Connie, and heard instead the excited babble of his sister Polly.

"Pete! Finally. It took me three calls to get you. I'm at Hughie's marina in Bradford. Meet me. It's the strangest thing. He says he's talked to Clem Rogers!"

"Clem Rogers? Are you loony? He died fifteen years ago."

"Look, will you just get over here? And *hurry*." She hung up.

Pete replaced the phone, stared at it, picked it up, called Connie.

"Hello?"

"Ah. Still alive, I see."

A loud crash resounded in the distance. "One of us soon won't be," said Connie. "Those were your work boots going down the stairs, by the way."

"So put her in her room."

"I tried that. She just opened her mouth and began to scream. I stood it for about five seconds. And where the hell are you?"

"This is the thing. I have to run to Bradford. Polly just called me. But stick to your guns. She can't scream forever."

"Thanks for all your help." The phone went down with a loud thump.

Pete winced. When he turned, he found Phoebe standing in the doorway watching him rub his temples.

"Most tension headaches stem from the neck," she said. She moved behind him and began to rub. Almost immediately Pete's head felt better. "How do you know these things?" he asked.

When she told him, he wasn't as surprised as he'd been the first time he'd heard it from the police chief.

Willy kicked himself as he drove back to the station. He should have thought of that damned boat before now. The perfect place for a man to disappear. No lease, no mortgage, no paper trail, and with a flick of the wrist you could pick up and move out.

Willy resorted to the phone for the preliminaries. His first call, to Polly, gleaned the information that she was out, but that anyone who felt so inclined could leave a message at the beep. "I miss you," he said simply. His second and third calls, to the federal and state marine registries, gleaned the information that there was no boat registered to Roger Coolidge, and that the registration on the *Rose* had long lapsed. While he was on the phone, for the sake of thoroughness, he inquired and found that Tim St. George, Hugh Peletier, and Nicholas Peck all owned registered boats. He next pulled the phone book up close and flipped through the yellow pages to marinas.

It was a long list.

When Pete walked into the Ship to Shore Shop he found Polly in the back office making coffee while Baby Hughie watched from a chair. When Polly saw Pete she abandoned the coffee and grabbed a paper off the desk. A credit slip. She babbled so fast that Pete had trouble catching the gist, so he took the slip from her and read. Clement B. Rogers. Weams Point. Could it be? No.

"He's at Eastside Marine right now," said Polly.

"Or he was this morning," said Hughie. "Now he's got his part he's ready to roll."

"Let's go," said Polly.

Pete went. Polly piled into the truck with him and rattled off directions like a cabby's worst nightmare. "I know where I'm going," he said crossly. "I'm not sure *why* I'm going, but at least I know where."

"What are you talking about? You heard Hughie."

"So I'm supposed to trust him, now?"

Polly giggled. "I wouldn't. But I'd still want to check out this Clement Rogers, wouldn't you?"

Pete gave up and drove. After all, considering the laws of probability, even Polly had to be right once in a while.

"Sure, Clem Rogers," said the woman behind the counter at Eastside Marine. "He's tied up in berth 4C. He's been stuck here five days now. He ran into some engine trouble, but that's all fixed. Good thing you came by now. He only paid up through today. He'll be taking off soon."

Pete thanked the woman and let Polly yank him through the door and onto the floating dock. The lights were good and bright where there were lights, but where there were none, the visibility was poor. They passed a wide variety of craft on the way to 4C—an ancient catboat, a modern houseboat, a new Chris-Craft, an old Boston Whaler. But as they approached 4C, Pete caught Polly's arm and held her back. The boat was long and low and painted dark green, but under the paint Pete could still faintly make out the carved name. *Rose.* It was everything Pete might have expected an old rumrunner to be, but the man on deck was no old rumrunner. He was in his early forties maybe, long-haired, thickly bearded, none of it even gray.

"It's Roger," Polly whispered. "Willy was right about that part, anyway. He's not dead."

Maybe he wasn't dead, but he was living off his

dead grandfather's name, credit cards and all. "I'll stay here and keep an eye on him," said Pete finally. "You go inside and call Willy."

"I tried that already. Jean acted like whatever I had to say to him should be said after hours. I'll stay here and keep an eye. You call."

Pete left Polly huddled behind the shadow of the Chris-Craft and returned to the phone he'd spotted outside the office door.

By the time Willy hung up the phone he'd reddened both ears and collected a dozen possibles, but only two were on the Hook—one in Elder Bay and one in Murray's Mills. The remaining boats were on the mainland. He hadn't called Hugh Peletier at all. He wanted to drop by in the flesh—the man was still setting off warning bells. So he decided to work one side of the Hook on the way to the mainland, the other side on the way back—Elder Bay and Bradford on the way out, Murray's Mills on the way back.

But the particular boat in question at Elder Bay was not in its slip, and when he got to Bradford Marina, the shop door was locked and dark. He surveyed the long rows of boat slips and decided to begin east to west. He hadn't gone far when he heard footsteps behind him and turned.

"What do you think you're doing?" said Hugh Peletier. This time he held what looked like a large marine radio antenna in one hand, a screwdriver in the other.

Willy described Clem Rogers's boat and counted to fifteen while Baby Hughie proved whatever point he was trying to prove by gazing silently at the first pale stars. "Nothing like that here," he said finally.

"Mind if I take a look?"

Oh, Hughie minded all right. But he pointed Willy at the dock and left him there.

As Pete dialed the Nashtoba police station he peered along the dock, trying to make out 4C in the mix of bright glare and black tar. He could see the Chris-Craft almost directly under a light post, but the boats beyond were obscured. He could see Polly, though—her small, straight form kilted sideways around the Chris-Craft, still watching. Finally Jean Martell came on the line, and Pete asked to be put through to the chief.

"Chief's not here. Gone out to buy a boat. Least I think that's what he said. Runs by here hundred miles an hour grumbling as he goes. I tell you—"

"Can't you reach him?"

"No siree. I already told your sister once today. I'm not supposed to crank up the radio unless it's an emergency."

"Crank up the radio," said Pete. "Tell him to get over to Eastside Marine in Murray's Mills. Tell him we think we found Coolidge, but he's not going to be here long. He'll want to talk to him."

"Oh, really? And where and what are you—"

"Call him, dammit, Jean."

"Just hold onto your britches, why don't you?" said Jean. "And I'll thank you to mind your language," but she left the phone, and soon afterward Pete heard some hopeful crackling. When she came back on the line she said, "Well, I tried, but I can't raise him. Dead air, that's all I get. I told him about these old radios. We're still in the Stone Age over here. Why, over to Naushon they've got—"

"Keep trying," said Pete. "Tell him Eastside Marine. Got that?"

"And who do you think I am, some ninny he picked up off the street?"

Some other time Pete might have enjoyed answering that, but not now.

Now, not only had he lost sight of the boat in 4C but he'd lost sight of Polly as well.

Polly watched from her hiding place behind the Chris-Craft as Roger Coolidge methodically moved a series of boxes and bags from the deck to the cabin. On the way down she could see him disappear as if he were being gobbled by an unseen monster—first chopped off at the ankles, then the knees, then the hips, then the chest. On the way back up he began as disembodied head, then grew neck and shoulders and torso like a large baby getting born. He made three trips. It was only when he hopped onto the dock and uncleated the stern line that Polly realized he was about to go.

Well, she'd have to do something about that. No sense dragging Willy all the way out here only to find Roger gone. She stepped out from behind the Chris-Craft into the ring of light, walking in the direction of the old boat, not looking at Roger Coolidge, but not looking away from him, either, letting her eyes fall on him casually. First she tried a noncommittal half smile, which he met and upped some, but with no recognition behind it. Next, she took a strong step forward as if she intended to move past, but halted mid–double take. She tried the smile again, got an even better one back.

"Excuse me for staring, but I think I know you. Roger Coolidge, isn't it?"

He continued to smile but shook his head, moving to the bow line. He untied it and hopped on board. Well, he couldn't go anywhere if she hopped on with him, could he? So Polly hopped on board. It was a nice feeling to know that these Coolidge types didn't intimidate her anymore. "Now don't go skittering away until we've solved this little mystery. I'm so sure I know you. We met on Nashtoba a thousand years ago. My name is Polly Bartholomew."

And finally a flicker of recognition. He held out his hand. "I'm sorry. Yes, of course. Polly. You've changed."

"So have you."

Roger smiled. "But not enough, apparently."

As the chief looked at the boats, Hugh Peletier looked at the chief. Willy could see him on top of a cabin roof two floats over, occasionally flailing around as if he were actually replacing the antenna, but mostly standing spread-legged, hands on hips, watching the chief. Some tough punk this was. When the chief finished he fluttered his fingers at Hughie and strolled toward the parking lot. He was halfway to his car when he spotted Polly's Renault.

He turned around, retraced his steps, kept going until he stood just below Baby Hughie on the dock.

"I see Polly Bartholomew's car out there. She's here?"

This time Hughie didn't even look up. "Nope."

"Any idea why her car is?"

Hughie straightened. "Why don't you tell me why you'd care? Then I'll see if I feel like answering."

Willy was a big man. He could have picked up Baby Hughie and chucked him like a harpoon into that inky black patch of water below, but Willy had a strong aversion to throwing his weight around. There were times, however, when it proved useful to let it show that the thought could cross his mind. He rested a foot on the deck of the boat and bounced. The boat rolled wildly. "Hughie," said Willy softly, "where is she?"

Hughie took just long enough to prove it was his own idea. "She called her brother. Left in his truck."

"And went where?"

"How should I know?"

"I don't know how you know, but I know you do. So why don't you empty that tiny little mind of yours? Or do you want me to climb up there and empty it for you?"

A much shorter pause this time. "Try Eastside Marine. And don't tell 'em I sent you."

"Thank you," said Willy politely.

Pete couldn't believe his eyes. Polly hopping onto Roger Coolidge's boat like she was about to take a pleasure tour of the harbor. Oh, he knew he should never have left her there. And now what should he do? He could just see the two shapes in the outer limits of the light, could see Polly talking away like she was a guest on the QE II.

And when he stepped around the Chris-Craft and moved toward the boat, Roger Coolidge saw him. Pete could tell by the way the man snapped to attention. Pete started to move forward, but almost at once he heard two sounds—the engine on the *Rose* throttling to life, and feet pounding the dock behind him.

He whipped around and there was Willy coming at him. Pete heard a throaty roar and turned again, but it was too late. Coolidge peeled away from the dock with Polly still on board, spewing twin rooster tails behind him.

22

PETE WAS ALREADY in the Whaler by the time the chief reached him. Since Willy didn't appear inclined to argue over the small matter of theft, Pete never had to use his hastily assembled speech about emergency maritime law. Willy vaulted on board. Pete guided them out of the slip and into the channel and opened up the throttle, but even over the noise he could hear Willy swear violently.

"What's the matter?"

"Damned radio. Dead spot, out of range, who knows." He swore again. "Piece of crap. Who is that, Coolidge?"

"Polly said it was." He didn't mean it to come out sounding skeptical. "Whoever he is, he's using the name Clem Rogers."

And whoever it was, he was running black. No lights. But as the waning moon danced out from behind thick clouds, it suddenly outlined the *Rose*, cut like a black arrow against the silver water.

"He's got twin Fiats up there," said Willy grimly.

Pete turned. "How do you know that?"

"That's Clem Rogers's old boat, I'd bet my pension on it. I've just been talking to his cousin Reese. Hundred horsepower, thirty-five knots."

And Pete had a fifty horsepower outboard behind him. But a smaller, lighter boat. Which still only meant twenty, twenty-five knots. He glanced at the hulking police chief beside him.

Maybe.

Don't panic, Polly told herself, but she wasn't such an idiot that she didn't know there was cause to. Why would Coolidge roar away from the dock the minute he saw the police chief? Because he was using his dead grandfather's credit card? Maybe.

Or maybe it was because Polly had recognized him, and Willy had been right all along.

That Roger Coolidge *had* killed Susan Jameson.

And now what? Polly decided, for now, she'd best continue as she'd begun. "Well, aren't you the impulsive one," she tittered over the sound of the engines. "Where are we off to, the south of France?"

"I seem to recall we had a trip to Gull Island planned."

Gull Island.

So don't panic. "Gull Island," she babbled. "What fun! I always regretted saying no the last time. But isn't that a long way to go at this hour of the night? And I do have this dog that will need to be let out soon."

But Coolidge didn't seem too worried about her

fictional dog's bursting bladder. "Who was that back there with the cop, your brother?"

"What cop? I didn't see any cop."

Coolidge smiled, white teeth against dark beard. "Never mind. Whoever they were, it doesn't matter. They won't catch this honey." He patted the wheel affectionately.

Involuntarily, Polly looked behind her. She could hear a boat, but she could see nothing but dark. She looked forward again. They were on Nashtoba Sound. She'd spent enough of her youth tacking around the island in the family sailboat to know that much. As a matter of fact, right now they were running parallel to Pete's beach, she was sure. She could see the long stretch of black shore, then the cottage lights, shining out all alone in the middle of the blank space that was the marsh.. But they were going so fast. They were going to leave it all behind. They were going to Gull Island. And then what?

Somehow Polly didn't think it was going to be Mexican omelettes.

Connie looked at the clock and then at the little girl and then at the plate of untouched food. She looked at the clock again. So why didn't she just give up and send her to bed? It wasn't like Lucy was going to eat any of that cold glop now. But Pete stilll wasn't back, and it was no day at the beach getting her to sleep without him.

Oh, well, nothing for it but to try. She stood up. "Time for bed."

"I want a cookie!"

Connie pointed to the almost full plate. "No dinner, no cookie. Now upstairs." To her surprise, Lucy got down from the table and ran up the stairs. Maybe being furious with Pete helps, thought Connie.

They even breezed through the washing up portion of the program, sailed straight through the pajamas, and actually landed Lucy uneventfully between the sheets.

"I want Leerie," said Lucy.

Connie picked up *A Child's Garden of Verses*, a copy that had once belonged to Pete, and watched it open automatically at the requested page.

"I want Pete to do it."

"Pete's not here."

Lucy kicked at the covers. "I want *Pete* to do it."

Oh, did Connie know this kid or what? She sat on the bed, irresolute, debating between the irresponsible, which was to let Lucy stay up till Pete deigned to return, or the responsible, which was a knock-down-drag-out that would take five more years off Connie's life.

"I'll make a deal with you," said Connie. "You promise to listen to your poem and go right to sleep afterward, I'll give you that cookie."

So sue me, thought Connie.

Polly shivered. The wind was like cold steel, much colder because of the speed. The boat was built for business, she could see that.

"Where did you get this boat?" she asked.

"It was my grandfather's."

Of course. Clem Rogers's old rumrunner. She remembered what Ben Fox had said about the speed of boats like this, how impossible it was for the Coast Guard to catch them. So Roger wasn't lying about that part, anyway. Polly strained her ears, but by now she could hear nothing but the wind in them.

"I'm getting awfully cold," she said finally.

Roger Coolidge pointed to the hatchway. "There's a coat down there."

Polly ducked through the hatch and felt for the ladder with her feet, just as the boat veered sharply. She lost her footing, pitched forward into the cabin, came to rest on all fours. She groped in front of her in the dark, felt slatted wood, metal, rope, thick wool . . . ah, yes. The jacket. She sat down where she'd landed and pulled it on.

And as she struggled to her feet she remembered something else Ben Fox had told her.

They were losing her. The Whaler was planing, snapping off the tops of the waves, the salt spray slapping Willy in the face, the smell of gasoline filling his nostrils, but still the Rose was slipping away. It was the second worst moment since Pete had broken the news about the marine radio. There wasn't one. Willy unsnapped his holster.

Pete's head swung around. "What are you planning to do with that, shoot out his tires?"

"Warning shot." But there was no chance. A thick, dark mass swallowed the moon, and the boat ahead disappeared from view. There was no way Willy was going to fire blind, not with Polly out there.

"Damn," said Pete, but he didn't throttle down. And suddenly there it was, the sleek dark hull, cutting sharply across their bow. Pete yanked the wheel hard to port, slamming back the throttle so fast that the engine stalled out. The black boat veered again and disappeared into the night.

Pete reached for the starter, but Willy caught his arm. "Wait. Listen."

They listened.

And Willy heard it. Already sounding like it was a million miles away, but clearly to the southeast. But, there was a second whine, coming from the west. *Damn.* There were two boats out there. Which one was the *Rose?*

Pete seemed in no doubt. He opened up in the southeasterly direction, but even so, Willy knew there was little hope of catching Coolidge now. He should tell Pete to turn back, call the Coast Guard from the dock. They'd been a couple of fools to try to chase down the *Rose* alone. Willy paused, uncharacteristically indecisive. All he could think of was Polly in the boat up ahead. If she knew they were there, if she heard them turn back . . .

Willy did nothing, and the Whaler roared uselessly on into the night.

The minute Polly emerged from the hold she searched again for the black stretch of land, the lone lights of Pete's cottage. Still there, but further off than before. Over the dull throb of Roger Coolidge's engines she thought she could hear a far-off whine, but as hard as she looked she could see nothing except black water. She snuck a look at

Coolidge's profile and could make out nothing but bristling hair. "When do we get to Gull Island?" she asked.

"We don't." And before she could move or duck or even gasp, he let go of the wheel, drew back a thick arm, and, still smiling, knocked her overboard into the cold October water.

❋23❋

" '*Now Tom would be a driver and Maria go
to sea,*
And my papa's a banker and as rich as he can be;
But I, when I am stronger and can choose what I'm to do,
*O Leerie, I'll go round at night and light the lamps
with you!' "*

The little girl's head lolled in the crook of Connie's elbow. She closed the book, slid her arm from under the soft down, kissed the smooth, untroubled brow. So who needed Pete? Granted, she was still going to kill him when he got home. She looked at the clock. Eight-thirty, and not even a phone call. Well, he wasn't going to find his food in the oven and his wife waiting up with open arms. Connie went down to the kitchen, put away the remains of the meal, cleaned up, doused the lights to further emphasize the point, crashed into bed, and lay there plotting her revenge.

* * *

Polly went down. It surprised her how far down. Her jeans and Roger's jacket seemed to turn into chains that dragged her toward bottom. But there was no bottom out here. She kicked and thrashed, and long after she'd run out of air and was sure she'd explode, she burst through. She couldn't seem to stop herself from thrashing uselessly upward, as if she could climb out into the sky and walk home. It wasn't until she was accidentally caught and carried on the crest of the wave that she remembered her old life-saving training. *Let the water do the work.* She took a large bite of air and eased back into it, facedown, arms extended. She exhaled, pushing down with her arms, and as her head came up nice and easy above the surface of the water she breathed in. Eased back down. Exhaled. Pushed. Rose. Breathed again. Drown-proofing, it was called. Four more times and she'd managed to quell the panic, but it didn't last long. As she looked around to get her bearings, she realized the friendly light that had glittered over the desolate marsh was now gone.

A sudden gust of wind pushed aside the thick batting that had covered the moon, and in a flash Pete saw what they were looking for—the *Rose*, closer than he'd expected. And getting closer still? Not possible. But true. As Pete closed the gap he saw why. The *Rose*'s engine sputtered into silence. She began to drop fast, going down by the stern.

Pete pulled into the lee of the *Rose*. Willy leaped aboard. Pete saw Coolidge come at the chief with a gaff in his hand, but toss it aside once the chief closed in. What had he seen, the gun? Some indecipherable words were exchanged. Suddenly Willy slammed Coolidge over the gunwale, cuffed his hands, bore down. Willy said something and got no answer.

Uh-oh, thought Pete. He saw Willy move, saw Coolidge's body jerk convulsively, heard a scream cut the air and it was done.

As Pete struggled to keep the boats abreast, Willy yanked Coolidge upright and tossed him through the air onto the floor of the Whaler. Willy sprang on board, cuffed Coolidge to the starboard rail, yelled to Pete, and suddenly the ugly little scene Pete had just witnessed began to make sense.

Polly.

Overboard.

She was too far out, already tired, long past cold. She knew she'd never make those distant lights on the mainland shore, and everything else was black. Nashtoba had to be out there somewhere, but where? She continued a hybrid mix of drown-proofing and treading, letting herself drift as she tried to think. There were two factors that would dictate where she'd likely end up—wind and tide—and neither was pushing her toward those distant lights of the mainland. So either they were pushing her toward Nashtoba, or they were pushing her out to open sea. She tried to remember which way everything had been facing when she'd been tossed overboard. She strained her eyes, trying to separate land-black from water-black, and failed both times. Polly was a good, strong swimmer—she had, after all, been living partly submerged since before she could walk—but there was no sense striking out in a direction until she knew which one was the right one. She couldn't, for example, buck the current straight on, but if she knew which way to angle, she could cut across it and edge her way toward the Nashtoba shore.

But which way was the Nashtoba shore?

And then she heard it. The sound of another boat engine. She had long ago lost any whisper of the *Rose*, which hadn't surprised her. She'd remembered Ben Fox's description of the sea cocks. She'd found the hatch in the floor, found the levers just as Ben Fox had described them and swung them open, had listened in amazement as the water flooded in from all corners faster than she would have believed possible.

But this was an even sweeter sound, now. Another boat. She pushed herself as high above the waves as she could and screamed at the top of her lungs, but she couldn't do it for long. It was a matter of corralling enough air to blow out while at the same time not letting any water flood in. After a few short blasts she stopped, gasping and choking. She listened.

The whine of the engine seemed closer. Much closer! She rested, breathed, tried again, listened again.

After the third time it was clear.

The boat had drawn close.

Passed by.

Left her there.

Willy McOwat gripped the bow rail and strained his eyes against the dark as Pete puttered slowly in the direction from which Coolidge had come. The chief didn't believe the tale he'd coerced from Coolidge—that Polly had, of her own volition, dived overboard—but now there was nothing to do but trust in Polly's good sense and Pete's seamanship. He could see Pete figuring Coolidge's path, factoring in tide and wind. After that, all they could do was pray that in the middle of miles and miles of cold, black water they'd spot a small, white face or hear her cries over the combined sounds of outboard, waves, and wind.

But after half a dozen futile passes Pete called him back from the bow. "This is no good. We have to go back, get the Coast Guard in."

"There was another boat out here. If we find it, divide up—"

Pete didn't say anything. Willy supposed there was no need. He nodded once. Pete throttled back and cut a smooth, wide arc for Eastside Marine.

Connie lay in bed, plotting the various methods of torture for Pete. Boiling in oil, keelhauling, or an up-and-coming favorite of hers these days—castration. There would be a few disadvantages to herself with that last, of course, but the way things were going these days, it wouldn't be that many.

The more play Connie gave to her grisly thoughts, the further and further away from sleep she drew, until finally, in desperation, she began to recite to herself what she could recall of Lucy's poem about Leerie. She got through the first few verses, but the final one escaped her. Something about a lamp outside the door. Pete, of course, had the whole thing memorized, but, need she remind herself, Pete wasn't here.

How did that damned poem go? It was driving her crazy. She'd be lying here thinking till morning. Maybe she should sneak into Lucy's room, nab the book, sneak out? No. She'd wake Lucy for sure. The kid slept as lightly as a night owl.

And speaking of night owls, had she heard something then?

Yes.

No.

Yes.

Polly heard them go. She heard the change in the engine, first slowing, then revving, then fading into the night. For a minute she thought she heard a similar, faint whine from the other direction, but then that, too, was gone. That was when Polly realized that she was numb-cold, dead-tired, raw-lunged. That was when she gave up, and that was when it happened, that thing that she'd never believed happened in the real world. Her life, up front and personal, like a video on fast-forward. There she was in the carefree little-girl years, running on the beach, leaping into the waves after Pete. Then the middle years, the silly boy-mad ones, the ones that could still make her feel hot and flushed despite the numbing cold. And the nightmare years, the years of all those walking testosterone mutations as Pete liked to call them. And what would her future have held? No big mystery there, not if she knew Willy. Finally, someone her brother actually liked, and she was going to toss it all away by going out and drowning. And why, now that she had no future, could she suddenly picture it so clearly?

Willy would buy the house down the beach that he'd
been renting from Connie. He would mow the lawn
every Saturday, paint the trim every five years, tend
his precious garden. He'd continue his work as police
chief, earning the love and respect of all who knew
him. They'd have a couple of kids. Willy wanted kids,
she knew. He'd said so one day after playing checkers
with Lucy. And he'd be great with them. Gentle but
firm. Patience of a saint. He'd still find time to treat
Polly like a queen, of course . . .

So what was wrong with this picture? Polly,
that's what.

She lashed out, in anger this time, thrashing
numbly against the weight in her arms and her legs.
She raised her face one more time.

And saw the light.

" 'For we are very lucky, with a lamp before the door,
And Leerie stops to light it, as he lights so many more;
And O, before you hurry by with ladder and with light,
O Leerie, see a little child and nod to him to-night!' "

"Again!" chirped Lucy.

She shouldn't, of course. She should get firm. Close
the book. Turn out the light. But the little girl was
curled against her, soft hair brushing Connie's cheek,
one hot hand holding Connie's finger tight. It was
nice. You needed a few of those, now and then.

Connie cleared her throat.

" 'My tea is nearly ready . . .' "

It couldn't possibly have taken them as long as
it seemed. Two calls, one to the Coast Guard, one

to the Murray's Mills police. The handover of Coolidge took the most time, but in the meantime Pete was busy scrounging things—blankets, hot coffee, a powerful searchlight.

They heard the Coast Guard cutter some time later, but by then they were already back in the commandeered Whaler, heading out across the sound for the second time that night. And the night had gotten blacker. But there was one change, Pete noticed. On the far shore, a light. *His* light. It was like a beacon to him, the symbol of the place and the people he loved best. If only Polly could have seen it. *Could* see it, he corrected himself, fast.

And then it hit.

What if she *had* seen it? If she had, she'd have struck out for it. Pete once again opened up the throttle, cutting across the sound like a dart.

"What are you doing?" shouted Willy.

Pete explained. The Whaler's shallow draft would allow them the leeway not afforded to the Coast Guard cutter. They could pull in close, run along the shore. And the tide was in full flood. If she'd headed for the light, if she'd gotten across the sound in the first place, she'd get swept straight into the mouth of the creek.

And the cutter certainly couldn't do what Pete did once he got there—nose his way through the clogging marsh grass, scouring the banks of the creek with the spotlight.

And that was where they found her, caught up in the weeds just inside the mouth of Rum Creek, small and white and stone cold.

24

CONNIE HEARD THE crash of the door as it banged into the wall behind it. She heard Pete's voice call to her. She leaped to her feet, scooping Lucy into her arms, answering the babble of questions with the same six words all the way down the stairs. "It's just Pete. It's all right."

But she could tell by his voice that it wasn't all right. When she saw Willy McOwat with the colorless Polly in his arms, a blanket twisted around her like a shroud, she was already mentally prepared for action. She put Lucy down and ran upstairs for more blankets. When she came back, the chief had set Polly on the couch and was efficiently stripping off her clothes while Pete made a fire. Connie went into the kitchen, but Pete had already put on the kettle as well as a can of soup. She put in a call to the doctor, Hardy Rogers, but the answering service told her he was at the hospital, delivering a baby. As she hung up she felt Pete's hands on her shoulders. "Try Phoebe Small."

"Phoebe?"

"She's a doctor. Or almost a doctor."

Connie opened her mouth, closed it, picked up the phone and dialed.

At first Polly felt nothing. Not the cold, certainly not the heat. She was mostly tired. And mostly she wanted to sleep. But they kept shoving things at her —cups, spoons, clothes. And it was only when she began to feel the warmth that she began to shake. It scared her, that shake. She couldn't control it, and she didn't know why she was doing it. So she closed her eyes and shook. She heard a distant voice explaining to someone that there was no cause for alarm, that this was normal, but she didn't at first connect the voice to any known person, or the words as referring to herself. After a minute she felt someone's hand on her face. She opened her eyes, and there was Tim St. George peering down at her. She closed her eyes and opened them again.

Still there.

"Am I dead?"

Someone cleared a throat. "Damned close." The voice was raw, gruff, unfamiliar. Certainly not Tim's. But it was close by, behind her, out of her line of vision. The trouble was, she was too tired to turn around.

But inside her line of vision there were other faces besides Tim's—Connie, Pete, Phoebe Small, even Lucy's tiny dark head.

"This is very strange," she said. She reached out and touched Tim's hand, which had by now left her face. It felt real enough. "What are you doing here?"

"I brought him," said Phoebe.

She brought him. That figured. Polly sighed and closed her eyes again. But it seemed there were other questions she should be asking. She opened her eyes. "Did you catch him? I tried to sink him. I opened the sea cocks."

She heard the raw throat sound from somewhere again, but it was Pete who spoke. "You sank him. We caught him."

Polly sighed and closed her eyes again. "I'm a little tired."

As she fell asleep, she heard a funny sound.

Laughter.

Pete looked from Tim to Phoebe and from Phoebe to Tim. The two doctors—one full-fledged and one on leave of absence mid-residency—sat in the matching rattan chairs like a pair of bookends with the fire blazing between them. Pete perched on the old sea chest they used for a coffee table. Polly slept soundly under a mound of quilts on the couch behind him. Willy McOwat had finally left Polly's side to deal with Roger Coolidge, and Connie had gone to deal with Lucy. Pete had already explained to Phoebe and Tim, to the limits of his own knowledge, the events that had led to Polly's swim. Any answers about Roger Coolidge would have to wait for Willy, but that didn't mean there weren't other questions.

Pete decided to go first. "So how did Factotum end up employing two doctors?"

"No big mystery," said Tim. "I met Phoebe during her rotation at the hospital."

"I confided my doubts," said Phoebe.

"About her direction," said Tim.

"And he told me he knew a place that could help me sort it out."

Pete looked from one to the other of them. "*Here?*"

"It's not uncommon in this profession to find yourself on one path, wishing you'd chosen another," said Tim. "Neither is it uncommon to find yourself with a good case of the proverbial cold feet. So I suggested that Phoebe take some time off, think it through for a while."

"Here."

"When your police chief hinted to me that you were hiring, I suggested it to Phoebe. I described this place to her."

Phoebe laughed. "And what a description. 'Lots of mindless physical drudgery conducive to soul-searching. Lots of crazy people to test your resolve.' Wasn't that how you put it?"

"The point was," said Tim, looking uncomfortable, "that I thought it might help her to take some time to think. Do something that would give her the room to think. And I thought this would be a good environment for settling one of Phoebe's biggest questions—whether she wanted to work with people or with paper."

Pete turned to Phoebe. "I hope it's people. You're good at it."

Phoebe flushed.

Pete faced Tim again. "So that's why you ended up here? Your own professional cold feet?"

Silence.

"Speaking of cold feet," said Tim finally. He got up and felt Polly's. "She's doing fine. She'll wake up tomorrow ready to swim back."

"Swell," said Pete.

✥25✥

FOR THE POLICE CHIEF, it was a long night, one
that ran straight through to Saturday morning and
kept on going. When Willy finally tore himself
away from Polly's couch and arrived back at the
station, he took a minute to make sure he'd regained his equilibrium. He was his usual cool, collected self when he pushed open the door to face
the man who had thrown most of his hope for the
future overboard. At least he thought he was. He
was surprised when Roger Coolidge took one look
at him and started babbling.

As soon as Willy could wrap up the necessary
details, he headed back to Polly's. As he got out of
his car he noticed for the first time that it was a
beautiful day—bright and blue and warm with a
hint of October crisp. Next he noticed two shapes
working their way over the marsh, one very tall
with a red plume of hair, one very small with a
few dark spikes bobbing up and down as it
skipped. He climbed the stairs to Polly's apartment

and knocked. No one home. He reversed direction and knocked and hallooed at Pete's door, where the response was better. Polly was there, sitting at the kitchen table with the other two Bartholomews.

"Did you see Lucy and Phoebe out there?" asked Connie.

"I told you, they're fine," said Pete.

"They're fine," said Willy. He ducked down to catch Polly's eye. "You too?"

Polly nodded, but her head remained tucked.

"Tim came first thing and checked her out," said Pete.

"Tell him the rest," said Polly.

"Tim's the one who sent Phoebe to apply for the job here. It seems working here helps these medical types decide their course in life."

"And tell the rest."

"Well," said Pete, looking funny.

"Tim's gay," said Polly. "Phoebe told us. So you can see my talent for picking men remains intact."

Connie winked at Willy. "If you ask me, you're getting pretty good."

Polly looked out the window.

Willy cleared his throat. This was not going the way he wanted. Time to get Polly out of there. But nobody would give him the chance. The questions flew at him from all sides. He finally gave up, pulled out a chair, and recapped his recent discussions with Coolidge.

There had been few surprises. The tragedy had indeed been born with Clem Rogers's deathbed allusions to something valuable buried at Rum Creek, augmented by Coolidge's own conviction that there was a rumrunner's fortune unaccounted for among his grandfather's effects.

Coolidge's own research had located the creek. It had taken only one look at his future sister-in-law, Susan Jameson, to realize that here was a weapon worth cultivating, and one look at the man who lived along the creek for Coolidge to figure where the weapon should be aimed. Willy tactfully skimmed over the precise how and why of Susan Jameson's conversion to the cause. From there it went much as Willy had speculated.

"Susan ferreted out the exact location of the old plank walk from you and Sarah," he said. "All the while remaining in touch with Coolidge."

"In intimate touch," said Pete.

Willy skimmed on. "Once they had the necessary information on location, it was a matter of getting you out of the way so they could dig around."

"So Susan led me on that wild-goose chase to Bradford."

"Parts of it. She called you, not from Bradford but from right here in town. Once you'd taken off for Bradford, she came back to the house with Coolidge and took him out to the spot on the marsh, equipped with one of your shovels. They'd expected to uncover a box or a bag or a barrel. They hadn't expected to uncover Manny Rose. When they did, according to Coolidge, Susan panicked. Became hysterical. Coolidge wanted to keep digging for the money. He gave me a good song and dance about that part, about how he couldn't see how a few more minutes would help or hinder the corpse and, after all, per his grandfather's will, it was rightfully his money. But Susan kept fussing at him, and finally, according to Coolidge, he whipped around in exasperation and caught her in the face with the shovel."

"Translation," said Connie. "She tried to light out to call the police and he coshed her."

"Or once she'd served her purpose by locating the right spot, Coolidge decided there was no need to split the take. Whatever the reason, there he was with corpse number two on his hands. The solution seemed obvious enough—one grave already dug, just add second body. He danced around some more about that. It wasn't his own neck he was protecting. Susan's death was an accident. He had no fear of facing his day in court. What he wanted to prevent was the discovery of that first body. By his grandfather's own admission, he'd buried whatever was in that marsh. He was merely protecting his grandfather's good name for posterity."

Connie snorted.

"And then Coolidge went back to the house, cleaned out her stuff, left that note on the Kleenex?" asked Pete.

"After leaving the message for you in Bradford that Susan had found a ride. And then he travelled to Weams Point and forged the postcard, doing a nice little balancing act—Susan's basic signature with Rosella's backward slant. He even spread the rumor that Susan was planning to come back to see Rosella. If Pete got suspicious at all, if he followed the trail to Weams Point, he'd uncover Susan's falling-out with her sister and, hopefully, the rumor that she'd been last seen headed in her sister's direction. Voila. Motive and opportunity. And no one but the dead Susan even faintly aware that Coolidge had been at the scene of the crime that night."

"That's what he thought," said Connie. "He failed to account for Baby Hughie's raging hormones, hot on the scent." She paused, looked at Pete, seemed to think better of what she'd been about to add. Something about somebody else's raging hormones, if Willy had to guess. But again, Pete seemed unrattled by the revelations thus far.

"So then what?" he asked.

"Then Coolidge really did blow town. He took off for the remotest but closest location he could think of, Gull Island, but even there he didn't feel safe. He realized he'd better hedge his bets, abandon his old identity. So he deep-sixed his car, set himself up with his dead grandfather's credentials, and took off, living on the boat. The perfect vanishing act."

"But why did he come back?"

"Because he still thought there was money someplace. When he got wind of the two bodies turning up, he crept back as close as he dared, waiting and listening for any new information, hoping to pick up that missing clue to the money."

"Idiot," said Connie.

"After fifteen years he must have figured he was safe enough. What could tie him to the crime at this late date?"

"What did happen to the money?"

"I had a long talk with the nephew, Reese. Some of it went into that boat. The rest of it went the same way as a lot of other ill-gotten gains of the era. Don't forget, the supply seemed endless. And for the first time in their lives, these struggling fishermen were in a position to live a little. So they lived. According to Reese, Clem developed some expensive tastes. Fancy cars. The New York speakeasies. A woman who liked jewelry."

"So there was nothing out on that marsh but Manny?" asked Connie.

"And Susan, eventually."

Pete pushed back his chair and left the room.

Connie followed him.

Alone at last, thought Willy, but still Polly wouldn't look at him.

"So you were right about Roger," she said finally.

"Believe it or not, there's usually no big mystery to these things. Look, could we get out of here?"

Without another word Polly got up and led the way out of the room, but they'd only gotten as far as the no-man's-land between her brother's home and hers when Polly's Renault wheeled into the driveway and Hugh Peletier jumped out. He sauntered up to Polly and tossed her the keys, ignoring the police chief, or pretending to, at least.

"You left these on my desk. And you left your car in my lot. Heard you decided to take the shortcut back."

Polly didn't seem to have any trouble looking at Hughie. She giggled. "I don't recommend the route. But thanks for the delivery, that was nice."

"No it wasn't. Whole thing's a kidnap plot. Now you have to drive me back." Hughie looked around. "Jeez, this place doesn't change much. Except for that." He pointed to the boat barn.

"That's where I live. I'm working for Pete again." She made a face, and Hughie laughed.

"Hey, things are tough all around So does the delivery boy rate a tour? Or am I interrupting some big interrogation here?"

"You're not interrupting anything. I'll show you around." She turned to Willy. "Want to come along?"

Maybe it was the eyes. Maybe it was Hughie. Maybe it was the fact that she'd even asked the question.

"I took the last tour," he said.

Connie came up behind Pete, where he stood looking out the window at the woman with the flowing red hair and the little girl with the fuzzy dark mop, still walking hand in hand.

"It's okay," said Pete. "She's still with her."

"What did she use, handcuffs?"

Pete turned around. "Didn't you hear her? She told her before they hit the door. Hold my hand or we'll have to go back."

"I *told* you. I *said* that."

"You may have said it, but you didn't mean it. When I heard it from Phoebe I was ready to make book on it. When I've heard it from you it's like you're saying, 'You take off and *boy* are we going to have a little chat.'"

Connie opened her mouth to retort, but she remembered a recent occasion when she had said it like she'd meant it and it had worked. She started to laugh. "Okay, okay. And you're Mr. Tough Guy, is that it?"

"No, I'm not. I'm talking to myself, too. We've got to stick to our guns."

"But I want her to like it here. To feel safe with us."

"So do I. But Reese Rogers said something to me that I've been thinking about a lot. He was talking about Prohibition. About why it was so out of control. He said a law should be something you can count on. I think Lucy will feel safest if she knows she can count on our rules. If she knows she can count on us to do what we say we will, bad or good. If we give her a clearly defined framework."

Connie thought. She had to admit it made sense. Still, it would be hard to do, especially at first.

"You think we can do it?"

"I think we can give it a better shot than we've given it so far."

Connie slid a hand into Pete's back pocket. Pete put an arm around her. They stood like that, looking out at the woman and the little girl for a long time.

"I guess it's time I forgive her her unfortunate hair color," said Connie, and just like that, the other conversation, the one they'd both been avoiding, spewed forth.

"Poor old Susan," said Pete.

"Generous of you, considering how she used you."

Pete withdrew his arm, swung around so Connie's hand was forced out of his pocket. "Right there. That's it. I couldn't figure out why nothing felt right. That's *it*."

"That's what?"

"It started with your *schmuck* attack. I didn't feel like a schmuck. I think it was because I was actually relieved when she left, but I couldn't admit it. When Willy told me that she'd been dead out on the marsh all this time I felt physically sick. I *wanted* to think that she'd left me. I'd come to the point long before that where I knew it was 'no go,' like the postcard said. And what did I do about it? Nothing."

"Because she was so hot in the sack. So you felt like you'd used her. And now that you know she was the one who used you, you feel better, is that it?"

"When Willy said that postcard was a fake, that she hadn't left, it was like it was my fault she was dead. Now I know I wasn't keeping her here under false pretenses to get her head bashed in. Does that make any sense?"

Sure, thought Connie. For Pete. "But tell me something. Why was it 'no go'? What was wrong with her?"

It took Pete a long time. "I don't know," he said finally. "She wasn't you, I guess."

Connie put her arms around him, pressed close, put both hands in both back pockets. "You're such a *nice* schmuck," she said.

✳26✳

WHEN RITA PECK got ready to leave work on Monday she got the second unpleasant surprise of the week, and from the same source. There was her ridiculous-looking ex-husband, leaning against that ridiculously huge, black Pontiac.

"We need to talk," he said.

"About what?"

"About us."

"There is no *us*."

"Aw, Rita, get off it. Lupo's. One drink. What's it gonna hurt?"

He opened his car door. Rita stepped past the brand-new Pontiac to her old Dodge Omni. "I'll meet you there."

He arrived first. He opened her door, ushered her inside, corralled a secluded booth, ordered the drinks without asking her preference. It might have changed, he could think. But as a matter of fact, it hadn't. So she accepted the white wine without comment and waited for him to speak.

"How's Max?" he asked.

The words took her off guard, which showed her how seldom he ever said them. "She's fine," she lied.

"Well, good. Because she's part of why I want to talk. Rita, all this Nicky-bashing of yours has got to stop."

Rita had been about to take a sip of wine. She nearly dropped the whole thing in her lap. *"What?"*

"I mean it. I've just about had it. The police chief was the final straw. Storms in on me and starts in about that redhead. You think I don't know where he got all that?"

"I merely said—"

"You merely said. I don't care what you merely said. What he came away with was me and that redhead. And for the thousandth time, I never touched the bitch. Now will you get off it?"

"You certainly did touch her. I saw you. That day she supposedly fell in that creek."

Nicky rolled his eyes. "Still the same old games, isn't it? You know and I know. That's not what either of us meant. She fell in the creek. I fished her out. So take it to the—"

"And there you are with your same old games. As if that's even the point. When we both know the point is, what were you doing out there on the marsh with her in the first place?"

"Boy, you've got some great memory. Turns on and off whenever you want. I was waiting for you, if you recall. I was supposed to be taking you to lunch. And you kept putting me off. Dotting i's. Crossing t's. It was damned hot waiting around in that office, so I decided to take a walk. And there she was."

"In the creek."

"Not in. Not at first. She was leaning over digging in the mud. I came up and scared the daylights out of her. Tumbled her head over heels into the water. You think I should have left her there, I guess."

Rita stared at her ex-husband. She had never bought that fell-in-the-creek foolishness, but knowing what she now knew, it began to make more sense. If Susan had been digging around for Clem's hoard and Nicky had stumbled across her, she might very well have decided to create a small landslide to distract him from the hole she'd been digging. But there was one other occasion that was as yet unexplained. "You said you met her when she came in looking for a car. A woman without two cents to her name."

"Happens every day of the week, Rita. How many times have I told you that? People like to dream. They get a new job, before the first paycheck's in they're down at the dealership, window-shopping for what they won't be able to afford for another fifty checks."

Rita supposed that even that made sense. After all, Roger Coolidge must have convinced Susan there was money coming or she'd never have jumped into the mess. But what didn't make sense was Nicky. "Is this what this little visit is all about? Your sudden, burning desire to put the record straight?"

Nicky slapped both hands flat on the table. "*Sud-*

den desire. You beat all, you know that? Didn't I tell you the same damned thing fifteen years ago? But that woman was only one on your list. And I told you then and I'm telling you now and for the last time. As God is my witness or any other oath you want. I never laid a finger on any woman but you the whole time we were married. I'll tell you what this visit is all about. After my little chat with the chief I saw red. As you know. I came around and bawled you out. But then I got to thinking. If you chose to toss away a perfectly good marriage on some unfounded suspicions, that was your choice. But if after all this time that's still what you think of me, what have you been telling my daughter? So that's why I'm here. I want you to straighten her out. You tell her the fact that she hasn't got a father is not my fault."

Rita tossed off her wine to cool her fury, but it seemed to have the opposite effect. She rose out of her seat, leaned across the table. "Let me tell you something, Nicky. If you think I left you because of some unfounded suspicions about other women, take another guess."

The look on his face was so comical that Rita almost laughed.

"What do you mean? What other reason was there?"

"Here are three to try out. Your total lack of investment in our marriage. Your total lack of involvement with our daughter. Your general irresponsibility." She sat back down. "But you know what? You're right about one thing. As long as there's a Maxine, there will always be an us. So on that note, let me promise you something, on whatever oath *you* want. I have never once said a bad word about you to your daughter's face. And I won't. Whatever she thinks about you, you've got only yourself to thank. And I've got news for you. Maxine thinks she does have a father. One who doesn't care about her much. If you want to do something about that, here's her number." She scribbled Maxine's phone number on Nicky's napkin. "Thank you for the drink. Good night."

As Rita drove away, she was surprised at how good she felt. Better than good. Lucky. Or maybe just plain old smart. She could have been stuck with that man for life. Oh, it was suddenly so clear. It had never been Susan Jameson. It had never been the marriage. It had been the man.

The wrong man.

And she knew where the right one was.

Willy McOwat walked up the slatted steps of the white house on the corner, lifted and dropped the brass knocker. He could hear heavy footsteps. He saw a closed blind to the right of the door flutter. He saw the tarnished brass doorknob turn, but this time, instead of the door opening onto a life doomed to darkness, it opened on what felt to him like a world gone reversed. Nothing dramatic, just a smiling Rosella with combed hair and clean clothes, and him with his guts kicked out.

"Remember me?" he asked. "Chief McOwat?"

Rosella nodded, opened the door further, stepped back. Willy went in.

She led him into a room with a TV blaring,

snapped it off, motioned for him to sit. He sat. He said what he'd come to say. That they still had Susan's bones. That she should collect them and do with them whatever she saw fit.

He wasn't sure she understood him until she said, "Do you always come in person to tell people this?"

Like he had unclaimed bones kicking around the station every day of the week. "It's not the kind of thing I like to do over the phone," he said. He didn't add anything about the lingering unease that had compelled him to check once more on her. What he did add was, "I'm sorry about your sister. It can't be easy to learn about something like this."

"It's better to know, I think. It was terrible, wondering what had become of her. I used to imagine. Sometimes good things, sometimes bad. Never . . . the worst."

"What kinds of good things?"

"Oh, different things. She wanted to become an actress. Most of the time I imagined that."

What the hell, thought Willy. "As a matter of fact, I believe she was an actress. According to the accounts I was able to collect."

Rosella's face lit up. "Really? I'm glad. What kind of work was she doing?"

"Ah, local productions."

"Really? I thought I saw her in the paper once. One of those outdoor theaters."

"I'm told some of it was outdoors, yes."

"Was she good?"

"I know she received some excellent reviews."

Rosella nodded sadly. "She would have been famous, I just know it. She was so beautiful. But now she'll stay beautiful forever. I suppose it might help to remember that."

Willy agreed that she would stay beautiful.

But as he drove home he wondered if Pete would ever think her quite as beautiful as he had thought her once.

When Willy got to the station he found Jean Martell in the middle of some sort of seizure.

"What, Jean?"

She continued to pantomime. Someone in his office.

"Who?"

She pretended to pull out a wallet and count money.

"Dammit, Jean—"

She mouthed a name. Feel Dirt? Filbert? Willy gave up. He pushed open his office door and there was Phil Clark, the chairman of the Board of Selectmen.

"Sorry to keep you waiting," said Willy.

The chairman waved away the chief's apology. Willy pointed at a chair, but Phil Clark elected to continue to stand. He handed Willy an envelope. Willy opened it up. He read the letter, folded it, slid it into his inside jacket pocket, and walked out.

❖27❖

PETE LEFT POLLY'S apartment and headed straight for the path through the scrub that led to the chief's house. He realized as he walked that not only his teeth but his fists were clenched. He deliberately unclenched. He had no right to be angry. And he certainly had no right to be surprised, since he'd predicted it in the first place. Maybe even caused it. He pushed through the last batch of bayberry, went up to the chief's door, and knocked.

It took the chief a while to get there. He finally appeared in a frayed pair of khakis, bare feet, and a sweatshirt that said Nashtoba Country Club. There was no Nashtoba Country Club. He led Pete into the living room, where Ray Charles was explaining how he didn't need no doctor. The day's *Globe* and the week's *Islander* lay scattered on rug and couch, along with an empty cashew can and a pair of dirty socks. There was an empty beer can on the coffee table, but something told Pete there might be a few others someplace else.

"Look," said Pete. "This is all my fault."

"Where do you get that? The minute I stepped onto that boat I assumed responsibility. I knew that."

Pete shook his head. "I just got through talking to her. She wasn't even going to mention it. Told me she was quitting. Moving out. That was it. I asked if you knew about this and after she got through the part about how it was none of my business, she said you two were quits. Then she told me. That she was moving to Bradford to work with *Hughie*. That it took her almost drowning to get her to see straight. I said something like, 'You call this straight?' And that was it. She went on the attack. On and on about how it was my big idea in the first place and if I thought you were such a great guy I should marry you myself. How she wasn't about to sit next door to me and try to live my life. How if she was going to make mistakes they were going to be her own mistakes. After that she stopped making sense. Something about how she may not be Susan Jameson but she was no Doris Day, either. Then something else about fish and horses. Gift horses with fishbowls in their mouths, to be exact." Pete stopped. "What boat?"

Willy got up, fished in his leather jacket, pulled out a letter, handed it to Pete. "I thought you meant this."

Pete unfolded the letter and read. *Effective immediately, pending further investigation, you are suspended without pay from all duties as Nashtoba Chief of Police.*

The letter elaborated. Reckless endangerment of civilians. Stolen property. Assault.

Pete crumpled up the letter and tossed it at the nearest plant. "No way. *Polly* jumped on board with Coolidge. *I* took that boat. *What* assault?" But just then he remembered the funny business on board the *Rose*. "You mean Coolidge filed assault charges?"

Willy nodded.

"I'll talk to them. I'll testify. You'll get your job back."

"I've already tendered my resignation. Don't worry, Coolidge isn't going to take anybody to court, his lawyer's going to be too busy trying to get him off the hook."

Pete sat, stunned. "And Polly?" he asked finally.

"Polly was right, it is none of your business. But it's also not your fault. Or your idea. It was mine. And I've had worse."

Pete refrained from asking him to name one. He stood up and began to pace back and forth. "I'll tell you what really happened. You treated her right. She doesn't know what to do with that. She thinks she should be shoved around, beat up, mouthed off at."

"It wasn't all Polly. I was out of steam. I couldn't take the little punk. I said things."

"Hughie. Christ." Pete paced some more. Stopped. "You know, you can't chuck one good apple into a barrel full of rotten ones and expect the stink to clear up like that. If she gets—"

"Forget it, all right? It's old news."

Pete sat down again. "What about the job? What are you going to do?"

"Give me a day on that."

"All right. All right. But look, while you're thinking it over, if you want something to do—"

"You can't help yourself, can you?"

"Come on, Willy. With Polly gone Factotum's down one. Or down a half, at least."

"I'll keep it in mind. And thanks."

"Yeah. Well."

Pete stood up.

And since Willy didn't act like he was too crushed by the move, he left.

When Pete emerged from the other end of the path he was greeted by the warm yellow arms of his own kitchen light. He crossed the porch, but paused before opening the door. There were Connie and Lucy, sitting at the kitchen table. He could hear the babble through the glass.

"Crackers, corn-on-the-cob, crullers," said Lucy.

"Crabmeat, crayons, chrysanthemums," said Connie.

"You can't eat kissandymums."

"And when was the last time you ate a crayon? No, wait, don't answer that."

Pete smiled for what seemed like the first time in hours. Days. Weeks.

Connie twisted around when she heard the door behind her. "What is this, a sneak attack?"

"I've been talking to Polly. And Willy."

Something there in the voice she didn't like. But when Lucy slid off the chair and ran to him he swooped her up to the ceiling without missing a beat.

"I hope you're not hungry," said Connie. "There's not one thing to eat in this house. Except all these crayons and chrysanthemums."

Lucy giggled.

Apparently the five minutes in her room half an hour ago hadn't scarred her for life. And it wasn't hard to chalk things up on the plus side. "Crawfish, cantaloupe, cat food," she tried, just to prove a point, and got a gleeful shriek.

"If those are the choices I vote for another bout of Lupo's pizza," said Pete.

Lucy yayed. Connie would have yayed with her, but she was suddenly overcome by the most powerful déjà vu she'd had in all these weeks . . .

"Hey," said Pete. "Look at the time. Better call it quits."

Connie reached for the remaining pieces of broken lamp. So did Pete. They bumped elbows awkwardly.

"Sorry," they said in unison, and laughed, also awkwardly.

"Look," said Pete. "It's Friday night. It's late. Everyone else has knocked off. I can clear this up."

"Tim's still here. By the way, why is he still here? I thought he was supposed to leave Labor Day."

Pete grinned. "He was. He keeps saying he's going to. I don't know what the holdup is. Not the great pay, that's for sure."

"Then it has to be the company."

"That's what I thought. But Polly left three weeks ago and here he is."

"I wasn't—" began Connie, but stopped. Maybe she was wrong.

"Speaking of which . . . here. Give me that." He took the pieces of lamp from her hands and put them down on the table. "I've been meaning to ask you. I don't suppose you'd want to stay on all year."

Connie feigned a look behind her. "Me? The one with the mouth?"

"Actually, you haven't yelled at me in months. I was beginning to wonder if you'd given up."

"It's you who's given up. Acting like a jerk. Since The Great Migration."

Pete didn't pretend not to understand. But then again, neither did he comment. Instead, he leaned against the kitchen counter, jammed his hands into his pockets, and flushed.

"Have you heard from her?"

"I wasn't expecting to."

Oh, really, thought Connie. But it was true that he hadn't seemed too broken up this past month.

"So what do you say?" he asked finally.

"All right. I'll give it a try."

"Good." One word, but it sounded like there was more in it. A long, awkward pause chose that moment to descend. If he'd only do something, she thought. Move away from that counter. Take a single, solitary step . . .

What he did do was to look at his watch. "I'm starving. What would you say to another bout of Lupo's pizza?"

"Will there be meteors?"

Idiot. Sap. Like he'd even remember that.

"You know," said Pete, still not moving, "I hated to

*leave here that night. I suppose that should have told
me everything."*

"Everything?"

"Something. It didn't tell you anything, I guess."

"Nothing I didn't already know."

Now that should bring him over the three or four
miles of kitchen floor, all right. But no. The only thing
that happened was the brown eyes widened. *"Since
when?"*

The door banged, and Tim St. George stuck his head
in. *"Oh,"* he said. *"There you are. Just wondered if
anyone wanted to—"*

"No, thanks," said Pete.

Tim looked back and forth between them.

"But thanks anyway," said Connie.

Tim left.

And Pete stood there. For two or three minutes, at
least.

The hell with this.

Connie stepped into the no-man's-land.

And didn't get back to the other side till the next
morning at quarter past eight, when they shared Wheat-
ies and bananas, sitting in the sun on the back stoop.

Pete stared over Lucy's head at Connie as he
heard himself speak. Those words. Would she remember them? No chance. But he remembered
them. *What would you say to another bout of Lupo's
pizza?* And she'd said . . .

"Will there be meteors?"

Meteors. Christ. So she'd remembered that night. And
here they'd been wasting all this time fixing lamps.

Okay, but this was no Susan Jameson. It was going to be up to him to get things moving, but he had to go slow, no scaring her off. Not after all this.

He did his best, held his position straight through the Tim St. George episode, but that was it. The second Tim shut the door Pete bolted across the kitchen floor, wrapped her into him, and didn't let go till the next morning at quarter past eleven when he got up, made them blueberry pancakes, and served them to her in bed.

✣28✣

Eᴅ Hᴇᴀʟᴇʏ and Bert Barker sat on the steps of Beston's store and shivered despite the sun. Or Bert shivered. With Ed it was more of a quake.

"Shame about the police chief," said Ed.

"I say good riddance," said Bert. "Hear we got a good one at last, from over Weams Point. Granville Foster."

"That right? What's he want to come over here for, I wonder?"

"Says he's getting sick of the rat race."

"Rat race! Wait till he sees this place. No word of lie, I saw five cars on Main Street just last week."

"Not all at once?"

Ed nodded grimly and quaked again. "Cold for this time of year."

"Chris on raft, Ed, it's November. What'd you expect?"

"Is it really, now? Well, that means old Ev's been gone near two weeks."

"Might never see him at all. Old fellow like him

287

trying to come up with a honeymoon performance, that's cardiac time, that's what that is."

"Well, I say more power to him."

"Well, you would."

"Better to die like that than like poor old Manny Rose, with a bullet through his head."

"*Old* Manny. He was twenty-five if he was a day."

"And that little redhead who used to run with Pete. She was even younger. Crying shame, that's what it is."

"Fool idiocy, that's what it is. Manny was bad enough. She was worse. Greed, greed, greed, that's what it is."

"And demon rum," said Ed. "It's been the ruination of us all. Ask me, they never shoulda got rid of that amendment." Ed looked up at the sky. "Looks like the sun's over the yardarm. Care to join me in a small libation?"

"Don't mind if I do," said Bert.

JUDY
MERCER

Praise for
Fast Forward

"One of the best suspense novels of the
year....inspired, provocative....makes John Grisham's
thrillers seem like the work of a rank amateur...."

— Les Robert,
Cleveland *Plain Dealer*

And look for

Double Take

and

Split Image

Available in hardcover

1331-02